not the ONE

A NOVEL

AMY DAWS

Copyright © 2015 Amy Daws
All rights reserved.

Published by: Stars Hollow Publishing
ISBN 13: 978-1-944565-01-5
IBBN 10: 1-944565-01-9
Content Editing: Stephanie Rose
Line Editing: Angela Pratt www.facebook.com/LilyRoseEditing
Contributing Proofing: DragonEditing4U
Cover Design: Amy Daws
Cover Photography: Megan Daws
Cover Models: Callie Wilson and Ethan Roepke

Dedicated to Kelly.
Your patience with me is astounding.
Thank you for London Lovering with me, always.

PROLOGUE

I met my first best friend when I was a twenty-three-year-old grad student. Most people have half a dozen best friends long before they turn eighteen. Not me. I was hell-bent and determined to not let anyone get too close. I liked my space.

However, the massive chip on my shoulder, and my weird loner tendencies weren't a problem for Marisa Clarke. She was going to be my friend whether I liked it or not. Thankfully for me, she was one of those people that you were drawn to, even if you swore you hated all bubbly blondes who giggled at everything. Her heart was so full of genuine honesty, love, and happiness that you couldn't help but want that around. She just made you feel good.

We were randomly paired together as roommates the first year of our masters program at Oxford. We clicked instantly over the lyrics to a song called *Love Life* by an American hip-hop band named Atmosphere. She was the only Brit I knew who had ever even heard of the Midwest rap duo. Our first night together in our dorm, we spent hours dissecting every lyric in the song, and eating our weight in Jaffa Cakes.

Looking at us, you'd never believe we were friends. We used to call each other Yin and Yang. Where she had white blonde hair and fair skin, I was dark haired and olive toned. Her entire appearance was luminous. Mine was dramatically darkened by my inked collarbone and shoulder. She was sweet and bubbly. I was straight forward and snarky. Even our clothing styles screamed opposites.

As our friendship blossomed, Marisa began texting me these epic rants about whatever was bothering her that day. It varied from her stance on overpopulation, to how a person walked their dog on campus. I couldn't help but sneak a peek at the texts in the middle of class because they were the best part of my day. I would literally have tears streaming down my face in the middle of a lecture because of her rants. They weren't even funny…that's what made them so laughable. She was so passionate and ferocious and adamantly serious about nothing. It was delightful.

I used to wrack my brain trying to figure out how to one-up her, because she deserved it. She deserved to feel that simple act of random positivity that she radiated out to everyone else in the world.

Marisa was perfectly traditional but gloriously unpredictable. Everything I wasn't.

Even my own mother loved everything "Marisa." She would visit us at Oxford and rave about how wonderful she was. She would even say things like, *"Oh Marisa, you have the loveliest skin…so perfect. Like Snow White!"* Of course, my mother would have to ruin the compliment by bringing the subject back to my *miraculous* existence. She would add, *"You should have seen Reyna as a baby. That's why her middle name is Miracle. She was the cutest, tiniest, most perfect creature. Her skin was so—"*

"Mom! Stop talking about my skin!" I'd scream like a petulant child.

She wouldn't even flinch. Her reaction to all of my outbursts was always just a proud smile. Even when I was a teenager and telling her that I hated her and wished she would die, she would never crack.

Marisa pushed me to be kinder to my mother. She pushed me to try to understand her better. And I'm not an idiot—I knew I was horrid. But I couldn't stop. I was a grown-ass woman and still begging for a reaction from my mother that wasn't her typical approving smile.

I wanted my mother to see me the way Marisa saw me. Flawed. Human. Not just the perfect miracle she named me after. If only she would get mad at me. Be disappointed in me. Yell for once! Lord knows I had done plenty of things to elicit such a reaction.

But she never did. She just continued to shoot that infamous Dr. Miller megawatt smile. It was the same one she served to all of her fear-stricken patients.

Even in times of complete distress, she carried a beam of hope and pride in her twinkling blue eyes.

She was perfect.

So was Marisa.

They were both so good to me.

And I hated it.

I didn't deserve it.

Because in my version of reality, I truly believed that goodness wasn't meant for me.

CHAPTER 1

"Name?" the man barks while pouring a pint of beer from behind the large stainless steel bar.

"Reyna Miller," I answer, shifting on the cold metal barstool.

"Sounds American," he huffs and takes a long drink.

"That's because it is." I'm momentarily distracted as I notice the perfectly symmetrical crease nestled between his two red eyebrows. A perfect, mirrored pair of S's.

"Christ, not another," he exhales heavily after chugging half the beer down. The bar is completely empty and apparently this is how they conduct job interviews here. He sets down his glass of amber liquid and strolls over to me. He's a tall, slender man with a mane of bright red hair that stands straight up on his head. It's coarse and curly and pairs well with the smattering of freckles across his cheeks.

"What brought you to London, love? Fancy getting wet?" he asks with a spicy smirk.

My eyes narrow. This guy is either a pervert or he's talking about the rain in London. I'm inclined to think perv. "A plane brought me," my face and tone serious.

"A smart arse on a job interview? Not bright, America. Not bright at all." He grabs his glass and takes another swig.

I cringe and look down. Damn, maybe I read him wrong. My sarcasm isn't always well received and it has a tendency to let itself out before I can think better of it.

Clearing my throat I add, "My mother's a high-risk neonatal surgeon. She got a job offer at the Chelsea and Westminster Hospital when I was a teenager."

"How old are you now?"

"Are you allowed to ask that?"

"I'm the one asking the questions here!" he shouts out of nowhere and slams his hand down on the bar.

I'd flinch at his outburst if it wasn't so damn funny. I bite my lip to conceal my giggle. It's glaringly obvious that laughing is not what this guy wants me to do right now. His tiny nostrils flare as his brown eyes bore into me. Someone really should tell this crazy red head that he is failing miserably at being intimidating. I may only be 5'4" compared to his six foot, but I'm certain I could take him if he came at me in a dark alley.

"You're probably trying to come up with a way to sue me right now, aren't you, America? Bloody hell, Lariza is going to kill me," he murmurs to himself. The lilt of his accent sounds posh, like he comes from an affluent area in London. He places his elbows on the bar and cradles his chin with his hands. "Come now. Be honest. Are you going to sue me?"

My face splits into a wry grin. I've got him right where I want him and honesty suits me best anyway. "First of all, I don't even know where to begin to look for an employment law barrister. Secondly, all of it sounds expensive and a huge pain in my ass. I'd rather just sit here and get the job instead."

"Are you blackmailing me to get the job?" His eyes widen with worry as his mouth drops into an O. "Fuck me…Do you even have bartending experience?"

"Yes," I answer, feeling a twinge of anxiety. "But continuing the honesty train…it's been a while since my last bartending job."

"How long is a while?"

"Three or four years-ish," I mumble that last part.

"Ish." He rolls his eyes dramatically. "So you take a break from bartending for three years and now you come crawling back to it? What's the story there?" He crosses his boney arms over his chest and looks down at my resume as if he's trying to crack the code. "You have a masters from Oxford? Are you joking?"

Contemplating how I want to respond, I pull my lower lip into my mouth, tasting the chalkiness of my deep purple lipstick. Releasing it quickly, I retort back. "You just asked me two different questions. Which one do you want me to answer?"

He rakes his hand through his hair and it springs straight back up to life. "Fuck me! You do have a degree from Oxford."

I sigh heavily. I didn't want to include my education on my resume, but it killed me to leave it off. Plus, this is a highly coveted job in the service industry and I hoped that it would get me noticed. I nod subtly, confirming his suspicion.

The red head suddenly whoops with laughter, clutching his narrow waist. "What is it with you Americans jumping the pond with your drama? You've got drama, don't you, America?" he asks, attempting to compose himself.

I glare at him. "Who doesn't?" My voice is flat and emotionless. God, I hope he doesn't press this.

"Touché," he replies, cocking his head to the side.

"Plus, the pay here is worth it from what I hear," I add, knowing full well that Club Taint is one of the highest paying nightclubs in London.

"Club Taint isn't your typical English Pub. I hope you realize this, Oxford."

"I do. I've been here before. I also know this isn't a gay bar." I rattle out the information I found online after deeply researching the establishment's history. This club has mistakenly been labeled a gay bar all over London for years.

His expression morphs from angry to impressed. "Oxford! You've put that education to good use, haven't you? I feel like I'm supposed to hate you. But, when you say accurate, lovely things like that, you make it bloody hard!"

I chuckle at the idea that such a simple research act could make this man's opinion of me change so abruptly. "Want me to insult your clothes so you can go back to hating me?" I ask as my eyes trail down his red lumberjack plaid shirt and land on his canary yellow skinny jeans. His clothing isn't a dead giveaway that he's gay, but it certainly doesn't help.

His face falls. "What is it with you Americans?" he shouts. "I suppose your all-black grunge look is supposed to be chic?"

I glance down at my choice of clothing for this interview. I dressed for the job I'm applying for. It is typical bartender attire—a black racerback tank, black skinny jeans, and black ankle boots. I slapped on a leather wrist cuff and bronze necklace, but other than that I wouldn't call it "grunge." When I washed my hair, I even curled my nearly black locks and left them loose and flowing down my back. It's far better than the messy way I typically wear it.

"Americans have absolutely no sense of style. Why the bloody hell do I always find…" He's mumbling to himself as he moves down the bar and lifts the partition up to walk over to me. "I think I'm back to hating you already. Let's get on with this shall we?"

He extends his hand in a motion for me to walk out onto the wide-open dance floor. The dreary London daylight is pouring in through the industrial skylights. There are several white techy-looking dance pedestals stationed throughout. I've seen go-go dancers and drag queens perform on them the few times I've been here so I know they illuminate several different colors when they are turned on.

"Since you've already got the job, I shall introduce myself," he sighs heavily. "I am Frank McElroy. My mate Larry Liza Minnelli, or Lariza, as I often call him, is the owner of this fine establishment. I am currently managing it for him while he's away on medical sabbatical." He cups his hand and stage whispers, "Lipo!"

I conceal a giggle as he continues. "As you already know, Club Taint is not the gay bar most stuck up west Londoners would like to believe it to be. It's what we refer to as a Welcome Bar. We welcome all people and we do not tolerate any type of discrimination. We are diverse, and we appreciate and celebrate snarkiness, sarcasm, and bantering. Think you can handle that?" He winks at me playfully. "Also, we are not a fan of the word bullying. It's turned into an overused, over-rated, sensitive-sally sensation of a word that exhausts the fuck out of me. We're adults for Christ's sake."

"Duly noted," I reply, taking in his exasperated tone. "I'm a straight shooter and bluntly honest, so I think I should fit right in."

"Let's not get ahead of ourselves, Oxford. Why don't you tell me first what happens the other twenty-three hours of the day?" He gestures down to the pocket watch tattoo I have on the inside of my wrist.

My hand instantly covers the offending design that's connected to an entire sleeve of ink, which snakes up to my shoulder on my left arm. I've had this collage for two years now and it still doesn't get any easier when people ask about the meaning behind everything. The truth is, the design came to me in a dream, so that's weird, in and of itself. I clear my throat and reply with the canned generic answer that I give everyone.

"Life," I smile politely. It's the only answer that isn't a lie but doesn't force me to dive into the truth.

He nods and his eyes drift up the rest of my sleeve. "Yes, 4:03 does seem like a good time to rest on. Shall we continue?"

We move through the club and into a long hallway on the far side with several red doors. Frank explains that Club Taint is a nightclub that has different hired acts perform on the pedestals each night. The performers vary from professional modern dancers, to street dancers, to drag queens. They even have one night a week for amateurs to perform. He's extremely insistent on the fact that no one ever strips. I honestly wouldn't have cared if they did.

He shows me the hair and makeup rooms, the master control room for sound and lights, and Lariza's office. At the end of the hall, he pushes through large metal double doors into a back alley.

"This is where you will take your breaks, smoke, whine about your drama, maybe finish designing your other sleeve."

"Um, no actually. This side is done." I touch my collarbone on my right side where I have only three black roses and cursive text that says "We All Die Young" woven intricately inside.

He nods his head approvingly. "It's stunning."

"Are you being nice to me, Frank?"

"Christ no! I'm just still smarting about that lawsuit drivel."

I laugh and we head back inside to Lariza's office. He sits me behind the desk and dumps a bunch of paperwork on my lap. "I'll be at the bar. Come out when you've finished."

When the door closes behind him, I bite my lip to restrain the triumphant scream I want to shout. Damn, I need this job. I can't keep sponging off of my mother, even though I know she'd give me money no matter what. This job is hopefully a means to an escape for me, a way for me to gain a little financial independence and try to forget about how crazy my life has become.

Just as quickly as the excitement comes, a pang of disappointment slides in its place, snuffing out my moment of celebration. I'm twenty-eight-years-old and cheering over a bartending job at a place named after a piece of skin within human anatomy. In fact, the name of the place is rather fitting considering I taint nearly everything I touch. How the hell did I let my life take such a dismal turn?

THREE YEARS EARLIER

Oxford

CHAPTER 2

"Guys, guys, guys! Our second semester schedules are posted! Our schedules are posted! Gosh, let's hope we got our independent study request approved!" Marisa squeals as she launches herself up from the futon, clutching her cell phone excitedly. She yanks my *Macbook* out of my hands and drops to the floor to begin frantically checking the Oxford email system. "It's our last semester here. Our whole future depends on this."

I'm draped lazily on my twin student-housing dorm bed and Marisa's boyfriend, Liam, is left stranded on the futon by himself. It's our final year for our masters program at Oxford and we requested an independent study to help us complete our bridal industry thesis. We have hopes of opening our own high-end bridal boutique in London when we graduate. Liam somehow got sucked into our business plan vortex.

I glance to Liam and he presses his full lips together to conceal his smirk as Marisa screams at the computer for being slow. His honey brown gaze drifts from her to me and we lock eyes knowingly, both wanting to burst out laughing at the tantrum Marisa is throwing.

Liam and Marisa started dating a few months ago. They met randomly at a *Subway*. Apparently, they were both standing in line and the sandwich-maker thought they were a couple. A few awkward shakes of the head and nervous giggles later, the two were splitting a twelve-inch and basking in each other's beauty.

And damn if they aren't beautiful.

Liam's tall and God-like in stature. Lean, roped muscles and an incredibly sexy, yet graceful swagger to his walk. His slicked over golden blond hair is handsome in that boarding school boy type of way.

Then you have stunning blonde and perfect Marisa. We looked like a pitbull and a poodle next to each other. But somehow our friendship worked.

"I can't bloody believe it. It didn't go through! This has to be a mistake. This can't be right!" She stands up and rakes her hands through her long, straight hair.

"Don't worry about it, Marisa. This is grad school. We're grownups, we'll be fine."

"No, Rey. No!" She jumps onto my bed and grabs my cheeks, squeezing them together until my lips form an elongated O. Her brown eyes pierce stormily into my gray. "Do not settle for the system. You are ma lady, you must know this! The system does not rule us. We are not bound by society's standards of acceptance. Who are they to tell us how to live our life? Who are they to tell us what is right and just? Normalcy is complacency. And I refuse to be normal or complacent. I want to shine for what we believe! I refuse to sit back and allow life to happen around us. I will go to the chancellor's office, grab him by his willy and we *will* have victory! And you will love it. You mark my words. I will make this right." In one bounding blonde flash, she darts out our door. Liam and I both look at each other and burst into belly-aching laughs.

"Her exuberance is astounding. How can you not love her?" I say, wiping tears from my eyes.

"I have no idea," Liam replies looking at me seriously for a moment. His intense expression causes the laughter to die on my lips. His mouth is pursed in a way that ignites something deep inside me. "Why don't I ever see a man in your life, Rey?" His eyes turn grave and pensive and they kill off the last few remaining giggles in my throat.

I roll onto my belly and tuck my hands under my pillow, looking at him cautiously. I hate when he looks at me like that. Like he can see right through me. Attempting to deflect with sarcasm, I reply, "I'm not made for loving, Liam. I'm made for being a loner."

"I don't think that's true." He lays down on the futon, mirroring my relaxed position, but never takes his eyes off of mine. "Tell me about your parents. What do they say about your loner tendencies?"

I sigh heavily. Something about Liam always makes me feel open. Vulnerable. And what's worse…I like it. I'm a painfully honest person about everyday things, but I keep the feelings I have about myself quiet. I've opened up to Marisa about some things, but Liam seems to reach me at a different place. And it scares me.

"Well, my dad croaked when I was five, so I don't really remember much. He dropped dead in the shower in our bathroom back in Indiana." I pause and release a shaky breath, avoiding Liam's severe expression. This is what I do when people push me; I get real to make them uncomfortable, hoping they'll stop.

"Fuck, Rey. What happened?" Liam asks, his voice deep and wary.

Liam never stops.

Rolling my eyes, I reply, "My mom found him unresponsive in the shower. She screamed at me to dial 911, but I was only five. I couldn't get past the fact that I was staring at my father, naked on the floor. She was draped over his body administering CPR and I just stood there, watching. I can't imagine dying that way. So *exposed*." Tears slip down the side of my face and I tuck my cheek against the pillow to hide them.

"Christ, you were just a child," he says, shaking his head.

I silently push away his sympathy. I don't want it. I don't need it. That day and that scene are mine and mine alone. "Anyway, it turned out to be heart failure. My mom was hysterical. It's the only time in my life I can remember her showing any kind of emotion like that. Like, *real* love. Seeing that kind of heartbreak sure messes with your urge to ever want to find love."

"It's okay to be vulnerable sometimes," Liam says, cutting into my horrifyingly painful memory. I look over and he stares back at me with an intensity that winds me. He purses his lips like he wants to say so much more but is holding back. "It's okay to let people in. Let them care about you."

"I have trouble letting people see me," I whisper.

He nods knowingly. "I see you."

PRESENT DAY

CHAPTER 3

Three years ago, I was preparing to graduate with my masters from Oxford in business management alongside my best friend, Marisa, and her boyfriend, Liam. The three of us had big plans to open our own one-stop bridal boutique in London. Marisa was going to do sales. I was going to do marketing and promotions, and Liam was going to do accounting. We had a business plan, financial backing, everything lined up and ready to go. The final thing we needed to organize was a commercial property.

Now I'm sitting at a nightclub and writing down bank account info for my paycheck deposits from a bartending gig. Memories start to creep unwelcome into my mind's eye. If I could take back one day, where would I be sitting now instead?

I shake off my walk down nightmare lane and finish up all the paperwork, shuffling it neatly back together. Heading down the long hallway and back toward the bar, I hear voices drifting through the empty club. As I round the corner, I see Frank standing behind the bar, talking quietly to a guy across from him. My eyes swerve to the guest and drink in his notable backside. Broad, chiseled shoulders are on display in a black, long sleeve shirt. The snug fit is showcasing his impressive triceps nicely. I continue my decent down to the sexiest pair of men's jeans that I have ever seen. They're a dark wash and they curve up against his sculpted behind in a way that makes you know he's packing more than just a hot ass.

Frank clears his throat loudly and my gaze shoots up to see him staring at me while I ogle this stranger's ass. My face flames and I smile sheepishly until I lock eyes with...

"Oxford, this is—"

"Liam," I finish, interrupting Frank. My face has to be the picture of disbelief right now.

"Reyna? What are you doing here?" The choked tone of Liam's voice matches my insides perfectly. His face reads like he thinks I'm here for him. My face reads like I'm going to be sick.

"I just gave Reyna a bartending job. How do you two know each other?" Frank asks as the tension grows uncomfortable.

Liam starts, "Reyna and I went—"

"We have mutual friends," I finish quickly, trying like hell to hide the insane emotional turmoil boiling over inside of me. I have no interest in reliving our time together at Oxford. My protective barrier is nowhere to be found. I need to get out of here before shit hits the fan.

Liam's shocked expression over seeing me again after so long now morphs into indignation as I minimize our previous connection. He huffs loudly and I find I have to turn away from his hurt expression. I can't let it affect me. I do not want to go there. Simply the sight of his golden, messily swept over hair and wide, worrying eyes causes a flash of a most unwelcome memory.

Avoiding his penetrating eyes, I begin to feel his gaze drift slowly down my body…like he's got to see every part of me to refresh his memory bank. I'm sure I look a great deal different than the last time he saw me. At the very least, I have a hell of a lot more ink now. Despite myself, I want to know how he's reacting. I glance back over to him as he finishes his perusal. His eyes shift nervously between my eyes and my mouth. The look on his face is so familiar I could cry.

I bite the insides of my cheeks, feeling this strange push-pull motion warring inside of me. It's been three years since I last saw

Liam. Now here he is, standing before me as if no time has passed, reminding me of a day in my life that I was trying desperately to forget. A familiar squeezing ache spreads painfully over my chest

"Do you need anything else, Frank?" I ask. My mouth feels like cotton and it is doing nothing to conceal my emotional state. I'm desperate to leave. My heart feels like it's about to rip out of the top of my shoulders and I can feel Liam's eyes boring into me.

"We didn't discuss when you can start," Frank says, the mirror S's returning to the center of his red eyebrows as he stares at me in confusion.

On shaky legs I lay my paperwork down on the bar, hastily trying to hide the tremble in my hands. "Yesterday. I can start yesterday."

"Brilliant. Be here tomorrow night at seven. We'll show you the ropes before we open at nine."

"Cheers." Offering a weak smile to Frank, I turn on my heel to leave. Blasting straight past Liam, I catch a whiff of his agonizingly familiar scent of cinnamon gum. It's almost more than I can take.

"Rey," he utters softly as if he has a direct line to my thoughts.

As I reach the door, I make the horrible, awful, stupid mistake of glancing back. The expression in Liam's eyes turns my burning ducts to actual tears. The painful remorse in his gaze slices through my heart. It's a look that I always seem to be on the damn receiving end of.

It's the look you get when you're completely shrouded in *loss*.

CHAPTER 4

I walk up the ramp out of the Pimlico Tube stop dabbing at the skin beneath my eyes. Luckily the Underground in late spring feels like a moist hot box, so my tears blend with the light sheen of sweat the other patrons are all rocking.

Running into Liam and having memories that I've locked up tight only to be released to the forefront took me by complete surprise. It immediately catapulted me back to the most miserable time of my life. I wonder how he knows Frank? I wonder what his involvement is at Club Taint? What if he works there? Could I handle that?

After crossing the street, I growl at myself for running off like a weak fool. If I would have stuck around I could have gotten answers and would know if this was a job I can keep or not. Working with Liam is not a possibility I will ever entertain.

Glancing through the lattice windows of the White Swan Pub, I throw a quick wave to Alistair. He holds up a finger for me to wait so I begrudgingly stop, but all I want is a drink and my bed. Who cares if it's only three o' clock in the afternoon.

But I'll wait. Alistair is in his mid fifties and the owner of the pub located a stone's throw from my flat. I met him when I first moved to this part of London three years ago. I ended up drinking so heavily the first night here that I passed out in a booth. He covered me with my coat and stayed at the pub all night until I woke up. He fixed me a full English breakfast and we talked for hours over tea about the difference between Americans and Brits. I'm pretty sure I was still drunk but I remember every ridiculous word of our conversation.

Ever since then, Al has been a staple in my life. I see him regularly and his presence is a comfort. His bald head gleams beneath the hanging lantern above the canopy entrance as he comes to stand eye to eye with me. At 5' 5" he's only an inch taller than me when I'm in flats.

"You get it then?" he asks eagerly, leaning in and dropping a kiss on both of my cheeks. His blue eyes crinkle at the edges with a wide smile as he balls his rag up in his hands.

"I did." I smile politely.

"Well done. I knew you would." He swats the rag at me playfully. "I'm still brassed off you wouldn't come here. You deserve to be doing a lot more than bartending, dear girl."

"Thanks Al. I'll keep you in mind. But this is all I want right now." I swallow a painful knot in my throat that's been present since I left Club Taint.

He looks sadly at me for a moment before he shakes his head and his mouth splits into a genuine smile. "Well, I'm chuffed for ye, lass." He swings the rag at me in a wave. "Pop by later if ye fancy some fish n chips."

"Will do. Later, Al."

"Cheers," he moves to head inside but turns back to me before he walks through the door. "You best call your mum and tell her the news, yeah?"

I half smile and say nothing as I walk the half a block to my building. Alistair is well-meaning, but calling my surgeon mother and telling her about my new bartending job is the last thing I want to do.

I reach my building and jump into the lift, punching the button for the fourth floor. My flat is located in a sweet, quiet neighborhood away from the buzz of tourism on every other street corner. I'm sure it costs a bomb here every month, but I don't pay a dime of it. My mother gifted me this place the day I graduated from Oxford. You'd think that would make me appreciative and grateful. I miraculously manage to resent her for it.

My mother, Doctor Elizabeth Miller, brought me to London from Indiana when I was seventeen. She received a prestigious job offer and research grant from the hospital and dropped everything to take it. Her research project on in-utero neonatal surgery was her life's work, aside from me.

She tried to sugar coat the move with promises of more European travel, a gorgeous townhouse in Chelsea, great education opportunities, anything I wanted. She also attempted to persuade me with how important her research was and how many babies she could save by accepting this grant.

At that time in my life, all I cared about was the fact that she was ripping me out of school before my senior year. I didn't have a lot of friends I was leaving behind. My frank honesty rubbed a lot of people the wrong way and since I just can't do fake, I avoided most of the kids I went to school with.

Regardless, I was a teenager and I wasn't going to go down without a fight. This move was literally the only thing that my mother did to me my entire life that wasn't the usual pampering I was always subject to. I had plans to move back to the States as soon as I turned eighteen. But when push came to shove, there was no way I could afford it all on my own.

Not to mention, I fell in love with London. It wasn't hard. The city breathes history and culture and opportunity. I had the world at my fingertips here. I took weekend trips to Paris, short flights to Barcelona, train rides to Scotland. I was the most well-traveled twenty-year-old I'd ever heard of. How could I leave it all behind when it felt like it was where I belonged?

My strained relationship with my mother didn't improve with my love for London. My entire life she treated me like I was made of crystal and would shatter at any moment. I was born a micro-preemie and she never stopped treating me like I could cease to exist at any second. I would do things to lash out at her and show her how strong I was. Anything to piss her off and evoke some type of reaction. Nothing worked. If anything, she treated me with kid gloves more during the times I was most horrid. It was infuriating.

She was so protective of me that she rented a flat across from the university I attended in London. She was close enough to be a helicopter parent, but far enough away that she didn't seem completely unhinged.

She finally let me move more than a few blocks away from her when I started grad school at Oxford. Then my graduation present was this flat located behind the White Swan Pub near the River Thames back in London. I thought she would have bought me a flat close to the hospital where she worked, but she surprised me with this one. It fits me perfectly.

I hop off the lift and head down the hall toward my door. I know he's here before I even put the key in my door.

"Hey, Hay," I say dryly to Hayden as I round the hall corner to find him perched on my kitchen counter eating a Flake chocolate bar. He's made himself at home like he always does. His messy, copper blond hair looks like it's due for a wash but he's still sexy in that relaxed, don't give a fuck way.

"I got you one," he says with a proud smirk on his face. There's a glass of red wine and two open bottles sitting next to him.

"You better have." I cross my arms and lean against the counter adjacent him. Hayden and I have been in a toxic whirlwind of shitty friends with benefits for almost a year now. Neither of us strong enough to put an end to it, nor happy enough with our lives to want more. "You'll never guess who I've just run in to."

"Who?" He wipes his hands on his jeans and sets the wrapper down on the counter watching me warily, clearly sensing a shift in demeanor.

"Liam," I say simply.

"Liam who?"

"Liam Darby. The Liam. Your brother's best friend. The one who was going to propose to—"

"Don't finish that sentence!" he snaps at me, jumping off the counter. His face is deathly serious. "Where at?"

"At my interview at that club I told you about. He apparently knows the manager, Frank." I shake my head still in disbelief at the odds. "I don't know if he works there or what."

"I don't think he does," Hayden says quickly. "Theo talks about him a lot at the shop. Liam works as a controller at some medical device facility or something. I'm quite certain."

I exhale heavily. Hayden works with his older brother, Theo. They own a high-end, custom furniture shop in east London. Theo does the creating and lives in the loft above the store. Hayden does more of the scheduling and client meeting side.

"Seeing him again was—" I start.

"Weird. I know. I've run into him a few times." Hayden looks out the plate glass door that opens to a small balcony off my kitchen. I can see that faraway look he gets in his eyes whenever his mind drifts back to the time that he wouldn't even let me mention. "What did you say to him?" Hayden asks, refusing to make eye contact with me.

"Not much. I pretty much got the hell out of there. He looked at me like…like I was…a ghost." I shake my head sadly, a look of disgust smearing over my face.

Hayden hands me his glass of wine and I take it and gulp it down in its entirety, relishing the instant warmth that shoots through my blood. I close my eyes and lick my lips, while handing him back the glass.

"I haven't seen him since—"

"Don't say it," Hayden interrupts.

I open my eyes and see him cringing as if in pain. He sets the glass down and snatches the bottle up off the counter and tips it to his lips. If he's this worked up over what he already knows, I shudder to think of how he'd react if he knew the full history of my past with Liam. This is exactly why I'll never tell Hayden. He can't handle it. And I'm terrified at what he'd do if he ever did find out.

After several swallows, he closes his eyes and lowers the bottle. "Easy there, sport." My voice has a menacing tone to it. "We both said we were going to cool it on the drinking."

"You just nicked my entire glass of red!" he retorts.

"You look like this isn't your first bottle, Hayden."

He sighs heavily and glares at me. His damaged, hard gray eyes searching my face for further argument. Mindlessly, he glances down to my chest and the lids of his eyes droop as heat flourishes beneath them.

I instantly know he's no longer angry about the wine.

He begins to stalk slowly toward me—his tall, wiry build gliding silently across the white tile floor. I back up until I hit the half wall beside the fridge. "We said we weren't going to do this anymore, Hayden." I hold my hand out, pressing it to his firm stomach to stop him from coming any closer. I want to walk away, but a larger part of me wants to stop thinking about Liam. And there's only one way to do that.

Hayden sighs and grabs a piece of my hair. He brings it to his lips. "You look sexy as fuck, Rey. I like your hair like this." He rubs the silky, dark strand against his lips. A playful smirk dances in his eyes.

"Nice key change, Hay. But you should take those fuck me eyes elsewhere."

He hunches over and nuzzles his mouth into my neck, licking and kissing a trail up to my ear. "Now why would I want to do that?" he whispers, his voice husky.

I can feel him grinning against my skin as goose pimples flare out on my neck beneath his warm breath. I ball up a chunk of his T-shirt into my fist for some semblance of control. His hands move to grip tightly around my waist and I could scream at my body as it arches into his embrace.

This is exactly what Hayden does to me. He makes me lose all sense of thought and purpose. It's part of the draw. He's a freaking mess like me and I ache for the pleasure I know he can grant me.

"We say a lot of words," he mumbles against my neck and nips playfully. "Let's do less saying…and more fucking."

His words send an instant shock to all my erogenous zones. Suddenly, he shifts his head and swipes his lips against mine in a painful, biting kiss. The taste of red wine passes back and forth between our lips and tongues. My eyes roll to the back of my head as I let his assault intoxicate me.

His tall frame is at an awkward angle, so he slides his hands down my butt and lifts me up. I wrap my legs around his waist and he slams me back against the fridge. The cozy press of his hard on against my center instantly has my groin thrusting into his.

"God, I fucking love your legs wrapped around me," Hayden growls and bites at my collarbone with his teeth as he carries me over to my rumpled mattress on the floor in my living room.

Fuck, I can't resist him. This is what Hayden and I do best. We fuck to forget. We're a mess of dysfunctional, codependent, sex-starved garbage together. And it is hot as hell.

I'm airborne for a split second as he drops me onto my mattress and stares down at me with those smoldering charcoal eyes. He begins unbuckling his jeans and I quickly ditch my own. I slide my panties off as he takes himself in his hand and slides on a condom.

He lowers on top of me and between my legs. His tongue plunges so deep into my mouth that I can do nothing but suck on it. Hard. I match his moan with my own as he slides himself deep inside of me.

"Make me forget," I whisper into his mouth.

"Always." He bites his lower lip and our eyes connect for one painfully hard moment. So many unspoken words pass between us in that one silent moment. So many memories. So much hurt.

We both ache to forget and fuck to ignore.

That's what we do for each other.

That's what we're good for…and nothing more.

Breaking eye contact finally, Hayden growls and begins slamming into me at a punishing pace, over and over. Our bodies making an erotic clapping sound every time he hits deeply inside of me. I slam my eyes shut and focus solely on the climb to the orgasm that I long for. The climb to ecstasy that grants me the oblivion that I need.

The oblivion that allows me to forget.

The worst part of our fucked up arrangement is the fact that Hayden doesn't even know everything about me. My normally, never-fail, blunt honesty is completely nonexistent with him all because I'm too afraid of losing him. If he knew everything about me, then I really, truly would be alone.

After what feels like only moments, his hands grip painfully on my thighs wrapped around him as we climax at the same time. He drops down beside me, and we both lie on our backs, sweaty, panting, and sated; naked from the waist down. Hayden and I stopped with the foreplay a long time ago. We fuck and we finish. That's it. No sexy strip teases. No undressing each other. No pillow talk. Just kissing and screwing. And even the kissing has grown nastier the past year in the hottest way possible.

The familiar self-hatred creeps slowly over me as my heart rate returns to normal. "You need to leave," I croak, my voice hoarse.

In the corner of my eye, I see him nod. He stands, pulling his jeans on as he rises. His sexy happy trail down his lower belly is on full display as he stands above me, his jeans still hanging open.

"You're still my best friend, Rey." He's twitching his jaw from side to side and refusing to make eye contact with me. The self-loathing he feels right now is as potent as my own.

My brow crinkles at his admission. I close my legs, roll on my side, and pull them up to my chest to lie in the fetal position. "And you're mine," I utter softly feeling my heart break over and over. "But you know this isn't good for us."

He looks down and sucks his cheeks into the hollows of his mouth. "I can't lose you, too." His voice cracks and he turns quickly, striding down the hallway and out the door.

I flinch at the loud slam. When I open my eyes, tears spill freely down my temple. I roll onto my stomach, crying myself to sleep, and praying for that freedom once more.

THREE YEARS EARLIER

Oxford

CHAPTER 5

"Bugger! Bugger! Bugger!" Liam shouts, storming into the propped open door of mine and Marisa's dorm room.

"What?" I ask, my eyes flashing wide. I'm spread out on my bed with a million textbooks.

"My parents are visiting from Kent and I completely bloody forgot. I was supposed to collect them from the station, but I have a midterm. Then I told the bloke I work with that I would cover for him for an hour at the lab desk. Christ, do you know where Marisa is?"

"Gone home to Essex, remember? She had that hen night with one of her friends from primary."

"Bugger, you're right." He rakes a nervous hand through his hair.

"Why are you flying off the rails, Liam? I'm right here," I say, standing up and straightening my long black shirt.

"What do you mean?" He looks at me, his brow furrowed.

"I'll collect your folks." I slip my feet into my boots.

"God, no. I can't ask you to do that. They're really…not easy."

"You didn't ask. I'm offering. Actually, I'm not offering. I'm insisting." I grab my purse and sling it over my shoulder. "They're a bit older right? Early to mid sixties?"

Liam's face drops briefly before replying, "Yeah. My mum is sixty-three and my Dad is sixty-four. Why?"

"Don't worry about it. Betha and Alden, yeah?"

"Yeah, I'm surprised you remembered. But honestly, Rey. They'll be fine. They can just stroll around the train station until I'm done."

"Liam! Shut up already. I've got this. Text them that I'll be coming to get them. They can wait here with me until you're done."

He huffs with laughter, "They don't text."

I stand up straight, eyeing him. "Well, send a carrier pigeon then."

He chuckles and eyes me curiously for a moment before I wave him off and head outside to grab a cab to the train station. I hate when he looks at me like that. It makes me feel so…exposed. Once I arrive at the station, I dash around frantically looking for an older couple that look lost. Liam said they rarely ever travel and this trip would be a really big ordeal for them. He even warned me that they'd probably be extra cranky because of his muck up.

I find them easily. Liam's mom is yelling at someone behind one of the ticket counters and Liam's dad is fanning himself with a newspaper even though it's a cool autumn day.

"Mr. and Mrs. Darby! I'm Reyna, Liam's friend. I've come to bring you to campus!"

They eye me with indignation, clearly noting my little bit of ink sticking out from the collar of my T-shirt. Liam's dad, Alden, is a tall, large-framed man with white hair and black-rimmed glasses. His mom, Betha, is short and slim, and dressed impeccably in a traditional British skirt suit. She and the queen would probably be great friends.

I shuffle them into the cab and tell the driver where to take us. "How was your journey?" I ask, attempting small talk.

"Just fine, except for the blabbering prats behind us," Betha whines. "You should have heard the vile things coming from their mouths."

I smile sympathetically. "Are you guys hungry? I know a great pub that has excellent food."

"I'm famished." Alden pats his small belly seriously.

I redirect the driver to the pub that I've been at a handful of times when my mother came to visit. It's located a bit off campus and features more of the locals from the village and less of a student population. I found it my first year here and fell in love with it because they have a board game or cards at every table.

We walk in and Alden's eyes grow wide when he spots a cribbage board on one table.

"How about that one?" I ask gesturing to his line of sight.

"A cribbage board, Alden!" Betha's tone is high and excited.

"This is a right nice pub I'd say." Alden looks to me and his grumpy expression from earlier morphs into cheerful.

I'm thrilled by their excitement over this…and over the fact that I know how to play cribbage. We order three baskets of fish 'n chips and I suggest they try the local ale they brew in house.

"I'm not much of a beer drinker," Betha says.

"You'll find it really smooth. If you don't like it, they have a great chardonnay as well." I smile, feeling a bit jealous of Liam. His parents are so normal. And expressive. It's refreshing.

We get our beers and I'm pleased to see Betha drinking hers appreciatively. Alden is ordering another before we finish ours, but I can tell they are enjoying themselves.

"Let's get on with it, shall we?" Alden says pulling the cribbage pegs out of the back of the board. "We can teach you how to play, love. Don't you worry."

"Oh, I know how to play." I smile at their shocked expression. "I learned from a nurse that used to babysit me when I was a kid. He worked with my mom at the hospital and whenever she was called in for emergency surgery, he and I would play. I've been playing cribbage for nearly twenty years. I hope you guys are ready."

Alden's eyes twinkle with mirth and I instantly see Liam in his expression and a fondness sneaks over me. Shaking it off, we all dig into the game. They're good, really good. They've even taught me a few tricks that I never knew before! Before I know it, over two hours has passed. I shoot a quick text to Liam, telling him where we are and to meet us here. I might need help getting Alden and Betha back. They like the local beer a bit too much I'm afraid.

Liam strides in a few minutes later with a worried expression on his face. When he sees the three of us deep in a game of crib, his wide eyes dart to mine. "I didn't know you knew how to play cribbage!"

"There's a lot you don't know about me, Liam." I say and offer a stoic nod to Betha.

"This bird is skunking us good!" Betha slurs and hoots with laughter as she takes another sip of her beer.

I purse my lips, silently laughing and hoping that Liam won't be ticked I got his parents soused. It's been a great afternoon, honestly. One of the best I've had in a while.

"Well, alright then. Finish this game, so that we can start playing doubles," Liam says excitedly with a determined twinkle to his eye.

And that's exactly what we do. It's actually really fun. I can't remember the last time I've laughed so hard. The banter that Liam has with his mother is comedy at its best. Grinning at each other, Liam and I seem to be having a silent conversation throughout most of the game. It's challenging and playful. Knowing, yet mysterious. It both excites and scares me because I don't fully understand it. I've never had this type of feeling with anyone before. Not even Marisa.

After Betha and I end up skunking Alden and Liam twice in a row, we all decide to call it a night. It's dark out now and I'm quite certain that if we let Betha and Alden drink more beer, we'll be carrying them home.

"Reyna, it was such a pleasure to meet you," Betha says, pulling me in for a surprising hug. My eyes turn wide when Alden wraps his big arms around both of us.

"We hope to see you again soon," Alden croaks.

"What the bloody hell did you do to my parents?" Liam asks, his tone tight with shock.

Alden pulls back and grins dopily at me. "Bloody fantastic afternoon, Rey. I think I like Oxford. And I know I like you."

I laugh and hold the door open for them. Liam grasps my elbow and pulls me back into the entry way as his parents fold themselves into the waiting cab. I look up and his serious expression sends butterflies off in my belly. "Rey, I can't thank you enough for taking care of them today. They're in such a good mood, I don't think they even cared I was missing."

"Liam, it was my pleasure. Seriously, it was fun. Your parents aren't difficult. They're cool. I really like them." I smile, pulling my lip into my mouth and grinning out the window at them.

"Bloody hell," he says and I glance back to find him shaking his head.

Liam's face looks completely awestruck, amazed even. By what I don't fully know. Rubbing his lips together, I can tell he's about to say something serious and I want to hurry out before—

"Rey," his voice is husky and low, "I love how you continue to surprise me."

All good humor from my face vanishes. I feel a coldness prickle over my skin as I snap back to reality. "I said it was nothing, Liam. Just leave it."

PRESENT DAY

CHAPTER 6

"Reyna, honey? Wake up, my miracle."

Loving hands stroke down the back of my head and rest at the nape of my neck, massaging gently, and repeat the gesture.

"Reyna Miracle Miller…It's time to rise…It's time to shine…For you are a beautiful, miraculous child of mine."

My mother's familiar song wakes me from my slumber and I groan loudly in protest. "Just let yourself in, Mom." I roll over to see her standing above me.

She's dressed in a white, linen blouse, and a black, pencil skirt. I glance down to confirm that hell hasn't frozen over and see her *Puma* tennis shoes planted firmly on her stocking covered feet. She always wears tennis shoes. Even with dresses and tights. I've told her how ugly it is, but she claims she does it because she never knows when she might be needed for a medical emergency. Evidently she feels more equipped in comfortable shoes.

I would argue that the skills of a high-risk baby surgeon probably aren't the best for an emergency response, but I know she would just smile happily at me and ignore my snide comment. Deep down, I'd never say those words though. She's a brilliant doctor…that I can't deny.

I crawl off my mattress and realize I'm still naked from the waist down. My mother's gaze flits down to my bare legs and I see the tiniest crinkle in her brow before she smiles. "Need pants? I'd love to grab them for you!"

I shift my gaze to assess what she's walked in on. My place is a mess of dirty dishes, empty wine bottles, and yes, even a used condom on the floor twelve inches from her feet. My flat is a studio layout with room for a living area and sleeping area, but I was too lazy to ever buy furniture. A big king mattress on the floor suits me just fine. Most mothers would nag their children until they purchase proper furnishings for a beautiful flat. Not my mother. My mother finds her daughter passed out, half naked in her bed next to a dirty condom and all she has to say is, "Need pants?"

"I can get my own pants, Mom." I amble over to my closet and rifle through the messy contents. I find a pair of pajama shorts and slip them on. I glance at the clock to see it's nearly seven o'clock. I must have napped for over two hours.

"I came by to see if you've eaten yet. Thought we could pop 'round to the pub. It's been ages since I've seen Alistair. I want to make sure he's still keeping an eye on you." She bends over and picks up the stray wine bottle off the kitchen floor, pausing momentarily as she notices the condom.

I wait for a comment. Instead, she simply plasters on that same annoying smile and walks over to the trashcan. How the hell did this woman give birth to me? Personalities aside, when it comes to appearance, the only similarity we have is our short, hourglass figures.

I hated my double D's and curvy hips when I was younger. I would cry to my mom about my body and she used to tell me that I was healthy and strong. She made me sound like a feeder calf being prepped for slaughter. She would continue by saying since I came into the world as a micro-preemie at only one pound, one ounce, I should be grateful for every single curve God gave me.

It wasn't until I met Marisa that I really learned to love my body. Marisa used to lie on our futon and whine about how clothes "wore her"—not the other way around. She used my body as an example, saying that everything I wore made a statement because I "wore clothes."

Marisa always did have a fabulous way of complimenting people that sounded way too specific to be bullshit.

I scrape my inky hair up into a topknot. I wear it long and tousled most days. My mother's is a short bob that stacks stylish in the back and is graying with age. I am told that I inherited my dad's grayish-green eyes, and it kills me to this day that I never noticed his eyes before he died.

"Are you going to wear that to the pub?" Her blue eyes blink rapidly as she stares at my extremely short, thin gray shorts.

My eyebrows rise as I wait on bated breath to see how this will go down. "Yes. I am. Is that okay?"

Her smile shifts into a genuine laugh. "I'm sure it's not the most shocking thing you've worn in front of Alistair. Shall we?"

I roll my eyes and follow her as we walk down the street and into White Swan. It's bustling with business types, two hours deep into a very happy, happy hour.

"My two favorite beauties," Alistair says from behind the bar, stepping up to the point of purchase machine. "How are my favorite Americans this fine evening?"

"Hungry," I grumble, leaning my elbows on the shiny bar top. Al leans across the bar and double kisses my mom and me on the cheeks. He shoots me a sardonic smile before he turns his twinkling blue eyes back to my mother.

"We are excellent, Alistair. So good to see you again," she says, formally clasping her hands in front of her.

"Good to see you, too, Elizabeth. You are looking well."

"You, too. Business looks good!"

"Aye, it is. It is."

The two of them smile awkwardly at each other for an embarrassingly long moment before Al finally breaks the silence. "Will ye be havin' the usual?" He begins typing into the computer.

"Yes, please. Is that what you want too, Reyna?"

I roll my eyes and nod. God, what is it about my mother that turns me into a sullen teenager every time I'm around her? Al hands us our glasses of white wine and we manage to find a cozy table on the elevated level right by the window.

"So, how did your interview go?" my mom asks, taking a sip of her wine.

"My interview at Club Taint?" I ask in a louder than necessary voice. She nods silently, unaffected by my lack of decorum. "Great, actually. I got the job. I start tomorrow."

She smiles proudly. "I'm not surprised."

"Well the manager, Frank, was." I pause to take three long sips of my wine. Seeing Liam earlier and then watching my mother ignore the shambles of my life on display in my flat have me holding on by a very thin thread right now. "Frank was shocked someone with a masters from Oxford would be applying at a nightclub for a bartending position."

Her brow furrows as she considers her reply. "You've had a tough year."

"It's more than a tough year, Mom," I snap. "Marisa died three years ago. And I started making fucking mistakes before she died, if you recall."

She swallows uncomfortably at the topic she knows I'm referring to, then shakes her head, revealing that same infuriating smile. It's the smile that was my constant companion growing up. The same smile that walked me to school every day until I turned sixteen even though I cried and cried to her about how embarrassing it was.

"Everyone makes mistakes, Reyna. You just need to be happy that you're alive. Marisa would want that." She nods, clearly pleased with this response.

I stifle an obnoxious laugh. "I think Marisa would want to know that her best friend in the world fucked her soon-to-be fiancé the night before she died."

My mother pauses mid sip. My eyes alight as the briefest look of shock flits across her face. I sense eyes on us from the people within earshot. She sets her glass down slowly and leans forward to speak quietly. She hesitates and a moment of regret crosses my mind as she looks around at the people staring. I know this is cruel to do to her. I can feel it in my bones and it kills me. But seeing Liam today has only reaffirmed how truly pathetic my life has become. And how truly out of control I feel.

"Life is a gift, Reyna. Mistakes happen." My mother says, finally. Her blue eyes and fair skin shimmer from the overhead lamp light as she attempts to drive her point into me. "We can't control life anymore than we can control the hands of time. They both continue without our intervention."

That was a funny example she gave considering the fact that I have a pocket watch tattoo stuck at the time of 4:03. "How can you say that we can't control life?" I ask, my voice approaching shrill. "You operate on tiny, one-pound babies, Mom! The hardest, most impossible cases in the world come to you for help. Hell, you operate on them when they are still in their mother's uterus! You intervene every day and you save innocent babies. How can you say we have no control over what happens in our life?"

Her eyes relax and she smiles as if she's prepared to answer this question. "Modern medicine can only take us so far. The rest we have no control over."

No control. She sure didn't look like she gave up control when she invited herself over to the first boy/girl party I'd ever been invited to. Telling the boy's parents that it's always wise to have a medical professional nearby made me turn around and jump right back in the car and refuse to go in.

Tears well in my eyes as the aching feeling of loss clouds over me. My entire life I've lived with this overwhelming emotion like something was missing, like something was wrong about my existence. It felt like there had been some horrible mistake in allowing me to be here.

"Do you ever wonder what it would be like if it were one of them instead of me?" I ask quietly.

"One of who?"

"My sisters."

Shock etches over her face and for the first time in forever, I see a new emotion on my mother's face. "Why would you ever say that? You are here for a reason, Reyna Miracle. You."

"Is that what you say when you pray to them?" My words fly out fast and hard and my eyes narrow in challenge. I feel no remorse for the conversation I know will follow.

She shoots me a schooled expression. "What I say to your sisters in my prayers is not for your ears."

I shake my head. "What about Dad? What do you say when you pray to him?"

"Reyna, please stop."

"Why, Mom? If loss is a part of life, why don't we discuss them ever? You know I can't remember Dad's gray eyes? You've told me I have them but it kills me because I never memorized them."

"You were only five when he died, Reyna."

"And I was even younger when they died but I can still *feel* them," I retort and I'm suddenly overcome with emotion. Feeling my sisters is something I've only ever told one person about. And now she's dead.

My mother's smile is pained and hurting. "I want to see you happy, honey. Let's just have a good dinner. You got a new job today. I don't want to upset you, Miracle."

"Stop calling me that, please!" I exclaim with a shrill edge to my voice.

"It's part of your name!"

"It's a constant reminder of how horrid I've turned out and how wrong life was in picking me."

"Reyna!"

"No, don't say anything. You don't want to upset me, remember?" I push back the wooden chair and stand. I turn to leave but come back and place my hands down on the table and lean into my mother. "I got a bartending job at a place that refers to the area of skin between a man's asshole and his ball sack, Mother. Newsflash! Life is pretty damn upsetting right now."

I down the rest of my wine and turn to leave again.

"Reyna, please stay. We haven't even gotten our food yet! You need to eat." I'm causing a scene and she still has that inane smile on her face.

I pause before walking away to say, "You think talking about the three girls that I shared a uterus with for twenty-four weeks is something that will upset me. Forgive me for losing my appetite."

THREE YEARS EARLIER

Oxford

CHAPTER 7

"So, what do you think of it?" Liam asks me, his eyes squinting with anxiety.

"It's beautiful." I smile and snap the velvet ring box shut and hand it back over to him.

"That's it? Just beautiful?"

I nod and look away, avoiding his gaze. Liam and I are sitting down on the futon in the dorm room. The three of us graduate in a couple weeks and we already have a commercial real estate agent lined up to show us properties in London for our bridal boutique. I should be feeling on top of the world right now. But the closer graduation gets, the more anxiety I feel.

Liam called earlier to ask if he could pop over to show me something he picked out for Marisa. Marisa was out of town, back at her family home in Essex. She was going quad racing with her siblings. Typically Liam goes home with her, but he stayed back at school because he had to work.

My nerves were all over the damn place as I waited for Liam to show up. I had a pretty good feeling I knew what he wanted to show me and that was also probably why I was halfway through a bottle of white wine when he showed up on my doorstep.

"You're full of shit, you know that," Liam says, nearly growling in frustration.

I stand quickly, heading over to my small counter space to replenish my depleting wine. I take a sip and turn to face him. "I'm not, Liam. It's a beautiful ring."

"I know it's beautiful, I bought the bloody thing!" he exclaims as he rises and begins pacing back and forth in front of the futon.

Standing before me now, he suddenly appears completely different without Marisa here. Liam has always been attractive but because he was in a relationship with Marisa, I never let my brain go there. Now I can't stop myself from noticing the way his broad shoulders angle down in a perfect V to his hips, or the way his jeans cling to his muscular thighs. He smooths his hand over his blond hair and turns his warm brown eyes back to me.

"What is your problem, Liam?" I snap, growing agitated by this fit he's pitching in my room and feeling a bit brave from the wine buzzing in my veins.

He throws his hands out at me. "You, Rey! You are my problem. You say you never lie, but I don't think you've ever once told me the bloody truth!"

My jaw drops and I want to argue with him but I remain silent. The strange dynamic between me and Liam has only grown stranger as his relationship with Marisa progressed. He made me nervous like no one ever had. I prided myself on being up front, but somehow, he's managed to call bullshit on me every time.

"Am I exempt? Am I exempt from the Reyna Miller honesty train? You can be straightforward with everyone but me. Is that it?" He props his hands on his hips, waiting impatiently for an answer.

"Liam! I don't know what you're talking about!" I exclaim feeling a rising tension between the two of us. It's thick and makes me crazy nervous. I fidget with my cotton shorts and shirt hem to distract my eyes. "It's a beautiful ring, Marisa will love it. You two are perfect for each other."

"And what about you, Rey?" He steps toward me until he's so close I have to crane my neck up to look at him. The aroma of cinnamon and detergent invades my nostrils. A strange combination, but on him it's positively swoon-worthy. "Who are you perfect for?" he asks, his voice husky.

"No one," I croak and turn my head to look away from him. "I'm not the one for anyone."

He steps sideways to catch my eyes with his again. My brow creases. "What if I call bullshit?" he asks, his voice growing scarily serious as his eyes glance down to my lips for several monumental seconds.

My eyes lock on his full lips for the briefest of seconds. They're a lovely peach flesh-tone and always rest in a seriously sexy pucker. "Don't call bullshit, Liam," I whisper while silently screaming at the desperate urge I have to taste his lips right this fucking second.

"Why not, Rey?" His words are like a cry. His eyes are back on mine now, begging and pleading for something that I can't give him. "I'm a fixer, Rey. It's in me to fix whatever this messed up situation is between us."

"I'm not worth fixing," I say, smiling sadly. Tears betray me as they well in my eyes. "I'm not the one, Liam…I'm no one's anything."

He grabs my face in his hands and presses his forehead to mine. His breath is warm and smells like cinnamon as he whispers, "Bollocks."

"This is so wrong, Liam." I swallow hard as tears slip down both of my cheeks. "You can't do this. I'm not worth it."

"The fact that you can't see that you are just shows what a fucking liar you are."

***

I wake to the sound of drunken voices hollering in the hallway outside my dorm room. I instantly feel a satisfying ache between my legs. Then my whole world comes crumbling down around me. Glancing down to see a hand draped over my back, I quickly turn my head to confirm that it's Liam, even though I already knew the answer.

No, no, no! This can't be real. This can't be happening. A sob escapes my throat and my hand flies up to cover my mouth. Liam jumps at the sound and his eyes fly open. When his gaze finds mine, it all only becomes more real. I leap up out of the bed, taking a loose sheet with me. I wrap it around my body and gasp back several more sobs.

I fumble to turn on my desk lamp. Golden light casts over my room and further points a spotlight on all the horrid things Liam and I just did. It's only four fifteen in the morning and I'm already having my first full-blown anxiety attack for the day. I pull the sheet up over my head, rubbing it quickly on my face as I try to clear the fog over my sleepy-hazed head.

"Rey, are you alright?" Liam gets up out of the bed and places his hands on my arms from behind me.

"Don't touch me!" I scream and turn to see him jump back like I'd bit him.

"What the fuck is going on?" His face is wounded and worried.

"Liam! How can you be so stupid right now? What's wrong? For starters, you're fucking naked! And I just fucked my best friend's fiancé."

His face drops as he realizes the cause of my outburst. He doesn't look impressed. "We didn't just fuck, Rey." He bends over and grabs his jeans up off the floor and pulls them up, sans underwear.

"My pussy says we did," I snap.

"Stop," he growls. "It wasn't just fucking. It was a hell of a lot more to me than that!"

"Oh my God, oh my God! This should have never happened." I begin pacing back and forth.

Liam's jaw muscle ticks violently as he stands there shirtless in his jeans. "I agree, we took this too far, but I don't agree that this never should have happened."

"Are you insane? This won't happen ever again. God! Did you not hear me before…before you…before—"

"Before I kissed you and told you I love you," he interjects.

"Stop!" I scream, covering my ears. The words spoken aloud cause tears to instantly well and fall. Those words aren't for me. Those words belong to Marisa. Beautiful, sweet words that belong to anyone but me. "Don't say that, Liam. You're making this all worse! You don't mean it. You can't. I'm so not the one."

"We've been through all this, Rey! I'm in love with you. I love you. I always have. I was just so utterly wrong before. You have—"

"Liam, no. Stop saying it. Don't ever say it again. Ever. I'm not kidding. You can't say those words to me ever again. Ever!" My voice is strident and panicky. "God, you don't even know me."

"Lies. Again! You know I know you, Rey. This isn't new between us. We've been feeling this for months. I know so much about you and yet I want to know even more." He charges over to me and traps me up against the wall with his arms. "The bottom line is that I know how you make me feel. And I know how I can make you feel. Don't fucking deny that!"

"No, no! You don't get it, Liam. I don't have a lot of friends. Any really. I'm not nice. I'm not bubbly. Most people don't get me. They think I don't care about anything or anyone, but I care about everything. I care what they all think. Marisa saw that. She saw that without even trying. She was my first real friend. The first one I ever told—" My hand reaches up to touch the three black roses on my collarbone as another sob escapes me.

Liam's arms wrap around me and I don't have the strength to push him away this time. I fold into him as his hands stroke lovingly up and down my back as he drops soft kisses into my hair. I let myself cry into his bare chest, melting under his touch. His painfully beautiful touch. It feels so fucking good. So fucking right. But my tears only fall faster knowing just how fucking wrong it all really is.

"I need somebody like her," I croak, my forehead resting on Liam's chest. I'm saying these words for myself more than Liam though. "Marisa makes me feel like I belong here. She fixed whatever was broken inside of me. I'm terrified of what I'll be like without her. I can't…can't lose her!"

He sighs heavily as his body turns hard and tense beneath my hands. "So we won't tell her. I won't say anything. I won't pursue you again. I'll pull out of our business plan." I push back and look into his hopeless eyes. They are glossy with unshed tears as he continues. "I care about you, Rey. I thought I could make you happy, but Christ, I can't be the reason for all of this. This isn't happiness." He looks at me with sorrow and a deep, burning ache that I know could ruin me.

I sniff hard trying to ignore the painful look in his eyes that reaches me on a level I've never been touched before. He looks completely bereft and ruined and I am the cause. These emotions, this angst…it's uncharted territory for me and it's frightening as hell. The crushed look in Liam's expression, and the thought of never telling Marisa what happened, hurts more than the fear I have if I do tell her.

"I can't lie to her," I say finally after mulling over Liam's words.

He closes his eyes and nods like he knew that would be what I'd say. A fleeting look of relief washes over him when he adds, "I'll tell her with you when she gets back tomorrow."

***

The sun is shining bright and beautiful as I sit atop a hill overlooking the Clarke's home in rural Essex. A makeshift wooden swing sways from a nearby tree, blowing in the light breeze.

"You're here," I say feeling her arrival behind me like a light sand storm with no sand.

"Turn around and see." Her voice is cheery and excited.

I turn and lay eyes on Marisa. Her luminous blonde hair is long and blowing in the wind. Her cheeks are rosy, matching her pink lips as her face splits into the widest, most welcoming smile. She's wearing a beautiful yellow sundress. It's so her.

"You have new ink." She gestures to a huge sleeve tattoo on my right arm. There's a large sugar skull tattooed over top of my tricep. It's colored with a deep emerald green and sits as the focal point amongst a bed of sunflowers swirling all around it. I look down at it confused. This is the first time I've seen it. It's stunning.

"Do you like it?" I ask nervously, holding my breath.

"I do." She smiles again as a halo of sunlight shimmers all around her. "But do you like it?"

I stroke it affectionately. "I love it. More than you know." A knot forms in my throat.

Her smile turns sardonic. "How do you know what I know?"

That elicits my first half smile. But it's a sad smile. "I'm terrified of what you know."

Her head tilts to the side and she eyes me curiously. Her long, blonde lashes fan the tops of her cheeks. An eerie silence grows between us and I feel the need to fill it.

"For what it's worth, I'm sorry." I take a tentative step towards her. "It feels like the worst two words I could ever say to you, but if I don't, I think I could die."

"Death would not become you right now." She takes one step closer to me. Her brown eyes gleam.

"I'm not so sure about that. I feel like death most days as it is." I wipe the path of an errant tear that escapes quickly down my cheek. I hate crying in front of Marisa. She doesn't deserve it. She doesn't deserve to watch me cry.

"Why did you do it?" Her eyes are still smiling but her lips are pursed as if she's deep in thought.

More tears fill my eyes. "I wish I knew."

"I think deep down, you already know." Before I can ask her what she means, she adds, "I have something for you."

She takes another step closer to me and holds her hand out. Nestled between her two fingers is a diamond engagement ring. I'd recognize it anywhere. It's the same diamond Liam showed me that he was going to give to Marisa after graduation.

My heart sinks. "That's not for me." I take a step back.

"I know. I need you to return it." She steps toward me again.

None of this is making sense. How does she even know about the ring? "I don't think I should."

"You must. You need to tell him I'm okay." Her tone is more urgent and serious now. "You need to tell him everything is okay. I need you to return this."

She moves to hand me the ring and I step around her away from the hilltop toward the wooden swing. "I don't want it, Marisa!"

"Well, are you sorry or not?" she snaps and her cheery face morphs into anger. A rare sight that I only ever saw when she and I disagreed over music.

"Of course I'm sorry! I can't begin to explain to you how sorry I am!" I scream loudly in her face.

Her face remains stiff. "If you tell me you're sorry I'm going to believe you. You don't lie, Rey. You've never lied to me. I know this about you. Perhaps you lie to yourself." She brushes her hair back and her eyes flash with determination. "So tell me then…Are you sorry for what you did?" she repeats again. "Are you sorry? Are you sorry!" she screams the last question and grabs my hand, slamming the ring down into my palm.

Like a gun went off I shoot up in a cold, dripping sweat. Panicking, I kick all the covers off my legs and shove myself up against the metal arm of the futon, panting heavily. I look around to get my bearings and find myself in my dorm room. The exterior security lights stream in through the curtains, barely illuminating the scary darkness around me. I wipe off huge, fat tears mixing with my sweat-slicked face. Mid-swipe, I pause as I realize my fist is clenched tightly like it's holding something.

Gasping, I look down at my hand, willing myself to open it, one terrified finger at a time. Blood rushes in my head as my final digit lifts and reveals my fist to be empty. No ring. Releasing a huge gust of air, I whisper softly, "Just a dream." Just a horrible, sick dream.

An icky sensation roils over me as I recall the image of Marisa's normally sunny face, screaming. Reality settles over me at the fucked-up insanity of that dream and the tears overcome me again. I frantically pat all over my bed, searching for my phone. Finally my hand clasps over it and I go to dial the only person I want to talk to in this moment.

Marisa's voicemail chimes on. "Hey, this is Marisa. Miss me already? Leave a message!"

I click END and dread washes over me at what I know is to come later today when she returns.

PRESENT DAY

CHAPTER 8

Stepping foot into Club Taint for my first night has my nerves on edge. I was certainly rocking a fierce version of resting bitch face on the Tube the whole way here. I have no idea what to expect with Liam. Going three whole years without seeing him and then having every gamut of emotion pummel me with Frank watching wasn't exactly the first impression I was looking for at this job.

Yes, this may be just a bartending job, but it's a business. And there's still pride to be felt in doing a job well. I may be overqualified with my education, but a job's a job and I intend to give it my all. The past three years I've been sponging off of my mother and doing the odd medical transcoding of her and her staff's audio tapes. It was something I could do from my flat and required zero human interaction—a necessity at the time.

But, now I'm ready to get out from my mother's continued, unfailing support. I'm not far from thirty-years-old. It's past the time for me to get my shit together. My life. My everything. Hayden and I are still a horribly dysfunctional situation, but I'll tackle one task at a time. One day at a time. And right now, Club Taint is priority number one.

As I stride toward the bar, a few random employees are hauling boxes of bottled beer from the hallway and stocking the coolers behind the bar. Suddenly Frank's face pops up from behind the bar and stops one of the employees.

He aggressively rips open the box and grabs a bottle as the young twenty-something-year-old guy stares at him in confusion.

"Don't fuck with me! I'm in a very fragile state!" Frank shouts at the boy who then scampers away once Frank begins chugging the beer. He stops drinking and pants heavily, attempting to catch his breath.

His eyes land on me and roll briefly before walking in my direction. "Lariza actually thought I could run this bloody club. What the bloody hell was he thinking? I'm not equipped for this. I can't handle the stress! These bottles weren't supposed to be here until tomorrow and we don't have the cooler space! This was supposed to be a new product I brought into the club to surprise Lariza with when he returned. It's going to be a hit, but it has to be served cold! The delivery bloke said since they are being delivered cold, they have to remain cold or they taste like shite. We're fucked up the arse we are! Though Christ, a good shag sounds like a bloody lot more fun than this drivel."

I glance back at the stacked boxes. "You open in two hours?" I ask. Frank nods, his face crumpling in worry. "What's CT's Facebook following again?"

"What the fuck are you going on about?"

"Club Taint. You guys have over a million followers last I checked."

"Get to the point, Oxford!" he snaps, the mirror S's between his brows crinkle into tight Z's.

"Open early. You have the staff, it looks like. Send out a social media blast, pay to boost a post to increase your reach. Call it…" I pause and grab the bottle out of his hand to view the label. "Ginge on Top, Early Bird Premiere." I pause and read the slogan below it: *Always just the right amount of red head.* I conceal a snort at the suggestive bubbling head of foamy beer on the label and continue, "Make a flashy graphic with a decent price point and a giveaway drawing for the first thousand that share or retweet the special."

Frank blinks at me slowly, clearly computing everything I spewed at him. "That's bloody brill, Oxford. Can you do it all?"

"You want me to do it?"

"Erm, considering I don't know half of what you just said, I think you have a better shot at getting it done than I do."

I let out a small laugh. "Okay, let's do this."

I make busy work of directing the staff—whose names I forget as soon as they're told to me—to take the beer that doesn't fit into the cooler down into the basement. If they place it by the water pipes or on the concrete, it'll keep it colder than if it were left sitting next to the hot exterior of the cooler behind the bar. I also direct them as to where to station the portable coolers. If we set up two flashy stations at the entry and get a couple of outgoing bartenders over there, Ginge On Top will be all anyone buys when they come in the door.

Frank then sets me up at Lariza's desk where I'm pleased to find Photoshop and the Facebook page open. After browsing through the analytics on the page, I get the demographic that primarily follow Club Taint and use that information to select the ad photo. A sexy, muscular, shirtless, male ginger with a few quick graphics and we're in business. I add a carousel ad with a sexy, redhead female to try to pull in the straight men as well. It's not the primary clientele at CT, but it's good to expand the reach and put the message out there that this isn't a gay bar.

"Now what?" Frank asks with wide eyes.

"Now we wait."

"Wait for what?"

"If you build it, they will come."

"What are you going on about?"

"*Field of Dreams?*"

He shakes his head still clearly confused.

"It's an American classic movie about an Iowa farmer who builds a baseball field because he hears voices."

"We don't have baseball here. We have cricket! Come off it, Oxford! How the bloody hell is baseball going to save my Ginge On Top?"

I bite my lip to stop from laughing at his worried state. "Look." I point to the screen and see that in only five minutes we've already received one hundred and nineteen shares. "They are coming, Frank."

His eyes light up. "Let's get out there, then!"

We head out to the bar and I'm pumped to see a few people coming in the door already; Ginger word travels fast apparently. They're all huddled around the Ginge on Top stand that's set up and looking awesome.

"Here," Frank chucks a black tank top at me as I follow him behind the bar. "Uniform."

I hold it up and in bold, white lettering, it reads, "Taint isn't for the Faint."

"Nice." I chuckle softly.

"Thought you'd like that. Go on, strip. We don't have much time."

I hesitate at first but shrug my shoulders and peel my black tee off. I'm wearing a pretty scandalous lacy black bra, but since I'm not Frank's type anyway, it seems pointless to be shy. A voice clears from behind me and I swerve to find Liam staring right at me with his mouth hanging open.

"Liam, my boy! What brings you here?" Frank crows from beside me. He's completely oblivious to Liam's scorching brown eyes locked on my chest.

My skin heats as Liam's gaze runs up the length of me and lands on my mouth. "Saw the Facebook ad. It looked exciting." His voice is hoarse and he swallows uncomfortably.

"That was Oxford's doing! Isn't she brill?" Frank roars proudly.

Liam finally snaps himself out of his obvious state and looks down smirking. He pulls his lower lip into his mouth and nods in a knowing way like he's sharing some private joke with himself.

"Did you get a Ginge On Top?"

Clearing his throat, he replies, "Not yet."

"Bloody hell! I'll hook ye up, mate. The salesman's name was Lionel…He wasn't even a ginger, but I got wrapped into his boyish charm, hook, line, and sinker! Wait'll you try this. Sit tight."

Frank strides around the bar and up to the entrance while Liam and I stand, staring at each other. A slab of stainless steel is all that separates us.

"You going to put that on or use it as a rag?"

My eyes widen in horror as I realize I'm still standing in my damn bra. I glance over to the doorway and see one of the younger guys looking my way now, too. I mumble some obscenities and turn my back, throwing the small tank top over my head and yanking it down to cover myself. Nice greeting, Reyna.

"How have you been?" Liam asks as I turn back around and find him perched on the nearest stool. He's dressed in a fitted white T-shirt and his hair is thicker and wilder on top than I remember it ever looking back at Oxford. In the three years since I've seen him he's only gotten hotter. His muscles are larger now too, more defined. And his face appears different somehow too. Less innocent and young, more chiseled and sexy.

All of it is making me positively sick to my stomach.

"I've been okay," I reply finally, squelching my desire to run. If I would have run into Liam a year ago, I would have bee-lined away from him so fast. No two week notice, no excuse, nothing. I would have run to Hayden, drank my weight in alcohol and fucked the pain away. But I can't run anymore. I have to start dealing with life again. "How about you?"

He nods thoughtfully, then looks down at my mouth and back up to my eyes. "I've been okay, too. I'm working. That's pretty much it."

Damn, he's still doing that mouth glance thing that he did in Oxford. Whenever he does that, it reaches a place in my lower extremities that makes it difficult for me to think straight. "Do you like your job?" I ask, my voice a bit huskier than I want it to be.

"Not especially, but it's a good company. I'm a controller for a medical supply company. Good benefits. All the good, boring, grownup stuff that you're supposed to care about when you're approaching thirty."

"I missed that memo," I say gesturing to my Taint covered chest. Somehow it seems so utterly frustrating that he's sitting here looking like a damn *Men's Health* magazine model and I'm here behind a bar. A pang of sadness hits me at the idea of our own dream jobs never being acted upon.

"Seems like you're impressing Frank. That's certainly no easy feat." His mouth curves up into a half smile that's genuine and sexy without even trying to be. Damn, I wish I wasn't noticing how much more handsome he's gotten since I last saw him three years ago.

I'm pleased at the compliment but I quickly shake off the warm and fuzzies as reality settles back in. "It's still bartending. Let's not disillusion ourselves into thinking it's something special."

He frowns. "We all do what we have to…whatever works for our own self-preservation." His eyes are piercing and knowing and I fucking hate it. Reading between the lines of that statement is far too painful.

"You still friends with Theo?" I ask, trying to test the waters and see how he responds.

"Yeah, I am."

I nod, unsure what to say next. "You guys have been friends a long time now."

"About three years." He watches me carefully like he wants to say something more but decides against it. "Theo's a great mate."

Silence grows between us as the last time I saw him flashes in my mind's eye. The words I spoke to Liam when I last saw him were so awful, so cruel. I was in hell at the time and leaving carnage all around me. Not wanting to be fake anymore, I ask the question I've wanted to know for the past three years. "Are you seeing anyone?"

His eyes bolt up from the spot on the bar top that he's been staring daggers in to. He cocks his head curiously to the side, and I instantly wish I could take the question back. "No. I'm not having the best luck there."

"Why's that?" God, Reyna. Shut up! Why are you pressing this? He has every right to tell you to fuck off.

Pursing his gorgeous lips together, he eventually replies, "My best guess is that I seem to find the girls who are broken and in need of fixing. Which isn't all bad. They do need fixing, but I'm not the man for the job. Someone else already is."

His candid reply shocks me. "Sounds familiar." Our eyes lock for a heated minute, saying so much more than words ever could.

Resolution flickers over his face. "I heard you were hanging out with Hayden a lot."

This feels like a bucket of water thrown in my face and that painful longing between us is immediately doused. My protective guard shoots up. "It's not a lot. Let's not go there, please." I busy myself with a rag on the bar, attempting to ignore his penetrative gaze on me.

"Why not?" He stands from his stool and I look up and Liam's face is wide and curious.

"It's nothing. Why do we need to talk about it?" I snap defensively.

"Why do we not?" Liam's arms cross over his chest in that annoyingly intimidating way he has about him. It's alpha and it's hot, but right now, it's just annoying.

"Because it's none of your business." I bite my lip nervously, trying to figure out why I'm getting so defensive over his questions about my involvement with Hayden. What am I to be ashamed of? Why can't I tell Liam we're friends? Because I know deep down, that's not all we are…and I don't want to lie to Liam.

"So you can ask me if I'm seeing anyone, but I can't ask you? That makes a lot of sense, Rey."

"You didn't ask me if I was seeing anyone. You asked me about Hayden." *Specifically!* I want to shout.

My reply stifles his next response and his angry jaw muscle flares out. He nods, his eyes hard and closed off. "I think I've heard enough."

He turns to walk away and I feel a panicky desire to find a reason to make him stay. It's confusing as hell. I've wanted to avoid this man for the better part of three years and now that he's leaving, all I want to do is reach out and grab him.

"Take care, Rey." His face is stony serious.

Unsure what else I can possibly say to save this exchange, I say the only thing I can say after all the pain I caused, "Take care, Liam."

CHAPTER 9

Nothing like being sprawled out over the top of a man's naked body and not totally remembering how you got there to make you feel like you've finally hit rock fucking bottom.

Lying on my back, I feel the rapid rise and fall of Hayden's chest beneath me. His quick breaths match my own. His sprinkling of spiky blond chest hair is scratchy on my sweat-slicked skin. Swallowing hard, I attempt to remember how we even ended up in this position? My body sprawled out perpendicularly over his on top of my mess of a bed. What kind of *Cirque du Soleil* shit did we attempt this time?

Maybe if I focus on the ceiling fan blades spinning painfully slow above us, something will come to me. I blink one eye and then the other to see if that helps. Now the five blades look like twenty. That can't be right.

"That was a new one, even for you Rey-Rey," Hayden says, his voice scratchy and hoarse from our exertions. He drops a kiss on my shoulder.

Shit.

I so can't remember. That can only mean one thing:

I'm drunk.

Drunk.

Drunk.

Drunk.

So very, very drunk.

The air of my apartment feels balmy after the rapid cardio workout we just performed. All that panting and moaning and groaning and screaming. Fuck. We were loud. I was definitely loud. I can remember that much.

"Shut up, Hayden," I groan and attempt to peel my sticky body off of his. His hands band around my waist and pull me back against him. He finds my breasts and begins kneading them playfully, tweaking my nipples in the process.

"Stop," I groan.

"I'm not complaining babe. That position was hot as hell." His breath is warm on my ear and reeks of beer and cigarettes.

When I continue to fight his embrace, he finally lets me get up. I stand, feeling stiff and sore in all the wrong—or right—depending how you look at it—places. I kneel over and pull the blanket up off the floor, searching for my clothes. A shirt, panties, anything. I'll take anything at this point.

"Is that one new? I don't remember it," Hayden drawls, rolling over on his side and eyeing my new marking along my ribs. "God your ink is sexy as fuck." He reaches out and gently scrolls his fingertips over the newly healed ink.

I defensively turn away from him to conceal the new quote I got from the song *Love Life*. It's a gorgeous, script font across my left ribs that says, "Just remember it all, the beauty as well as the flaws." I so don't want to talk to Hayden about the meaning behind a quote from mine and Marisa's favorite song. It's too personal and it's too deep and just…no.

Feeling annoyed by his heated perusal, I snap, "Don't look at me. You shouldn't even be here." I hate that he calls my ink sexy, too. It's not sexy. It's…it's the opposite of sexy.

"Why don't you stop saying that and come back to bed."

I stand up and stare at him incredulously. God, this is a new low, even for me. Hayden and I swore we'd stop whatever it was we were doing. Why do we keep coming back to each other? The answer to that scares me.

I frown at him and finally catch a glimpse of my shirt beneath his feet. I walk over and grab it, quickly yanking it down over my head. Fucking crop top. Real helpful. He grins dopily at me.

"I want you to leave, Hayden."

His answer is a scowl, appearing momentarily wounded and then shrugs his shoulders, tossing me a flirtatious grin. God those fuck me eyes of his. If I wasn't already half naked, I'd feel like it by the way he looks at me sometimes.

Hayden is bad for me. I'm even worse for him. We're both damaged and fucked and nearly unrecognizable to our families. I know this. Why do I keep coming back to it…to him?

Here I am…continuing to fuck up our lives at any cost. Maybe if I wouldn't have been drunk myself, I could have been stronger. I could have said NO when he showed up hammered on my doorstep.

God, I'm weak.

God, I'm pathetic.

God, he needs to leave.

"You have to leave, Hayden," I say, tossing his pants at him. "Go to wherever you were on your way to and get out of my apartment."

Hayden throws his legs off the side of the bed and sighs heavily. "What's the point?" he asks sadly. "We always end up right back here." He pats the bed gently with both his hands and flops back onto his back, his softened erection showing renewed signs of life.

"Go! I don't want you here," I shout again and toss his shirt at him to cover up his dick. I'm sick of looking at it. I'm sick of fucking it. Why do I keep doing this shit?

"Rey," he hiccups and sits up, blinking slowly. "Stop treating me like some dick you just fucked from the club. You're…Fuck. Sometimes your honesty just bloody hurts."

I groan, dropping to my hands and knees, searching beneath the mounds of sheets and blankets for my shorts. "It's the truth, alright? We are the worst best friends to each other ever. I mean, we aren't even fucking for fun. We're not fucking for love. We fuck for all the wrong reasons. Sick, dark reasons. We suck so much, Hayden."

He grabs me by my arms and hoists me up so I'm perched on my knees and eye level with him. "You don't suck. I suck. I'm pathetic."

"We're not playing the pathetic game again, because no one ever wins. We're both shitty. Let's just try to be a less grade of shitty for once in our lives."

"You don't see it." His eyes lazily look over my entire face before he sighs and mumbles, "I don't want to be anything."

"What do you mean by that, Hayden?" I ask him seriously.

"My family is throwing a fucking suicide benefit in a couple weeks. A benefit that they started because of the serious nothingness I have become. Do you know how sickening that is? Do you know how pathetic that makes me feel? Has your mother started a charity focusing on the lowly, degrading, nothingness of your transgressions?"

I flinch at him mentioning my mother. "The list is much too long I'm afraid. There's no clear category for 'disappointing child turned tattooed, slutty back-stabbing rebel' for her to start a benefit around. Though if I give her enough time, I'm sure she'll find a way to make it into one so it looks good on stationary."

"Whatever fucked up shite we have going on here is the only time I feel anything. The rest of it…It's all just too much, Rey."

"Hey!" I shout at him and his droopy head snaps to attention. "You're not being an idiot are you?"

He frowns at me. "No more than normal. You?"

"No more than normal."

"Fair enough," he nods solemnly steeling himself to look more alert. "I need to go anyway. No need to kick your best mate out." We both stand and he clumsily dresses back into his clothes. His tall muscular frame looks hunched and run down. He needs to stop drinking and start exercising again. We both do.

"You're taking a cab right?" I ask seriously as I guide him to the door. "We don't need another incident."

He flinches and snaps, "I'm not going to fucking kill myself, Rey. Leave it the fuck alone!"

"Hey!" I shout at him. "Don't talk to me like that!" I eye him seriously but try not to be too rough with him.

"I'm sorry," he grumbles. "I hate that shite though and you know it. I get it enough from my mum, I don't need it from you. You're supposed to be my escape."

I swallow the knot forming in my throat. "I know, Hayden. But we can't escape everything forever. We've got to get back to our lives and stop doing this. We're toxic. Our pathetic-ness knows no limits! We have to set them."

"Limit our pathetic-ness? Sounds impossible. There's too many reminders of it everywhere." He glances over to the picture I have on the entryway table. I flinch at the location of his gaze.

"Please go, Hayden," I quietly echo again.

He nods sadly and turns, pulling me into a hug. My short frame barely reaches the bottom of his chest. He kisses me briefly on the forehead and then slumps off.

Closing the door, I mindlessly walk over to the picture frame on my hall table. My heart aches before I even look at it. I pass it every day and every day it aches. I thought eventually it would ache less. It doesn't. It continues to ache every day and I relish that ache. I hope it never stops. And anytime I feel the ache lessening, I get new ink to remind me why I crave that constant ache.

That ache is my reminder of how I fucked everything up so monumentally.

THREE YEARS EARLIER

Oxford

CHAPTER 10

Explosions.

That's what it feels like my life has been full of. A series of monumental explosions that have shaped and shredded every single part of me. Up until today, the explosions weren't entirely self-inflicted.

Now, they are.

After my horrid nightmare of Marisa on the hillside, I still can't manage to get myself up and clean the wreckage all around me. I can't even answer my phone that keeps ringing and ringing. All I keep doing is envisioning Marisa coming into our dorm room and having her whole life come crashing down around her.

She's going to lose her boyfriend.

She's going to lose her business partner.

She's going to lose her future.

She very well may lose her best friend.

I've fallen from grace, but I will devote my entire life to coming back if she'll let me. I know loss and I know she'll need me to get through all of this. As strange as that sounds—especially considering I'm the one who caused all of this—I'm the only one that can be there for her in the way that she'll need.

If she grants me the opportunity to atone, to make amends for what I did. Just two little words are all I'm asking her to hear from me.

I'm sorry.

I just need two teeny, tiny, simple words to make all of my guilt and anxiety and dread over what I did to be forgotten.

And if I'm lucky…forgiven.

Loud pounding echoes through my room. "Reyna. Rey! Open up," Liam's voice shouts from the other side of the door.

What's he doing here? We decided I would tell Marisa by myself once she returned from her parent's place. If he's having second thoughts, I don't want to hear them.

"Rey, it's an emergency," his voice cracks on a painful whimper.

I jump up instantly and wrench open my door, my eyes wide and worried. On the other side is a disheveled mess of a man who resembles Liam. His face is white and coated with a sheen of sweat. His jaw is slack and his eyes look like they are about to roll into the back of his head as he blinks slowly, looking anywhere but into my eyes.

"It's Marisa," he says, his voice rising in panic at the end.

"What?" I ask, instantly on alert and somehow knowing at the same time what he's about to tell me.

"She…she…" his words cut off as he struggles to say them. "She's gone, Rey. There was an accident and…" His face crumples, as he can't bring himself to finish the sentence.

Outside, my fearful expression morphs into a flat, emotionless statue. My eyes pull back into tight slits. My hunched posture stretches so I'm standing erect, my posture perfectly straight.

Liam's voice continues, "It was…there was a quad accident on the property. They said she was gone when the medics arrived."

Inside I'm crumbling.

Imploding.

Shredding.

Disintegrating.

I nod solemnly as if he's just told me the day's homework assignment. Finally, I hear my voice reply, "I'm so sorry for your loss, Liam." I turn my lips down into that sad expression that I remembered seeing at my father's funeral when I was only five-years-old. All these people kept patting me on the head and saying the same thing over and over. All their faces looked the same. Wrinkled and contorted in a way that was anything but sympathetic. It was disgusting. And here I was doing the same thing to Liam.

I blink and two hot tears escape down my face. I wipe them, confused at how they formed and fell without my allowance. I didn't permit them to fall. I didn't permit them to exist! Damn these tears. Damn them to hell. My chin begins wobbling and more tears join the first betrayers. Feeling suddenly woozy, I reach out to grab the doorframe to steady myself.

For the first time Liam looks straight into my eyes and that's when he really loses it. He releases a strange guttural noise that doesn't sound human. He reaches out to embrace me and I put my hand out to stop him. I shake my head no over and over and over. My vision blurs from how fast my head is shaking back and forth. Feeling a painful crescendo within my body has me retreating back into my room and away from him. I need space. What's coming is scaring the daylights out of me.

He follows me inside and reaches for me as I turn away and drop down hard on my knees. My mouth opens in a silent cry. Thick spit clings to the back of my throat as I ball my fists up to my chest and scream a loud, blood-curdling scream.

This has to be a lie. This has to be a nightmare. One that I'll wake up from any second now. Life was bad enough before this. I don't need more added to it. I need to get to that point in the dream. That point in the dream when it becomes so intolerably scary you don't think you can take another second of it. That point when you think if you don't wake up soon, you're truly going to die inside the dream and be gone forever.

Two large arms clamp down around me and rock me back and forth, sobbing alongside me. All the noises seem like they are coming from someone else. They don't sound anything like me. Who's making all that noise? They must be going through something really tragic right now. How sad for them.

"I'm so sorry, Rey. I'm so, so sorry."

Liam's voice cuts into my internal warring and I glance over my shoulder to see him holding me in a weird, squatting stance as I sit in the middle of my room on my knees. This is real. Those sounds are coming from me. This isn't a dream.

This is yet another explosion.

This one so much worse than the others…because of what I did. Because of what Liam and I did.

"I need to be alone, Liam," I grind out on a painful cry. I stand up, pulling out of his hold.

He stands in front of me, reaching out cautiously like I might explode if he pushes the wrong button. Slowly he replies, "No, Rey. I don't think you should be alone. I want to help."

"No Liam, I need you away from me." I step back and duck over to the door, opening it for him to walk out.

He scrubs his hands down his tear-stricken face and says, "Please, Rey, let me hold you. You're not the only one hurting."

"I don't give a shit!" I scream, "I need you out of my life. Don't you get that? I'm a walking explosion, Liam! Get the fuck out of my wake…and get the fuck out of my life."

"Please, Rey," he walks toward me.

"Go!" I cry out and shove him out the door. "I want nothing to do with you. Nothing." And the last thing I see before I slam the door in his face, is that look.

That haunted look of remorse.

***

I never got to say those two little words. I never got to get them out. I completely and utterly betrayed my best friend and I was fully prepared to grovel and spend a lifetime trying to win back her trust.

Because she was worth it.

She was worth trying to win back. Her friendship was that special. And now she was dead.

"Reyna, honey. Have you eaten?" my mother croons into my ear as we stand in the living room of the Clarke family residence in

Essex. The same place that Marisa died. How utterly morbid to have the funeral here.

I cringe away from her touch and shake my head in disgust. "I'm not hungry."

I glance over to her and she's giving me one of those pinched, awful smiles that I despise. It's the smile that she gives me when she wants me to do something but I refuse and she doesn't want to look upset.

My mother is dressed in a simple black, long-sleeve dress with black tennis shoes. I'm dressed in a pair of black leggings and a long black shirt that goes down to my thighs. I couldn't bother doing anything special to my hair, so it's pulled back into a messy ponytail. I don't even remember the last time I truly brushed it.

"I understand you not wanting to eat. You lost a very dear friend. Marisa was so special, but so are you. You need to remember what a true miracle your existence is my love—"

"Mom! Stop!" I snap loudly and everybody's eyes swerve over to me. Staring at me is a room full of idiots in black, all offering that same ridiculous pinched smile that's shaped like a downward pointing crescent.

One set of brown eyes stand out from all the others. Liam is standing out on the porch next to Marisa's older brother, Theo. He eyes me through the open doorway and then looks away just as quickly.

I blink and tears begin to fall down my face. I storm past my mom through the house and out the back door by the kitchen. I burst out into a gray and dreary day of drizzling rain.

"Fuck me!" I exclaim, feeling instant relief at being out of that hotbox hell of a house. I take in the Clarke family property. Their backyard consists of several acres of rolling English hillsides. It's gorgeous countryside, even in the rain. So green and lush with various strips of hay rows scattered throughout. I tip my chin up to the sky and allow the mist to moisten my already wet face. Maybe it'll rinse the tears off and give my heart a break for a minute. "This is all such bullshit," I say quietly.

"You can say that again," a voice says from a distance.

I look around and see Marisa's brother, Hayden, sitting down on the ground beneath a small overhang and leaning against an old stony wall side of the house. Marisa had three siblings. Her older brother, Theo, her younger brother, Hayden, and a teenage sister named Daphney.

I'd met Hayden once before the funeral, when I came back home for a long weekend with Marisa. He was four years younger than me and seemed a bit like a wild child. Playful, even. Marisa was so desperate for me to see where she grew up and meet her siblings because she said it was so magical. And she was right, it was. So magical I never came back.

"You look like you need a drink," Hayden states, shaking a bottle of wine in front of him invitingly.

I walk over and slide down the stony wall to sit down. He hands me the bottle and I tip it back to my lips and take a generous drink. The warmth it spreads in my throat is a welcome contrast to the raw ache I've been feeling for the entire week since finding out about Marisa's death.

"You're the roommate, right?" he asks as I press my sleeve to my mouth and hand him back the bottle.

"Yeah. And friend…kind of. I'm Reyna."

"I'm Hayden." He reaches out and shakes my hand formally. He then pulls out a pack of cigarettes and offers one to me. I shake my head so he lights one for himself and takes a long drag. "We've met once, right?" he asks, blowing out smoke while talking.

"Yeah I came out to visit with Marisa once. It was a couple years ago. I haven't been back."

"Why not? Because it's all bullshit?" he winks playfully at me.

"Actually, no. I loved it here." Being honest, I add, "It was just too perfect."

He arches one brow sardonically, so I continue.

"You and Daphney got in this huge argument over the kind of pie your mom was going to make for dessert. You told Daphney she was a prissy baby and she started to cry." A maniacal giggle escapes my mouth mid-sentence. "Sorry. That's mean of me to laugh."

"By all means, be honest!"

"No…I mean…it's a compliment really. You guys just all argued and fought and teased each other mercilessly. There was tons of drama…never a dull moment. I was so envious of it that I avoided ever accepting another invitation from Marisa to come visit again."

"Blimey. That's messed up." He offers the wine back to me and I take another swig. "So you know the boyfriend then? You were all at Oxford together, right?"

I nearly choke on the wine. "Liam? Yeah, I know him."

"My brother, Theo, and Liam have been talking I guess. Have been ever since Marisa…died." He swallows uncomfortably. "Theo says Liam was going to propose. Is that true?"

His gray eyes pierce me with an urgency that shows he's basing a lot of weight on the answer to this question. I take one more drink of the bottle and hand it back to him, nodding a silent yes.

He sighs heavily and takes a pull from the bottle with the same hand that's holding his cigarette. "Life is fucking bull shite is right."

PRESENT DAY

CHAPTER 11

"My brother is fucking seeing someone."

I pause, mid swipe of a glossy black polish I'm applying to my toenails. Hayden appears from the hallway. He's dressed in a pair of dress slacks and a wrinkled dress shirt.

"This is a bad thing?" I look back down and finish my final toe, then screw the lid on tight and stretch my legs out in front of me. I give them a little wiggle to help them dry.

His face morphs into indignation. "Considering I know fuck all about her, yeah. I mean, why does he think he can just—"

"Date?"

"It's more than dating," he grumbles. "The prat is acting like he's in love. It's maddening."

"Why?"

"You know why, Rey."

I pause and take in his slouched stance and defeated expression. I know exactly why Hayden is upset, even if he won't say it out loud. For the past three years, the Clarke family have all been living in a state of darkness. Still stuck in an endless grief of mourning over the loss of Marisa.

The Clarkes are an affluent family, so they're very private about their struggles in some ways, but public in others. For example, Hayden's mother self-medicates with charity work. They have a suicide gala coming up that they do every year. It's an extremely sensitive subject for Hayden because without actually saying so, he's the reason they do it. His history with booze, pills, and reckless driving can't be denied. He has a track record. I try not to come down on him about it. He already isn't trusted with a car from his parents. I just make sure he's safe and never driving when I know he's been drinking.

Which is most days to be honest.

If anything, I'd call Hayden a high functioning alcoholic. He drinks to oblivion at night but is up and working every single day. Working doesn't mean he doesn't have a problem, but at least he can't be blamed for ruining the family furniture business

Hayden's sister, Daphney, struggled in school after Marisa's death. She was flunking in several classes and eventually had to drop out and take an entire year over. Daphney texts me on occasion. She's not even twenty-years-old and worries about her brother. She knows that I see a lot of Hayden, so I think she feels closer to him when she keeps up with me. Hayden's older brother, Theo, is the most mysterious. Definitely a silent mourner. He's very standoffish and I've probably had one whole conversation with him in the five years I've known the Clarke family.

Hayden says his family is living in "the darkness." I tell him that's called depression. And I fit in quite well with the sorry bunch.

"When I see Theo smiling, it makes me so, so…" Hayden's jaw clenches down and his fists ball up. "Do you have anything to drink? Something hard."

I nod and he helps himself to my liquor cabinet. He pours vodka into a glass of ice and adds a splash of club soda. This is obviously upsetting Hayden. I suppose Theo dating would be a sign of him moving on without the rest of the family. This shocks me even because Theo has always been the silent, cryptic one I could never figure out.

"Let's go out tonight, Rey," Hayden says buoyantly.

"Out?"

"Yes, out. What time are you off work?"

"Midnight actually."

"Perfect, I'll just come to the club and wait for you. There's a new twenty-four hour place I've been wanting to check out."

I want to argue with him and tell him we shouldn't go out clubbing after midnight when we're supposed to be trying to cut back on our reckless behavior. Logically, I know what we're planning is bad for us. But it's so much easier to give in to the temptation of oblivion than to deal with the reality that Liam is around and looking better than ever.

The attraction I still feel for him feels like the largest bubble of guilt resting heavily on my chest. I didn't expect him to look so good. I didn't expect him to get even more attractive and more intriguing. There was always something special about him in grad school, but because he was with Marisa, I never even entertained the idea.

That was until we both went way too far.

The sharp tightening in my chest is returning. It's that same painful feeling that was my constant companion the days following Marisa's death. So many memories of her are coming to the forefront of my mind now that Liam and my pain are back.

Instead, I agree to Hayden's plan and he hangs out and watches me get ready, annoyingly commenting on every selection I make as he sips his V&T. I load up on my makeup, prepping for our night out after I get off. My eyes are an unusual gray. At times, they look olive-green; other times they look emerald green. I can't help but wonder if my father's did the same thing.

I pair my black CT tank with olive green skinnies, and then tuck a glittery black top into my purse to change in to later. I throw on my favorite black ankle boots and Hayden walks me to the Tube stop, telling me he'll stop by later. He kisses me on the forehead and turns to flag down a cab.

I briefly worry about how much more he'll drink before I see him again. Then I relax when I see him fold his tall frame into a cab. He's getting in a cab, Rey. He's being smart. He's got this.

Back at Club Taint, I'm in the process of re-stocking the liquor bottles that are running low, combining the ones with less than half inside and replacing the empties. My first night last night went better than I expected. After Liam left, Frank passed me off to a large fellow named Callum to show me the ropes behind the bar. Callum is a towering 6' 6" and has dark skin, black hair, and a goatee. He's hefty but loaded with muscle. Honestly, he looks more like a bouncer than a bartender, but his thick Turkish accent is positively panty-melting to the loads of hen parties that come in every night.

"Oxford, you came back for more pain, did ye?"

I roll my eyes as he tosses a bar rag at me. "Callum, you can call me Reyna. I wish Frank would."

"People can wish lots of things of Frank that never come true. That man cannot be controlled."

"What's his story anyway? He doesn't seem to be too keen on bar management," I ask, pausing my work and propping my back against the bar.

"This is true. Frank is not very familiar with working in general. He is…as you say…very posh. His family is quite famous in London high society."

"Interesting. What do they think of him managing a place like Club Taint?" This makes me feel like Frank and I have more in common than I realized. A little rebellion against the parental units is something I'm very familiar with.

"Aye, Frank doesn't really talk much about them, but I don't think there are good feelings with his family. He seems to call his friends his family and spends all of his time with them. His roommates especially. I've met them all at a Tarts and Vicars party not so long ago. They are very special indeed. There's a dynamic in that house unlike any I've ever seen before."

"You talking about me, Callum?" an American female voice says from behind me. I turn around to find a gorgeously tall brunette with the most stunning blue eyes I've ever seen.

"Finley!" Callum strides past me, pops the bar top up, and engulfs her in a huge hug. "I haven't seen you in ages."

"I know!" Her smile is so genuine I can't help but smile along with her. I realize what a complete loser I must look like so I quickly wipe the grin off my face.

"And where is this Brody? I have still not met him. Frank raves about him, though. You might want to have a word with him about that. He seems to somehow know very intimate details about your husband."

Finley laughs heartily and shakes her head. "God! Frank and Beans is too much sometimes. He has a bit of a man crush on my hubby after getting an eyeful during an unfortunate hallway incident. I'm glad to hear my husband's reputation precedes him, though!"

"That it does. Oh, Finley, this is Rey, our newest bartender." Callum gestures to me and she raises her eyebrows, taking in my tattoo sleeve briefly.

"Hey, Rey!" Finley reaches her hand out and I take it in a firm shake. "Nice to meet you. Frank is your boss right now? Girl! I feel sorry for you!"

I can't help but smile. "Oh, he's not all bad. Just a little…challenging."

She giggles and winks at me. She looks around cautiously and when she decides the coast is clear she leans across the bar and speaks in a hushed tone, "You're totally right. He's actually one of the best. But you'll survive a lot easier around him if you go toe to toe. Start with calling him Frank and Beans. He'll love that." She tweaks her eyebrows playfully.

"I can do that." I grin back at her.

"Fin Bin!" Frank suddenly cries from the back hallway. "I'm back here!"

Finley shoots Callum and me one last stunning smile and saunters back down the hall. I watch Frank embrace her in one of the most genuine hugs I've ever seen and can't help but wonder what it's like in that house that Callum says they all live in together. What would that sense of family friendships be like? Would I have that with Marisa and Liam if things hadn't all gone so horribly wrong?

Callum makes himself busy, continuing my training and before I know it, it's eleven o'clock and I'm slinging drinks like a seasoned pro. The clientele at Club Taint is varied and unique, but I feel like I fit right in. My tattoos were never something I did to stand out. They were memorials that I felt compelled to represent. They were such a large part of me that I couldn't imagine myself existing without them. But it's always the first thing people notice on me.

I watch a group of girls down a row of shots I mixed and am clanking the glasses together to throw into the washer when a voice slurs from above me. "You look positively shag-worthy back there."

I look up and see Hayden's familiar droopy expression gazing down at me from the other side of the bar. "Well, you've shagged me so your opinion is a bit biased," I reply, shooting him a sardonic half smile.

He slumps down into a barstool and slaps a ten pound note on the bar top, "Beer me, wench!"

I shake my head and grab him a Ginge on Top bottle, popping the top off with my bottle opener attached to the loop on my jeans. I set it down in front of him and see that he's well on his way to completely fucked up.

"You look like you've been having a good time."

He smiles dopily at me. "I was just round the pub from my flat. Just had a couple." He squints as his fingers form an inch of space in front of his eyes. "You ready for a night on the town?"

"Yeah, I guess so."

"You guess so?"

"Well, it doesn't seem quite as exciting when you're already three sheets to the wind."

"Please, Rey. I'm hardly wasted. I'm ready for a night of fun. Don't start with the nagging."

His comment stings and I won't tolerate it. "Don't fuck with me like that, Hayden. I *nag* you about one single thing and you know exactly why I do. I'm on your side, always."

He glares at me. "You could have fooled me. You've been different lately."

"That may be true, but I still don't deserve to be categorized with everybody else. That shit hurts."

"Well, why don't you tell me why you keep pulling away from me then?" His gray eyes are hard and crinkled around the edges as he stares me down.

"I'm not pulling away!" I cry in shock. Hayden's words are a clear indication that he is drunk. He never gets this personal unless he's well on his way to hammered town or unless he's comforting me after one of my many bad dreams.

"You are, Rey. You're pulling away from me and leaving me alone. I can feel it." He props his elbows up on the bar and cradles his head in his hands. I could cry at the sad, desolate state of him.

"Hayden, listen to me. You are still my best friend. None of that has changed. I'm just trying to help us get out of this darkness, too."

"The darkness is my home. It's where I belong. Maybe forever." He moves to stand up.

"Hayden," I reach out and grab his wrist. He looks down at my hand on him like it's the kiss of Judas. "Stop!"

"I'm suddenly not up for going out anymore, Rey." He pulls his hand free and pushes past the crowd of people heading toward the door.

"You good?" Callum asks, appearing beside me.

Without diverting my gaze from Hayden, I ask, "Do you think you could follow him out and make sure he finds a cab and isn't driving?"

"Consider it done." Callum hustles out of the busy bar area and in the direction Hayden is heading.

I want to run after Hayden. I want to hug him, comfort him, help him forget whatever demon he's fighting with right now. But I can't. Whatever's warring inside of him has a lot more to do with him than it does with me. I just need to know he's being safe.

CHAPTER 12

I'm asleep on a firm surface and wake to find voices arguing above me. "Research shows that allowing multiples to co-bed in the NICU improves their health. There are fewer episodes of bradycardia, better thermo-regulation, and lower oxygen needs."

"Dr. Miller, I appreciate your vast knowledge, I do. But, the risks of co-bedding all four of them are too great. We risk infection since Baby D isn't on nasal cannula oxygen, exposing her—"

"Reyna! Her name is Reyna! Use her damn name! She's lying right in front of us." My mother's voice is screaming as she breaks out in loud sobs. "They need to be together! They're dying! They are all dying right in front of me and none of you are doing anything!"

My father's voice hushes my mother's, but she only screams louder, "No, James, no! I can't stand by when I know I can save them. I can save all four of them! Just let me touch them! I need to hold them. I need to feel their hearts on my heart…Please!"

Her cries echo in the large NICU. Nurses and other doctors all stop to watch the scene unfolding. "Dr. Miller, please. These kinds of emotions aren't good for your babies—"

My father's voice interrupts, "Honey, please, you're going to pull out your stitches. You need to sit back down in the wheelchair."

"I can't. I can't sit here any longer and watch these idiots kill all of my babies! It's my fault they're in here. I shouldn't have been operating. I should have been in bed. I should have known better. I should have done things differently. God, please! Please, no," my mother cries more and I blink my eyes open for the first time and stare at her through the foggy plastic incubator.

Finally, my eyes aren't taped shut anymore. Finally, I can see the voice that's been nurturing me from the outside of that cozy place I was inside not so long ago. Her hunched over frame is blurry but I'd know her voice anywhere. It's my mommy. My mommy is sad. My mommy is upset. Why is she upset?

I manage to move my head over to look the other way and see three other incubators next to me. My sisters. Those are my sisters. I can feel their hearts beating with my own. I can feel their emotions. One of them is awake like me and she's scared. She's scared hearing our mommy scream like that. The other two are sound asleep, their hearts weaker and more muted than ours. I want to be close to them. I want to be next to them. If I was, I could help them. I could help their heart beats increase so they could wake up more. They just need me. Listen to our mommy! Please!

I begin flailing inside my incubator, fighting against the straps holding my hands down. I need to get to them; I need to be close to them. My heart rate increases and a beeping alarm suddenly chimes loudly beside me. All of the sudden, several faces are looking down at me.

"Doctor, she's in tachycardia. What do you want to do?"

"Check her BP, where's it at."

"It's elevated."

"Reyna?" my mother's voice cries from behind all the masked faces. "Reyna Miracle…Don't honey. Calm down…Be still, be safe my love."

"We need to sedate her. Push ten of Propofol."

A funny taste explodes in my mouth as a cool liquid pushes through my veins. Instantly, my eyes begin to feel heavy. Just before I close them, I see Marisa floating above me. But it's not the Marisa I knew as an adult. It's the child version of her. Six or seven-years-old maybe.

She's looking down on me with a serious expression. Her voice is like an angel. "Now do you see? Now do you understand?"

Before I have a chance to ask her what she's talking about, my mother's voice is whispering in my ear. "You're just going to take a nap, Reyna Miracle. Just a nap. I'll be right here. I'm not leaving. Don't leave me sweetie. Don't you dare leave—"

My eyes fly open and my pillow is soaked in tears and sweat. I sit up to find myself lying on my mattress in my Pimlico flat. My throat and chest ache like I've been bawling for hours. There's a strange metallic taste in my mouth that reminds me of the taste I had when a nurse pushed morphine into my IV as a teenager. I had to have my tonsils out after an abscess got infected on one and it was brutally painful.

"What in the hell?" I croak out. My voice hoarse like I've been screaming in my sleep.

As realization settles over me as to what I just witnessed in my dream, anxiety overcomes me. I jump out of bed and rush into the kitchen, searching for alcohol. Something, anything to numb this overwhelming sense of sickness raking through me with sharp, defiant strokes. My hands wrap around a bottle of vodka. I unscrew the lid and put the bottle to my lips. At the same moment a painful ache seers across my chest.

"No!" I croak out loud to myself. "Not this. Anything but this."

I check the clock to see it's nearly five o' clock in the morning. An anxiety attack is coming, I can feel it. I replace the lid on the vodka and place it back in the cabinet. On shaky legs I return to my mattress to find my phone. I dial the one person who can always talk me down from these attacks.

"Rey?" he says groggily.

"This one was bad, Hayden," my statement causes a loud sob to erupt.

"Another dream?"

"So much more than a dream, Hay," I cry into the phone and begin coughing violently.

"Calm down, calm down. I'm on my way. I'll stay on the phone with you until I get there."

"You're not driving, right?" I ask nervously. Even in my frazzled state, nagging Hayden about driving is like a reflex to me. It was only a year ago that I spent weeks watching him in the hospital after he wrapped his car around a tree and nearly killed himself. The whole ordeal nearly killed me, too. I wasn't eating over the stress and the crippling fear that I was that close to losing him, too.

"I'm not driving. Stop with that shite, will ya? I'll be there in five."

I slide down the hallway wall and ball myself up against the wall, trying desperately to stave off the impending attack. Having no idea how much time has passed, I'm startled when warm arms wrap around my shoulders and squeeze tightly. Hayden begins swaying me back and forth slowly—dropping soft kisses into my damp hair. He removes my phone from my ear and sets it on the floor beside him.

His right hand reaches around and squeezes the base of my neck in long, pain-relieving grips…exactly the way he knows helps me.

When the sobs subside, he lifts me up into his arms and carries me to the mattress, lying me down and tucking himself in behind me. "Do you want to tell me about it?" he asks, squeezing me protectively into his chest

Still unsure how to process it all myself, I can't possibly imagine telling him everything now. How can I dream of a time when I was a newborn baby? Was any of that real? Or was it all just a dream? Did my mother actually say any of those words that day? All I know about my birth is that I was one of four girls born when she was only twenty-four weeks pregnant. I was the only one that survived the NICU.

That's it.

My mother doesn't talk about them and neither do I. Regardless, I've always felt this strange connection to them. Like they are a part of me. Like I'm missing a part of myself every day of my life.

Hayden doesn't know I was born a quadruplet. All he knows was that I was born a micro-preemie. Marisa was the only person I ever revealed the strange pull I still feel to my sisters' short existence.

I roll over to face him. "Marisa was there," I say quietly to his chest, trying to give him some nugget of information to understand my attack. My face is tight from the salty tears that have dried now.

He squeezes my neck again and I tuck in even closer. "I figured." The smell of alcohol on his breath is strong.

"I'm sorry about earlier at the club," I say, feeling guilty that he's here taking care of me right now when I know he's hurting deep inside.

"Don't even bring it up."

"I'm scared, Hayden. I'm scared we're stuck in this place that we'll never get out of if we don't change. If we don't do something."

He sighs heavily into my hair. "I miss her too, you know."

I pull away from him to look into his drooping eyes. "Hayden, why do you only ever talk about her after my dreams?"

He shakes his head and turns away from me to lie on his back. "I don't know. It just feels like there's a safety in the night. You can go back to sleep and sort of start fresh the next day. Things just feel different at nighttime." The security light from outside my window streams in across his face, illuminating his profile as he stares up at the ceiling and continues, "And…because I think she's listening."

"You do?" I'm stunned by this admission. "You've never told me this before."

His face turns to me as he stares seriously into my eyes. His voice is barely a whisper. "I swear I feel her all around me after I see her in my dreams. Don't you?"

A prickling sensation cripples over my skin as I sit up to look into his eyes more fully. Nodding I reply, "I feel like she's always trying to tell me something."

"Me too. But it's so hard to figure out."

"Yes," I reply, relieved to feel like someone finally understands what I'm going through. "She was the best friend I ever had."

"She was the best sister, too."

"It's been three years, Hayden. When will it ever get easier?"

"I don't know. Christ, I wish I did. This darkness is bloody wretched."

He pulls me down onto his chest. His fingers draw lazy circles around the sleeve of my tattoo. Both of us lie there for a while…awake and silent, mourning the loss of his sister…mourning the loss of my best friend.

In the darkness that seems to have no end.

I wake several hours later to find Hayden has left. It's not surprising. It's usually what he does after opening up to me about Marisa. Opening up isn't exactly what our relationship is about, so he always gets awkward when we do. I sigh cursing to hell what an awful night that was. Drunken oblivion was easier than this.

This has to get easier.

It just has to.

THREE YEARS EARLIER

Oxford

CHAPTER 13

Graduation day at Oxford was upon us. I was capped and gowned and standing outside Sheldonian Theater. I stared sullenly into the camera of my mother's phone. Her face twinkled with hope and possibility and just bullshit everything.

"Can you at least try to smile, my Miracle?"

"Can you at least try to stop pretending I'm a miracle?" I bite out meanly.

She smiles at me. "Never." She places her hand on my wrist in a comforting gesture and I flinch away from her. "Sorry, I forgot."

I roll my eyes and lift the enormous sleeve up of my graduation robe to inspect my new ink. A pocket watch on the inside of my wrist set to the time of death that the medics called Marisa's death. Four o' three pm. She was dead for three hours before Liam was able to get a hold of me to tell me the awful news. The second skin bandage is still firmly in place, so I cover it back up and turn my back on my mother.

It's been two weeks since Marisa's funeral and two weeks since I've actually eaten anything worth mentioning. I wanted to skip graduation all together but despite my continual resentment toward my mother, I couldn't deny her this moment. She's paid for every single bit of my schooling and I do not take that lightly.

Since sleeping with Liam and learning of Marisa's death, I've slipped into a depression unlike any other. I've completely sabotaged every other relationship in my life. I may as well walk across that stage today in my cap and gown and hold onto the scraps of the mirage that is my mother's love.

It's also been two weeks since I've seen Liam. The real estate agent called to confirm our appointment to look at commercial properties in London, but I canceled everything. I took Liam's absence and silent treatment as no longer being interested in a future with me of any kind.

Not that I wanted one with him anyway.

"I'm going to go inside and take my seat with the other parents. You look beautiful, honey." She kisses me and disappears into the theater.

I look down at the enormous and elaborate academic robe and red sash across my neck. I adjust it uncomfortably and then my eyes trip over a familiar figure. I focus quickly in on a furious looking Liam. He's pushing through the hundreds of other robed students to get to me.

"Christ, I hardly recognized you," he seethes, the angry bulge in his jaw bone ticking violently. He grabs my arm firmly and pulls me off the concrete steps and into a covered archway away from all the other happy students. "What the fuck, Rey?"

"What are you talking about?" I ask in utter confusion.

He reaches beneath my chin, grabs the zipper and yanks it down harshly. I shove his hands away as my robe is yanked open.

"Fuck, Rey! You're skin and bones!" Liam's face is tortured and sickly. Dark circles reside under his eyes but he still looks gorgeous as ever.

"Don't be ridiculous." Grabbing the edges of my robe, I cover myself back up, protectively. I'm wearing a short blue shift dress that used to hug every one of my curves but now hangs on me like a potato sack. I know I've lost some weight since Marisa but I'm not about to let him scold me like a child over it. "I'm a twenty-five-year-old adult, Liam. I don't need you chastising me over this."

"Rey," he says my name on a sigh. "How can you expect me to ignore this?" His eyes are pleading and pained as they flash between my eyes and my mouth in utter agony.

"I'm not your concern!" I push back my dark hair and squeeze the back of my neck to try to gain some of my control back.

"You made that perfectly clear when you shoved me out of your dorm room. Fuck. How did we get this so utterly wrong?"

"Just leave it, Liam."

"No." He grabs my shoulders and turns me to face him. "Don't you miss me? At all? I miss you like crazy. I feel like I'm mourning two deaths instead of one. It's like you died on me two weeks ago. And now I see you today and it makes me sick to my stomach that I've left you the way I did!" His eyes are shimmering with tears and pain, only adding to the self-loathing I've developed the past fourteen days.

My eyes are dead and cold, my voice flat and unaffected. "I told you I wanted nothing to do with you, Liam. I meant it."

"You're lying to me. Again!" he roars, angrily punching the concrete wall beside my head.

I flinch and yank myself free from his hold. "You need to leave me alone. None of this is right. It's fucked up, is what it is." I turn away from him, and cross my slender arms over my chest.

"What's fucked up? You and I staying friends? Marisa dies and our friendship has to die with it?"

Her name on his lips so close to my face is like a dagger through my heart. I turn to face him, resolute written all over my face. "Yes, Liam. Our friendship ends. That's what happens after you betray someone. Shit ends…badly. Leave it alone."

"Bollocks, Rey. You've gone completely mental. You need help!" He rips his cap off his head and shoves his hands through his hair. "I can't just watch you wither away!"

"You don't have to. We're done with school. We'll never see each other again. Stop worrying about me. This is how it has to be, Liam."

"Why? Why, Rey?" he's shouting again. His brown eyes are dancing passionately between my two gray ones.

"Because—"

"I still love you, Rey." His words cut me off as his shaky hands cup my cheeks. He leans down to catch my downward cast eyes. "You have to stop pushing people away. This can't be how this ends."

"It most certainly is," I say, pulling back from his embrace. Pushing people away is what I'm good at. Keeping everyone at an arm's length is rudimentary for survival. Marisa was the only exception.

"No, it isn't."

"I don't love you, Liam!" I scream the lie at him and the words echo of the concrete walls. "I never have! Whatever you think this is, isn't worth it."

My words have the instant effect of turning his passionate expression to stone. He drops his hands from my face and steps back, releasing a shaky breath. Unable to watch a single second of him hating me, I shove past him, leaving his bereft face in my wake as the final, lasting memory I have of Liam Darby.

PRESENT DAY

CHAPTER 14

"I need you to do more of that marketing magic, Oxford. I just checked the books for the week and that night you did all that work for Ginge on Top was our highest grossing night of the entire week by double!"

My brows rise as I lean against the doorway of Lariza's office. Frank is seated behind the desk in a white tailored blazer rolled up his slender forearms. His red hair is gelled so much it looks like he's just come from a shower.

I've been working at Club Taint for about two weeks now and am finally starting to not feel like a newbie. I've been able to focus and take in extra shifts since Hayden has been MIA. This isn't the first time he's disappeared on me. Whenever he opens up about Marisa, he always pulls away after. It's during these times that I text with his sister Daphney to make sure he is being safe.

Just thinking of the nightmare I had that night shoots chills up and down my spine. I've had dreams of my sisters before, but nothing that involved our time in the NICU. That dream was bone-chilling.

I refocus on the flailing ginger in front of me. "Tune in, Oxford. I'm talking here!"

"Am I a bartender or a marketing rep?" I ask cheekily with a wry grin.

"You are whatever I bloody well want you to be. Don't get smart, Oxford or I'll send you to Brixton to pick me up the latest vintage porno that just arrived."

"Say what?"

"That's what I thought. Get over here." He grumbles beneath his breath and I can't help but laugh at the utter randomness that is Frank McElroy. This guy is a breed all to himself. I make my way over to his desk. He has an Excel spreadsheet graph open and points out how much higher our income was the night of Ginge on Top. I'm impressed and even a bit pleased.

"Now, we can't open early every night. But I'm quite interested to see if you can increase our business with any other marketing ideas that don't require a change of hours. We have a great clientele here but I'd love to show Lariza that I'm not a posh, spoiled tosser with no work ethic."

"So you want to exploit my mad skills to make yourself look good?" I arch one plucked brow at him.

"Precisely," he replies without shame.

"What's in it for me?" I lean back in the wheelie office chair and cross my arms over my chest.

His eyes turn to slits and he props his chin on his fist, looking me up and down. "What did you have in mind? I have to say, I'm intrigued. This is the first time your badass ink actually matches your attitude."

Tightness forms in the pit of my stomach as my nerves kick in, but I school my face to look strong and confident. I've been dying to ask Frank this since the day of my interview, but never had a good opportunity. Now seems like the only chance I'll get. "I just want a bit of intel. Shouldn't hurt too much."

Leaning back, he waffles his fingers over his flat stomach. "Fire away, Oxford."

I glance back to the computer, unable to make eye contact as I ask, "How do you know Liam Darby?"

Frank releases a small puff of air with a knowing laugh. He kicks his foot against my chair, swirling me to face him head on. His cocky grin is maddening, but I match it with one of my own, refusing to lose my poker face.

"Liam's a good bloke. We've become proper mates in the past year. He had a bit of a rendezvous with my flat mate, Finley, when she first moved here from the States."

"So what happened?" I ask, trying to mask the green-eyed emotions overcoming me. Jesus, Rey. You didn't expect Liam to sit and pine over you for three damn years.

"Finley's heart was never on the market…no matter how much she wanted it to be." His words sound painfully familiar. "And then Liam does what he always does. He plays the part of the nice boy and tried to fix everything."

"What do you mean? What's wrong with that?"

Frank looks up at the ceiling thoughtfully for a moment before replying. "The boy has trouble asserting himself. I know that something in his past gutted him to the point where he just seems to let life happen around him. He seems to cope with obstacles by being a pawn for someone, instead of a rook or a bishop. Instead of taking charge and going at it head first himself. He's a helpful lad. But that kindness of his never seems to get him anywhere." Frank pauses and grins cheekily. "I think he just needs to grab a good 'ol handful of hairy balls and man up."

I cringe at his choice of phrase when he suddenly leans forward, piercing me with his brown eyes. The two crinkles rippling perfectly between his brows. "As I said, Liam is a good bloke."

"Agreed," I reply dropping my chin to return his glare.

"I don't want to see him hurt."

"That makes two of us." My voice is hard and flat. I don't take kindly to threats, but I know that deep down Frank is just trying to be a friend. And a large part of me is glad that Liam has someone looking out for him. Even if it is a crazy ginger.

Frank's eyes search mine for a moment and he cocks his head to the side, seeming to find what he's looking for. "Excellent!" Frank sings cheerily, snapping me out of my reverie. "Now, let's see what that horribly underused education can get my Taint."

I shake my head, "I just might have some tricks up my sleeve for your taint."

"Saucy minx! Let me see." He snatches my bare arm up and brings it to his eyes, closely inspecting every stroke of ink on my skin. I giggle as he pulls a face like it smells. "What's with all the sunflowers?"

"They're kind of a tribute to a friend."

"Was his name Sonny? Oh my God, are you a Sonny and Cher fanatic like me?" Frank's eyes alight and I honestly can't tell if he's joking. "This is a serious question, Oxford. Don't toy with my emotions!"

"No, I mean…I don't mind them, but that's not what this is about."

"Bugger!" He rises from his seat. "Right. I've got a delivery coming. Get to work, Oxford. I expect that big brain of yours to make magic happen tonight."

In an attempt to get the last word, I mumble quietly, "Later, Frank and Beans," as he strides out the door.

His narrow frame reappears in the doorway. "What did you just call me?"

I school my face to remain serious. "Sorry, what's that?"

"What did you just say…just now…as I was walking out the door."

"I don't know what you're talking about. I'm putting my brain to work. That's all." My eyes are wide and innocent.

He squints at me suspiciously. "Alright then. As you were."

As he rounds the doorframe I say a bit louder this time, "I could really go for some Frank and Beans."

"Bloody hell, I knew it!" His face is back and I can't hide the ear to ear Cheshire cat grin splitting across my face. "It was fucking Finley, wasn't it? I swear to God, Oxford…if you start calling me Frank and Beans…"

"I have no idea what you're talking about!" I bite my lip playfully. "I was just thinking about what I feel like for lunch!"

"That's a load of codswallop and you know it, you cheeky cow! I'm going to murder Fin-Bin." I hear him continue to mumble obscenities as he makes his way down the hallway.

Just as my giggles subside my phone pings a new text notification.

Hayden: Hey…Sorry I've been MIA. You good?

Me: Yeah…I'm good. At work now.

Hayden: Cool. I might pop by later. I miss you. x

I clutch my phone to my chest feeling grateful that Hayden reached out again.

Me: Perfect. I'm off at 9.

Hayden: Right, I'll swing 'round and pick you up. Not driving, don't worry.

Me: Not worried…and that sounds great. xx

CHAPTER 15

After some strategically placed ads and social media blasts, plus a call into a huge nightclub vlogger, I feel pretty chuffed when I see a line out the door of Club Taint. We don't open for another ten minutes.

"Well done, you." Callum offers me a high five as I walk out the door and I proudly take it.

Grinning like a loon, I stride out the door expecting to see Hayden's face. My breath catches when I see Liam's tall frame leaning against the nearby bus stop bench. He's dressed in slim gray jeans and a sexy, white, long-sleeved ribbed Henley. The sleeves are pushed up, revealing sexily firm forearms beneath.

"Hiya," he says as I pause awkwardly looking at him.

"Hey…Are you waiting on someone?" I ask, looking behind me.

"You, actually." He pushes himself off the bench and slides his hands into his pockets. "I was wondering if you wanted to grab a coffee or tea or something."

"Now?" I ask, looking down at my Club Taint tank and black jeans. "I'm not exactly dressed for it."

"We could go to my flat. I don't live far." He nervously gestures down the sidewalk and looks back at me hopefully.

Anxiety creeps down my neck and over my shoulders. This is what I wanted. I wanted to see how he was doing. I wanted to make sure he was okay. Why am I suddenly crippled with fear over the idea of being alone with him?

"It's been three years, Rey…Surely you can stand to be around me for a cup of tea." His hand finds its way to the back of his neck and scratches nervously.

I purse my lips together at that pained statement. "It's not that, Liam. I—"

"Reyna?" Hayden's voice cuts in from behind me. I swerve and see him standing a good ten feet away from me. He's dressed in a pale blue button down and gray trousers. His copper blond hair is disheveled as his gray eyes are hard and penetrating the air beside me. "Liam," he adds stiffly, looking past me.

I step back and see Liam's posture instantly rise and I swear his chest puffs out. "Hayden. I haven't seen you in a while. How are you?"

"Fine," Hayden's reply is clipped and serious. "You here with Theo?"

Liam shakes his head no. "No, I was just here to catch up with Rey."

"That sounds nice. I'm just here to *pick up Rey*." I frown at Hayden's tone and feel instantly annoyed at what I see going down right now.

Liam nods and glances back to me, his eyes briefly drift to my lips and then he smiles. "Got it. I'll let you get to it then."

He turns to leave and it's when he rounds the corner that my feet develop a mind of their own. I turn, walking backwards, "I'll be right back, Hayden."

Ignoring his exasperated expression, I round the same corner and see Liam's long strides have taken him halfway down the block already. I jog to catch up to him. "Liam!" I shout, finally within earshot.

He instantly stops and turns to watch me approach. His face is marred with confusion. Once I reach him I suddenly feel ridiculous and slightly out of breath.

"Did you want something from me tonight?" I ask, finally.

"What do you mean?" His eyes squint.

"I mean, the tea. Why did you want to get tea?"

"I just wanted to catch up, Rey. I thought, stupidly, that maybe after some time had passed perhaps you and I could become friends again. Catch up. We were pretty good at being friends once upon a time."

"I agree," I reply, honestly.

"But, I'm not looking to step on anyone's toes."

"You're not," I reply, cutting him off. "Hayden and I are friends. Mostly. I just…didn't want you to think…" My voice trails off, feeling uncomfortable at finishing that sentence.

His brow furrows. "Why do you care what I think?"

"I just…I didn't want you to think I was lying to you before. When you came to the club last week."

He nods seriously. "It sounds more complicated than that."

"It usually is when it comes to me," I offer self-deprecatingly.

He half smiles, "This I already knew."

A moment passes between the two of us and I swear I can hear his thoughts echoing in my head.

"I won't keep you." He leans in and brushes my cheek with his lips and his smell fills my chest. A wanting ache fans out beneath my skin. "Have a good night, Rey," he murmurs into my hair.

All too soon he backs away, pulling his lips into his mouth to lick. His eyes flash to my mouth before he stuffs his hands into his pockets, turns on his heel and continues down the sidewalk.

I watch him walk for longer than appropriate before turning and running back around the corner to my own personal complication.

CHAPTER 16

I find Hayden slumped against the side of the building. His gray eyes are glowering at me as I approach. Silently he pushes himself off the wall and flags down a cab. He opens the door and steps back, waiting for me to enter. The cab ride is quiet and tense. Hayden tells the driver to drop us at the White Swan Pub instead of in front of my flat.

"I need a drink," he says to my questioning eyes as he slides out of the cab. I follow in his wake, stepping inside first as he holds the door open for me. Alistair gives me a cheery wave as he's busy tending to a large group of men.

"Are you hungry?" Hayden asks, avoiding eye contact with me.

"No, I'll just do red wine," I say timidly.

He nods and heads over to the bar to get our drinks and I grab a cozy red, leather booth by the latticed window. After a few minutes he's walking back toward me with our drinks.

After a few awkward sips, I finally break the silence. "What's got you in such a mood?"

He glares at me and tips his beer back, drinking nearly the entire contents before replying. He licks his lips and penetrates me with a hard look. "Perhaps it has to do with the fact that I came to pick up my best mate from work to find her flirting like a slut with my dead sister's ex fiancé."

Fiery rage unleashes in my veins. Pure, undiluted rage. Gripping my glass of wine, I toss it in Hayden's face and yank myself out of the booth. I storm through the pub, ignoring the cheers and heckling at the scene I just created. I slam my hands into the door and fly out into the crisp, summer evening. How freaking dare he?! I turn and make my way up the dark sidewalk toward my flat.

"Rey!" Hayden shouts after a few seconds. I don't slow a single step as he calls out again, "Rey!" His voice is laced with anger this time.

I stop just steps from my building door and turn around and pummel him with the nastiest glare I can muster. "I wasn't sure I should answer to anything other than slut!" I exclaim, shoving his chest hard as he moves to touch me. He barely budges and it just frustrates me further.

"You alright, love?" Alistair says out of breath as he jogs up to our ridiculous scene and out of breath. His top lip curls up as he glances over to Hayden. He turns and eyes me seriously, waiting for the go ahead.

"I'm fine, Al. Nothing I can't handle."

He nods and turns to face Hayden. Staring up at him, Alistair says, "If you were any other bloke, I'd have you by the neck and on your knees crying out in pain right now."

"Alistair, you don't know—" Hayden starts.

"And I don't want to know. You make that right." He points back at me without breaking eye contact with Hayden. "You make that right," he repeats ominously and strides back down the hill toward the pub.

Hayden scrubs his hands over his still damp with wine face before looking at me. "Fuck me…I'm sorry, Rey. I'm just knackered and upset. I didn't expect to find you with him." His blue shirt is covered in dark purple liquid. "Then you have the nerve to run after him right in front of me. How the bloody hell am I supposed to feel?"

"He used to be my friend, Hayden! I haven't seen him for three years and he looked hurt by seeing you and me together. I didn't want him to get the wrong idea."

"What's the wrong idea, Rey?" he scoffs. "That you and I are together? Last I checked you've been shagging me for the better part of a year."

My eyes turn to saucers. "Did I miss the part where you asked me to go steady, Hayden? Let's not make our relationship into more than it actually is!"

"Oh, so I mean nothing to you?" he sneers.

"Of course you do! You're my best friend! You mean everything to me. But, friends are all we are and you know that."

"Do I?" His jaw drops in utter shock at my grand statement. His tone drips with sarcasm. "Oh please, Rey…do tell me what I apparently already know since you seem to know it all."

"Stop, Hayden. We both said we were going to stop sleeping together over a month ago."

"And how's that been working out?" He steps closer to me so I have to crane my neck up to look at him. His gray eyes are determined slits as he breathes heavily down on me.

"Not well," I croak. His close proximity confuses me as attraction swirls between us.

"Exactly. So you should forgive me for not taking kindly to seeing you fucking tart around like you're single."

"I am single!" I slice my fingers into my hair. "You haven't spoken to me in a week, Hayden! Do you know how that makes me feel? Do you know how much that makes me worry? Do you even care?"

"You know better than anyone why I do that!" he roars.

"Exactly! And *that* right there is exactly why we said we were going to stop shagging a month ago. We don't work, Hayden. We've discussed this. We just keep each other down. We're a stifling, suffocating, sickness together. We aren't good for each other."

"And you think you can be good with Liam. My dead sister's almost fiancé?"

"Stop talking about her!" I scream, covering my ears. "I can't take it right now! It's killing me!" His arms wrap around me as tears spill freely down my cheeks. "It's not fair, Hayden. You never bring her up and the one time you do, you do it to hurt me."

"I'm sorry. I know," he murmurs into my hair. "I'm fucked up. But, honestly, Rey…Why him?"

"There's nothing going on, Hayden," I groan. "He just wanted to catch up. As friends."

"I know how good of a friend you are," he thrusts his pelvis into me.

I cringe and push away from him. "You fucking pig!" I scream.

"I'm sorry…bad joke." He holds his hands out defensively. "Bloody awful."

"You need to leave," I say seriously, barely able to even look him in the face.

"I'm not leaving. Come on, Rey. Let me come up." He tries to approach me again. "I want to make this right."

"No," my voice is low and menacing.

"I have a key," he replies in challenge.

I arch a single brow. "And if you force yourself into my flat right now, I'll be taking that key back from you. I need you to leave, Hayden. Now. Respect that."

He runs his hands through his hair and looks at me with wide, worrying eyes. "I'm sorry, Rey. I don't know what's gotten in to me."

"I know you're sorry. And we'll be fine. But you're not coming up. Not tonight. Please leave."

"Fuck!" he screams and throws his fists into the air. After eyeing me for a moment, he turns to walk back down the sidewalk toward the pub.

I exhale a shaky breath and let myself into my building. When the lift doors close, I slump down to the floor and completely lose what little reserve I had left.

CHAPTER 17

My dreams have always been poignant. My entire life I've been able to remember them really well, which I'm told is rather rare. About a year after Marisa died, I went to a psychic who claimed she could interpret dreams. She was located in a dodgy part of London, but I was curious enough to check it out. It was all a crock of bullshit. She started talking about dreams being windows into our soul from the dead and I panicked, threw my money on the table, and ran out of the room.

But ever since that day, I've always wondered.

Tonight's dream is no different.

I'm standing in the most stunning wedding dress I've ever seen. It's a fabric that feels like it's made of clouds. I turn, looking around for reassurance from my loved ones, but no one is there. I'm in the middle of a plush hotel room with a huge breakfast buffet spread with mimosas, coffee, and various presents. But still, no one is around.

I catch my reflection in one of the large mirrors above the bed and see that my dark tresses are pinned up in a beautiful up-do with swirling tendrils framing my face. My makeup is dark and seductive. My lips a deep shade of purple. My tattoos are on full display and I look like I belong on the cover of Alternative Bride magazine.

Suddenly, my mother appears behind me. "Where is everyone?" I ask her, turning and taking in her ivory, lace mother-of-the-bride dress.

"Who do you mean?" Her smile is beaming. I don't think I've ever seen her look so genuinely happy.

"My friends…my bridesmaids?" I stop myself just in time before saying 'my sisters'.

Her smile falters for the briefest of seconds. "Honey, you know Marisa was kidnapped three years ago."

"Marisa's dead, Mom," I argue, feeling confused.

"Miracle, no. We can't give up hope. She's just gone for a while."

She's not dead? She could still be alive? Just as my dreamlike mind begins to race with possibility, the double doors into the hotel suite fly open.

"I'm here!" Marisa's voice sings before I finally lay eyes on her.

She rounds the corner as the sun peeks out from the clouds and blasts the room with its fiery rays. She looks the picture of health. Her blonde hair is curled and flowing down her back. She's dressed in a floor-length peach gown and her lips are smeared with a shiny nude gloss.

"How Marisa? How did you escape?"

Her laughter peals through the room. "I didn't escape. I just left!"

"You just left? How did they let you just leave? Who had you?"

She shakes her head knowingly. "I was in the most beautiful place I've ever seen."

"Can I see it?" I step toward her, but my actions don't seem to have any physical results. I remain planted in front of the bed. I glance around for help from my mother to find that she has vanished.

"You don't need to see this place, yet. I'm just so happy I made it for this big day. Ma lady is getting married."

Hearing her call me 'ma lady' sends immediate warmth through my chest. She always called me that in grad school. Ma lady! I was anything but that most of the time, but she couldn't be convinced otherwise.

"Marisa, before we go out there, I need to talk to you."

"What's up buttercup?"

Stealing myself I begin the speech that I've rehearsed for three years now. "I've betrayed you in the most dreadful way and all I need to do is say—"

"Is this about Liam?" she interrupts haphazardly.

"Yes, I—"

"Oh, yeah. Sorry, sweets. I have to stop you right there. We can't have this conversation." She moves down the small corridor and opens the door.

"Why not?" I ask, following behind her.

"Because you don't deserve it yet." She nods her head like her decision is final.

"Then what do I deserve?"

"To walk down that aisle. Let's go!"

She rushes me out the door and I step into the lobby of the hotel where hundreds of strangers stand forming a makeshift aisle. I nearly burst into tears at the sight of my father reaching his hand out for me to take.

"Dad?" I utter, nervously. The word feels weird coming from my mouth, but I run to him anyway. The same issue happens where I'm running but there is no physical result of the action. "Dad!" I shout as he turns and walks away. "No! Marisa, help me!"

Marisa appears beside me, smiling and laughing. "I wouldn't worry about him. He'll be back. Let's get you married."

I begin gliding effortlessly down the aisle and see a tall, blond figure with his back facing me. His hair is mussed and my heart begins thundering a strange rhythm. We stand two feet from him but he still won't move.

"Why won't he turn around?" I whisper.

"Because you won't let him, Reyna."

"What do you mean? I'm not doing anything."

"That's just it, Rey. You're not doing anything except hurting. Hurting and aching and crying and not moving."

"What do you mean? I am living! I got a new job at least."

Marisa giggles affectionately. "Sweetie, get your shite together. I can't do this forever." The sunlight around her begins to fade and I feel her drifting away.

"Can't you just wait, Marisa? Please? I need you. I need you to get through this. You're the only one I can do this with. I just…I need you."

"Needs are always necessary. Wants have a way of surprising you." She smiles and disappears along with everything around me.

I wake to a crusty dryness on my cheeks like I'd cried in my sleep…again. I blink slowly, looking around my dark flat and trying to make sense of what that dream was about. Normally I would grab my phone and call Hayden to post mortem every detail. But after last night, he's the last person I want to talk to. I grab my phone and see I have zero text messages from Hayden. Not surprising. I'm sure he's going to vanish on me again.

What was last night all about anyway? Hayden has never been jealous in the past. He's seen me completely wasted at nightclubs, grinding on random blokes and never even batted an eye. Now that Liam shows up he turns into a territorial prick?

And Liam. What am I interested in from him? What was it that made me run after him to make sure he knew I wasn't with Hayden? At first it was just a strong desire to make sure he's doing okay…not a walking zombie like me. Now I fear that feelings are becoming involved and I do not know how to process any of that, yet.

My phone begins ringing in my hand and I see my mother's picture pop up on the screen. I silence it and drop it down onto the bed. I've been dodging her calls all week and blaming it on work. The fact is I can't face her after that messed up dream I had of the NICU. The woman she was in my dream that night is like nothing I have ever seen. That woman was ferocious and a mess. Real and authentic. The woman Elizabeth Miller is today is none of those things.

I heave myself up off my mattress and make quick work of my messy clothes, tossing a load in the laundry and putting away the ones that I'm pretty sure are clean. Busy work is what I need right now. Mindless tasks to keep my mind off whatever it is that I seem to be trying to work through in my REM cycles.

After a boiling hot shower, I'm feeling mildly human again. I rub some lotion into my ink stained arms and throw on a clean Taint tank and jean shorts. After a miserable night of sleep, the last thing I want to do is work at Club Taint tonight. But I'm slated for a full bartending shift and I can't let Frank down. I've worked eight shifts in a row now and my dogs are barking at me for a break. Marisa's words about living echo in my head and I know that calling in would only smother all the progress I've made so far.

I hop off at my Tube stop, making my way to the doors of Club Taint. Night has fallen and it's drizzling rain. Again. London seems to always be crying. I cross my bare arms over my chest in an attempt to protect myself from the cool rain.

"Rey," a voice calls from somewhere in the distance.

Glancing over, I see Liam emerge from the side alley across the street. I stop and slick the hair of my topknot with the newly added moisture. "Liam, what are you doing here?"

He stops right in front of me and stuffs his hands into his denim pockets. His face is squinting against the light rain and I can already feel little hairs clinging to my cheeks.

"I wanted to catch you before your shift," he answers, his voice deep and purposeful.

"How did you know when I was working tonight?"

He tweaks his brows knowingly. "How do you think?"

Frank and Beans! What a mouth he has on him. I guess that protective friend vibe he gave off yesterday was all just an act.

"I'm sorry how last night went down, Rey. I wanted to talk to you seriously, but everything went a little haywire. I think I got spooked."

I sigh and lick my lips thoughtfully. "Just leave it, Liam. All of this is too hard. Maybe catching up is a bad idea."

"Give me one weekend," he chokes out suddenly.

"What?" I ask, blinking rapidly against the mist. "The weekend! What happened to tea?"

"I'm asking for one weekend, Rey. Surely you can grant me that." He's rocking back on his heels nervously.

"Why would I grant you anything?" I groan out. Gosh, all of this seems intense. So deep and twisted and confusing. The last time Liam and I had a real, genuine conversation I was screaming at him to stay out of my life.

"Because, Rey." He leans down to lock his eyes on mine. They flash briefly to my matte red lips. "You and I used to be friends. Once upon a time you used to be kind. Sweet. Funny even, in your own rude, dry way. We were friends. No matter how much you want to diminish that or pretend that it was only you and Marisa, I was there too. I was there for nearly a year, watching you live. I know you. And you know I know you. I want a weekend."

His speech floors me, but it doesn't change anything. "Liam, it's just too painful and it doesn't change anything."

"I know it doesn't change anything. That's why I want a weekend. A weekend to prove to you that we can be friends again. I miss you, Rey. I miss our friendship. I miss your smart mouth. Please."

He puckers his lips the same way he did in grad school when he was concentrating hard on something. His eyes look so hopeful that I can hardly believe it when I ask, "When?"

His face lights up. "Tomorrow."

"Tomorrow? I have to work."

"Frank owes me a favor," he replies hurriedly.

"Where would we even go?"

"My parents have a place in Cambridge. We'll have it all to ourselves." His tone is rushed. He's been thinking on this for a while.

"Cambridge? But you're an Oxford boy!"

"I know," he huffs with a laugh. "It pissed off my father so much when I told them I was going there." His grin is devilishly proud.

I push my wet strands back from my face, returning his smile. "But I thought you were a good boy."

His grin disappears. "Even good boys know how to be bad sometimes."

My stomach swirls at the intensity behind his words. So few words have ever said so much. "Just friends though, right?"

"'Course. Friends."

CHAPTER 18

What in the bloody hell did I agree to? A weekend? A whole weekend with Liam Darby? How do I even pack for something like this? I mindlessly stuff random clothing into a duffle bag and forget what I'm doing only to look down to see that nothing I've packed even remotely resembles something wearable. I jog into the bathroom and begin tossing toiletries into a sack and bring that out, shoving it in with the mess of mismatched clothes.

"Oh fuck this," I say and head to the kitchen, ripping open my fridge and finding a half empty bottle of white wine. After smelling it and deciding it must be safe, I take a cooling sip. "Holy shit!" I cry out, looking accusingly at the wine. I run to the sink and dump the remaining wine down the sink. It didn't taste bad, but it tasted like a huge mistake.

Wiping my moist chin, I shake my head as I recall exactly how I felt the night Liam came over to show me the engagement ring he bought for Marisa. "I drank a whole bottle that night and look how that turned out. That's not what this weekend is about. I can't be repeating my mistakes. I can't."

Needing some air, I pull open the kitchen floor-length window and step out onto my small wrought iron balcony. All that sits out here is a metal chair and a flower pot of dirt where Hayden's cigarette butts lie. I hunch over, holding onto the railing and take in large gulps of air. "Get a grip, Reyna!"

"Or just get out of your head and get down here!" a voice calls from below. I look down and see Liam standing at my building entrance. He's dressed in a pair of gray shorts and a light gray plaid shirt. A large backpack rests at his feet.

"I'm not sure I'm feeling well enough for a weekend away, Liam. Maybe another time," I croak out and smile painfully down at him. I'm not even on my way there and already towing the line of a full blown panic attack.

"You're just getting squirrely like you always do." Liam shakes his head knowingly. "Rey, there won't be another time. I'm asking you to do this. Now."

Throwing my hands on my hips I reply, "Now or never? Is that seriously what you're saying?"

"I'm saying that I'm not going to wait down here forever." His voice has a finality to it that scares me.

I nod shakily and pull my hand up to my mouth to chew on a hangnail. "I'm coming. Stop griping at me, would ya?"

I hear him chuckling as I move back into my flat to grab my bag and purse. Curiosity over how Liam is takes precedence and evidently my mind is choosing now over never. Striding out of my apartment, I feel suddenly foolish over him witnessing my little meltdown on my balcony.

When I walk outside, Liam smiles brightly at me. "Can we pretend that didn't happen?" I ask shoving the sleeves up on my red, lumber jack shirt.

"Don't even know what you're moaning about. You look great, by the way," he says as he leans in and kisses me on the cheek. When he pulls away he reaches for my bag.

"I can carry my own bag."

"I know," he says and takes it anyway. He struggles for a moment as he slips his backpack on and throws my bag over his shoulder.

"You look ridiculous."

"I just said you look great and that's what you've got for me?" I nod simply and he grins. "Nice to know some things haven't changed."

The gleam in his eyes is so familiar that I can't help but feel calmer as we make our way to Victoria Station. We grab the eleven o'clock train to Cambridge. It's an unusually sunny day and it has everyone in London busting out the tank tops and shorts and looking extra chipper.

Sitting across from him on the train, I watch Liam as he places an order for two coffees from the snack cart. I take the opportunity to inspect every little thing that's changed about him since Oxford. His blond hair is longer now and he wears it in a stylized mess on top of his head. In college he did that slicked, swept over look that was so trendy at the time. Back then it looked like he was probably trying too hard to look like an Oxford boy instead of just being himself.

The way he is now is decidedly sexier. His morning five o'clock shadow is darker than the hair on his head. It gives him a mature look that I can't blame the cart attendant for noticing when he speaks to her. He hands me my cup and we sit in comfortable silence, listening to the hum of the people chatting around us and taking in the English countryside.

About the only thing that hasn't changed on Liam are his eyes. They're a gorgeous deep brown, but it's not the color that draws you in. It's how they look at you. His gaze has this way of penetrating through all of your secrets. Then he does that thing where he glances down at your lips and a simple look turns into a sexual thrill coursing up your spine.

After a while, we begin smirking knowingly at each other. It's odd the comfort I feel with him already. In grad school, we always did have a certain undeniable connection. I wouldn't say it was sexual…just synced. Like he could hear me and I could hear him and we never had to say a word out loud. Neither of us would ever admit it to anyone, though. It was this private secret we shared.

After he catches me staring at him again, I finally break the silence. "How didn't I know your parents had a house in Cambridge?"

He pauses mid sip and begins coughing. "Erm…about that."

"What?" My eyes widen with alarm.

"Nothing to fear. It's just…well…I may have exaggerated when I said they had a cottage. You'll see." He's smirking and watching me out of the corner of his eye as I mull the possibilities over in my head.

With everything that's happened since Marisa, I thought things would feel awkward…different. But they don't. They feel natural. Fun even.

When we finally reach our stop, Liam hails a cab outside the train station and gives the driver the address. I slide in, chewing my lip nervously. I've been to Cambridge a few times before and it's stunning, but we seem to be heading away from the city center. In only a few moments we're driving right alongside the River Cam. The cabby takes a few sharp turns and we pull back into a secluded, private mooring. A decent sized hunter green houseboat rests just off a small dock.

"What are we doing?" I ask, confusion marring my face.

"This is it," Liam tweaks his eyebrows playfully and leaps out of the cab.

My jaw drops as I take in the scenery around me more fully. It's an exquisite, isolated little piece of property. No homes or neighbors within eyesight. A weeping willow rests in the center of the large grassy lot. Alongside the moor is a quaint garden house. I hop out for a better view and I about gasp when a flock of swans swim past us down the river.

"Is this all your property?"

"My parent's property, but the boat is mine. She's not seaworthy yet, but she's more comfortable than the majority of hotels, I can promise you that."

Liam pays the driver and grabs our bags, gesturing with his head for me to follow him. The smell of field roses permeates the air as we walk past the garden house. It's a gorgeously designed, three-season shed of some sort. Large, overflowing pots of pink flowers line the decent sized wooden deck attached to it. Old, period French doors are propped wide open inviting you in to a brightly designed interior. The inside walls are painted a bright turquoise with various empty frames hung crookedly throughout. It's bursting with charm. Two cushioned patio chairs are nestled amongst several more clay pots of greenery and produce plants.

We pass by the building and step onto a wooden dock. He hops down into the boat and sets our bags down. He then turns and holds his hand out to me with a bright, boyish smile. I reach out and tentatively take the first step when his other hand wraps around my waist and pulls me down the length of his body all the way to the wooden boat floor. He continues to hold me as he looks into my eyes with a salacious grin that says so much and yet nothing at the same time.

"Thanks," I murmur and pull away from him, denying that familiar spark of attraction.

"Let me show you inside," he says, twining his fingers with mine.

Ignoring my inner turmoil over whatever feelings are reigniting, I let him pull me through the wide-open deck of the boat toward two wooden doors. He spins a code on the lock and pushes the sliders open to reveal a plush and welcoming living area.

"It's bigger in here than I expected," I say, walking past him and stepping inside.

The décor is all creams and browns and wicker accents with pops of Aztec-colored rugs and throw pillows. A long, comfortable-looking oak-trimmed couch rests on one wall. Across from it is a brown leather chaise. Past the seating area is an attractive kitchen with glossy wooden counter tops and stainless steel appliances. A separate island rests in the center with two wicker barstools.

"This is ridiculous!" I say and continue through the kitchen into a narrow hallway, passing a small bathroom. "It even has a tub!" I exclaim and hear Liam's laugh close behind me.

I turn to find him watching me with wide, excited eyes. He's proud. He's proud of his houseboat. He should be. It's stunning. I continue my perusal past the bathroom and find myself standing in front of a large king sized mattress with several colorful throw pillows scattered over a lush, white duvet. Three round porthole windows are above the head of the bed.

"You can sleep in here. That couch is actually quite comfortable."

I frown briefly and then turn around and sit at the foot of the bed. "This is amazing, Liam."

He sighs and sits down beside me. "I'm glad you think so. It didn't look like this when I bought it, that's for sure."

"Well, you've done a great job with it."

"So you're okay with staying here?"

I nod taking note of the long, horizontal mirror on the far wall. I gaze at our reflection for a moment. Watching Liam watch me is an odd feeling. It feels like I'm witnessing something he wouldn't want me to see. Nerves take flight in my belly and I break eye contact with our reflection. "So what are your plans for the day then?"

His eyes flash down to my lips and then return to mine before answering, "Well, Stourbridge Common is just across the river. I thought we might head over there for a bit. Walk around maybe? I had the fridge stocked and planned on a barbeque tonight, if you're alright with that."

"I'm a vegetarian now, Liam," I say flatly.

His face falls. "Oh, Christ. I didn't even…shit…um—"

I silence him with my laughs. "I'm joking, you prat."

He grins and nudges me with his shoulder. "Come on. Put on some comfortable shoes. We've got to row over."

CHAPTER 19

After a quick lesson on rowing, we make it across the river with ease. I actually ask if we could row around a bit longer before heading to the commons and Liam is more than happy to oblige. It isn't the type of rowboat where the girl just sits there while the man does all the work. It's a two-seater, racing rowboat. A mini version of what you see in competitive rowing. It's fun!

Once we reach the Stourbridge, I'm warm from our efforts so I shed my plaid shirt and tie it around my black shorts. I'm now in a simple white tank top that reveals the straps of my purple bra beneath. I notice Liam's eyes on my ink, but he surprises me and never asks about them.

We hike and muddle around the grounds, taking in the beautiful English landscaping. We make small talk about Frank and our jobs. It feels relaxed. Liam speaks kindly of his work but it's obvious it's nothing he's passionate about. I can't say much considering I'm working as a bartender.

For the most part, it's easy with Liam. We avoid the heavy subjects and that helps. After first running into him at Club Taint, the only thoughts that pummeled my mind were the physical acts of our betrayal. That and how utterly awful I was to him after Marisa died. I expected this weekend to be heavily laced with thoughts of her. But right now, my mind is wondering what it would have been like if the two of us would have opened that bridal shop up after Marisa died. If we wouldn't have slept together, maybe we could have proceeded with our plan?

He seems happy and in his element here but Frank's words about Liam just letting life happen around him keeps echoing in my mind. Perhaps on paper, Liam is doing well, but with relationships he's just as messed up as me.

After the sun begins to set, Liam indicates that we better head back to the houseboat before it turns dark. "There are no lights on the row boat." He winks at me.

Once we cross the river and enter the moor, I have to stop rowing just to take in the grand sight of it all. The moor is a small, private cutout from the river so no waves or wake even touch it. The glass-like water is glittering in the golden twilight as Liam continues to slowly slice the oars into the smooth surface.

"It's magical here," I say, turning in my seat to show him my face of wonder. "It feels ethereal."

He pauses, staring at me curiously. Slivers of warm sunlight shine through his messy blond locks as his gaze falls to my arms. "They suit you."

"What suits me?"

"Your tattoos. The sleeve." I cover my arms self-consciously. "Don't cover them. I mean it, Rey. You had the roses back in Oxford, but not all this." His eyes move down my arm and pause on the pocket watch. "They're gorgeous on you. Like they should have always been there."

My posture straightens at his sincere words. "Thanks. You have any?"

"Nope…Not yet." He begins rowing again.

I turn and start rowing again. "So you want one?"

"I've had an idea for one for a while."

I glance over my shoulder. "You should get it. What's stopped you?"

"Life, I suppose."

As we pull back up along the backside of the houseboat, I see a blank space for a boat name. "I see there's no name on your boat. Don't guys like to name their boats? You referred to it as a 'her' though, so do you have a name in mind?"

Liam looks introspective for a moment. "I keep waiting for something to come to me…but so far, nothing quite fits. It's always felt like a 'she' though." He smiles fondly and helps me scramble off the rowboat.

I excuse myself to take a shower and Liam says he's going to get dinner started. A short while later, I'm in a pair of skinny jeans, a black, loose vintage tank, and flip-flops. My hair is wet down my back and my face is bare. I step onto the deck of the boat and the night sky is twinkling with stars. I smile, taking in the view. You never see stars in London.

Light music drifts down from land and I look up to find Liam standing at the grill by the garden house. He's changed into a comfortable pair of jeans and a white fitted t-shirt. His hair is mussed and glowing in the Edison bulbs hanging from the wooden lattice overhang. The entire deck is illuminated in a soft, magical glow.

As I approach, Liam looks up and smiles softly. His eyes graze down from my face to my body and the intensity in his gaze makes me stop just before the deck. I feel suddenly sick with nerves. Stepping onto this deck right now feels terrifying. It feels like an important decision. One that I'm not sure I can trust myself to make.

Liam continues to look at me expectantly so I close my eyes to search my mind for the answer. When I open them, he's standing above me with his hand stretched out. I look at it and then back into his warm, brown gaze.

Reaching out, I place my hand in his and a comforting warmth casts down over me as I step up onto the same level as him. He guides me over to the entry of the garden house. Inside is a small, rustic end table where he has most of our dinner prepped and ready.

"Would you like a glass of wine?" he asks.

I nod and accept the pre-poured glass of red sitting beside the grill. I sip it slowly while walking around and taking in the various produce throughout. "You've been busy. Who maintains all this when you're in London?"

"A neighbor," Liam answers, pulling the chicken off the grill and striding into the building. "They live just around the bend."

"How often do you come out here?" I glance out the etched glass at the twinkling water and feel star struck at the splendor of it all.

He shrugs and sets the chicken down next to the bowl of grilled veggies and a loaf of crusty bread. "Once a month. Maybe more?"

"Have you ever brought anyone out here?" Curiosity is taking over and I'm unable to stop my forward questioning.

He pauses as he plates our food, pursing his lips in the way he does when he's trying to be careful with his words. "No," he finally answers.

God, I must be glutton for punishment. "Why not?" I hear my voice ask honestly.

My question looms silently in the air around us as he pulls the chairs up close to the table and gestures for me to sit. He begins eating so I tuck into mine to be polite.

After a few moments Liam stops eating and takes a sip of his wine, eyeing me over the rim of his glass. "I can't seem to get close enough to anyone since…since—"

"Marisa?" I ask, finishing his sentence. Speaking her name out loud adds a heaviness to the air. But it's a heaviness I've been feeling already. Marisa is a huge elephant in the room whether we want to admit it or not. May as well just lay it all out there.

Liam's eyes squint briefly. "Yes. Something like that." I pause mid chew and swallow as he continues, "I don't know…this place just seems sacred somehow. I bought the boat on a whim just after graduation and poured all my efforts into making it livable."

Our eyes connect as the memories of our words exchanged at graduation loom between us. This. This is one of those moments where Liam and I seem to share an entire conversation without even speaking. My eyes are saying I'm sorry and his eyes are saying he knows.

"So yeah, it was quite a mess when I got it. Theo came out and helped me refinish all the woodwork. That's how we became so close."

I nod and take another sip of my wine. "It's funny how we both became close with someone related to Marisa. It's like we couldn't fully give her up."

He cocks his head and watches me for a moment. "Did Hayden help you…cope?"

His question should have been expected but the confusion I feel over my answer is unexpected. Did Hayden help me cope? Did anything Hayden and I give each other have any positive effect on us?

"That's a hard question to answer," I reply, honestly.

"How did you two start hanging out?"

"About a year after Marisa's funeral I ran into him at a pub in London. He was wasted and picking a fight with the bartender. I wasn't much better. We just both seemed to be in the same shitty place at the same shitty time feeling the same shitty way. I don't know." I shrug.

A steely expression fleets over Liam's face. His jaw muscle ticks and I have to look away from him. The pain I see behind his eyes is too much. I know what he's thinking. He's thinking he wanted to be there for me. He wanted to help me. But I did what I do best. I pushed him away with all my might.

He stands up and grabs our empty plates and sets them alongside the grill. Without a word, he walks out to the end of the deck and sits down on the edge, staring out into the darkness. His shoulders are slumped and I could kick myself for the sight of him.

I stride over to him and sit down beside him, letting my legs hang down into the grass. "What is it Liam?" My voice is shaky as my bare arm grazes his. I can feel a change in him and I hate it. I know what's coming.

He turns to face me with a determined look in his eyes. "Can I ask you a personal question, Rey?"

I arch one brow. "I thought we already were." The Edison bulbs cast a glow across his eyes as he chuckles sadly.

"I want to know about your sleeve. Every part of it."

That surprises me. And relieves me in some ways. I glance down and rub my hand over the colorful skull located right over my tricep. "It's a sugar skull. Have you ever heard of Dia de los Meurtos?" He shakes his head and turns so he's facing me. He grabs my arm and traces his fingertip lightly over the design. The sensation is thrilling but morose at the same time. The design feels so personal and intimate.

"It's the Day of the Dead. Mostly it just means death, spirituality…remembrance. It's on November first. It's like the Mexican Halloween sort of. The Mexican culture makes these clay molded sugar skulls on that date. They paint and decorate them really beautifully and then on the forehead they would write the name of the departed. You put the skull on the gravestone and it encourages the departed to appear on that day."

"Does it work?" Liam asks.

I shrug my shoulders. "I've never actually made one. Just the tattoo."

"And the sunflowers?" he asks moving his finger around the bouquet over my arm.

Swallowing against the butterflies that his touch causes, I reply. "Marisa has an uncanny way of appearing to me in my dreams…like a lot. And every time she shows up…it's always sunny." I laugh self-deprecatingly.

"Really?" His brown eyes are swimming with wonder.

"Yeah, in fact, I had a dream of her and this entire tattoo design before she even died. Crazy, right? Do you ever dream of her?"

His lips purse, deep in thought, as he touches the pocket watch on my wrist. I'm sure he doesn't need to ask the meaning behind that one. He knows Marisa's time of death just like I do.

"I've only dreamt of her once." He looks away suddenly, dropping his head down to his chest.

"What's wrong, Liam?"

He clears his throat. "Nothing. I'm just suddenly feeling very tired."

"We can go to bed if you want."

He nods and gets up to turn off all the lights. Once he's closed everything up, he comes back over to me and watches me from the deck. His whole body is tense with something major.

"What is it, Liam? Just tell me!"

He shakes his head. I can barely see his eyes in the dark. "Do you ever just feel like you've lost so much time, Rey? Time that we can never get back?"

"I don't know, I guess. I've never really been good at managing much in my life…Definitely not time."

He shakes his head, a flicker of disappointment marring his handsome face. "Let's just go to bed."

We head back to the boat and it's a charged silence as we both quietly get ready for bed. Whatever thought Liam is battling isn't something he's interested in discussing and that's probably for the best. This weekend is about rekindling a friendship…not raking each other over the coals for our poor life choices.

"Are you dressed?" Liam's voice asks from the doorway.

I pull down my long white T-shirt that hits mid thigh. "Yes."

He emerges in the doorway in a pair of shorts and nothing else. My mouth feels dry as my eyes flick over every corded ripple of muscle on his abs, chest, and arms. Looking away nervously I begin pulling down the covers on the bed to distract myself.

"Do you have everything you need?" I glance up and his eyes are sad and watchful on me. I nod silently. "Alright," he moves toward me and for a minute my heart takes flight up into my throat. He leans in and kisses me on the cheek, pausing by my ear. "Sleep well, Rey."

I clear my throat and nod woodenly. I watch him walk out and nearly drop to the floor at the overwhelming urgency I have to taste that cinnamon smell on him.

It's going to be a long night.

CHAPTER 20

I'm walking down a narrow set of stairs to a dingy and dark basement. There's old carpet tile squares scattered haphazardly around the floor revealing concrete below. An overweight guy with a long goatee is sitting on a stool in the corner playing with a tattoo gun and smoking a cigarette.

He looks at me expectantly, exhaling a huge cloud of smoke. "What do you want?"

"Reyna wants a tat," Jessica answers for me. Jessica was a girl I knew from school that dropped out two months ago. We were both only fifteen.

"How old are you?" The man glares at me knowingly.

"Eighteen," I answer confidently.

"Got cash?" I nod and hold out a large wad of twenties that I had stolen from my mother's purse.

"Know what you want?" he barks.

I nod again and hand over a sketch I designed myself.

"I only do free hand," he grunts.

"Works for me."

He didn't wear gloves and he never cleaned the needles. He just propped me on a stool and began carving into my collarbone like I was a damn Halloween pumpkin. I cried the entire time. The pain was so intense, my entire body was shaking. He'd scoff at me and ask if he needed to stop and I said no every time.

Suddenly, my mother appears right beside me, looking down on the ink being sliced into my skin. My eyes alight with determination.

"Look, Mother! Look! I got a tattoo," I cry excitedly.

Her face splits into a large smile. "What does it say, my Miracle?" she asks, her voice calm.

Anger explodes in my fiery veins at her less than desired reaction. I glance down to find the man has disappeared and my ink is complete. Three beautiful black roses wrap around the words: *We All Die Young.* It was stunning.

This tattoo was meant to be the ultimate fuck you to my mother and here she is smiling at me! "What does it say? It says we all die young, Mom. It says I'm dead inside."

"Reyna Miracle, that's an interesting choice. I'm glad you've found a way to express yourself."

"Express myself? That's it? That's all you have to say?"

"Yes honey, I'm proud of you…always!" Her smile remains.

"Fuck you!" I scream. "That's what you should be saying! You should be screaming at me for being an idiot! For getting a tattoo from a dirty guy in a crack house who didn't wear gloves and didn't wash his hands!"

Suddenly the room around us disappears and it's just my mother and me in a cloud of smoke. I glare into her blue eyes and yell, "You should be saying that you wished I wasn't the one that lived! You should be saying that one of the other babies would have been a better daughter than me."

"Reyna, no. You are my miracle always."

"I'm not, Mom! I'm not a miracle. I'm a fifteen-year-old who just got her first tattoo!"

"That doesn't take away your specialness."

"I hate you! I hate you for looking at me like I'm a miraculous survivor. I wish I would have died with them!"

I jolt up, screaming in agony as the sensation of a needle pierces through my collarbone. I swear I can still feel the residual pain of the fresh ink.

"Rey, are you alright?" Liam says looking groggy and out of breath as he runs up to the bed.

"Holy shit," I say breathing heavily, looking around and realizing I'm back in Liam's houseboat. I'm no longer a fifteen-year-old in a basement. "Holy shit…it was a dream but…but…it hurts."

"What hurts?" he asks worriedly.

"My collarbone." I touch the three black roses. "I just dreamt that I got the tattoo and I swear it still hurts." I check for scabs or any signs of freshness and there's nothing.

"Just a sec," Liam says, leaving me and going into the bathroom. I hear him turn the water on and glance at the clock to see it's one in the morning. He returns with a wash cloth and climbs up on the bed next to me, placing it on my ink.

"It's so weird," I croak out, my knees bent as my elbows rest on them. My head is dropped between my legs as I attempt to come back down to reality.

"Vivid dream maybe? Just residual memories?" Liam offers helpfully, stroking the cool cloth over my skin. "Do you want to tell me about it?"

I exhale a shaky breath. The truth is…the dream wasn't far from what really happened. I was fifteen when I got the roses. It was in a dingy basement and the guy told me he only did freehand. And, despite the dreary surroundings, the man had created art on my skin.

"I was fifteen when I got this tattoo," I croak, wiping a light sheen of sweat off my forehead. "I was dreaming of that."

"Fifteen? I bet your mom flipped."

I shake my head. I was practically begging to get into trouble and she just smiled at me. "That's the thing…she didn't. She didn't even punish me. Nothing."

"What's the meaning behind it? You never told me earlier."

Steeling myself I reply. "I'm a quad. I was born a quadruplet with three sisters. We were born super early and basically lived in incubators for months. I was the only one who lived." As soon as the words tumble from my mouth, I'm shocked.

"God, I had no idea. You've never said."

"You only know what I want you to, Liam. I've never told anyone I'm a quadruplet…except Marisa." The sound of her name brings a calm to me in that moment. I'm momentarily distracted by the idea that I've never even revealed this much about myself to Hayden. What is it about Liam that makes me want to open up so much?

"So the three roses represent them? Your sisters? But what about the text?"

I can feel Liam's eyes on me but I can't bring myself to look at him. This question isn't as easy to answer. My whole life I lived feeling like someone else would have been better here instead of me. When you have your choice of four and you end up with me, it doesn't really leave you thinking you hit the jackpot.

"My mother gave me a love that I couldn't understand. I couldn't believe it. It wasn't unconditional like most would think. In some ways it felt entirely conditional."

"How so?"

I remove the cloth from him and toss it to the floor. I touch the roses tenderly. "Her love was completely based on the fact that I survived. And that was it. I was the one of four quadruplet girls that lived. Her love didn't feel personalized for me. Just for the miracle that she said I was. She even made Miracle my fucking middle name."

"I never knew that either. How is that possible?"

"It's not something I tell people. It's embarrassing. Then my dad died when I was five, as you already know. And it's like she snapped. I could do no wrong in her eyes. It didn't matter what I said or did, how naughty I was as a child. Or even who I was as a person. She was going to love me regardless because I lived. That's it. That was the only condition for her love. I was the most perfect being ever created.

"But the problem was—my outsides didn't match my insides. If anything, I feel like I was twenty-five percent of a person…No miracle. And no matter what I did growing up, no matter how hard I rebelled, how awful I was…my mother always just smiled.

"This tattoo was just the beginning of my ink obsession. The pain I felt getting them done was almost as meaningful as the image that was represented. The ache of the needle digging in over and over was blissful agony to me. It was the most alive and imperfect I had felt in my entire life. The pain made me feel real. Un-miraculous."

"But what's so wrong with being called a miracle?" he challenges.

I roll my eyes and turn to face him, sitting criss-cross. Moonlight shines in from the three portholes above the bed, casting a blue glow over the white linen sheets. "It isn't reality, Liam. Loving someone like that just because they exist. It isn't fair. I was so awful and the more awful I got, the more I felt like I shouldn't have been the one. I shouldn't have been the one to survive."

"That's crazy, Rey."

"It's not crazy!" I snap defensively. "I've dreamt of my sisters, Liam." My voice cracks on his name and two errant tears slip down my cheeks. I swipe them away angrily. "It's like I feel them with me and it just makes me feel like I cheated destiny somehow."

"Rey, how can you say that?" He reaches out and cups my face so I can't look away from him. His thumbs slide along the wet paths as his eyes swim with emotion. "Do you not see yourself for all that you are?"

I shake my head and feel completely transparent in front of him right now. Surrendering, I reply, "It's a painful thing not living up to other people's standards of you. It's an even more painful thing when you're not even surprised."

"Fuck," he growls.

Staring at my lips, Liam's mouth follows his gaze. I pull back before our mouths touch, but he doesn't release my face.

"Liam. We shouldn't."

"I have to, Rey. I have to kiss these lies off of your mouth or I will die."

The intensity in his scrutinous expression is breathtaking. Seconds tick by and my eyes continue to rapidly shift between each of his, seeing no flicker of doubt. "You can't, Liam. You just can't." My vision blurs with tears.

"Try to fucking stop me." He connects our mouths and the taste of his words and the utter feeling of devotion in his embrace is all encompassing.

His grip on my face loosens as I begin to return his kiss. I'm powerless against it. It's like nothing I've ever gifted myself before. Even when we slept together in college, it wasn't like this. It wasn't this pure, this powerful, this demanding.

He moves to lie over the top of me, never breaking our lips. I can taste his cinnamon toothpaste and it's everything I've fantasized about for years since our first night together. I spread my legs as he pushes himself up against me.

He releases my lips and looks down at me with wide, fearful eyes. "Rey, I need you not to think about this. I need you not to stop this. We both need this and I'm begging you to just live in it with me. Please."

His lips pucker in that seriously seductive way as he waits for my answer. Unable to find my voice, I nod shakily and he rushes my mouth again. We can't get each other naked fast enough. After stripping my T-shirt and yanking down his shorts, we slide our bare bodies together, moaning breathlessly at the erotic sensation of our skin gliding along one another.

He pauses our motions and drops his head down to my sleeved arm. Running his cheek up from my wrist to my shoulder, a low grumble echoes in his chest that has my pelvis thrusting up greedily towards his. He pauses and moves across my chest, dropping a feather light kiss on each one of my hardened nipples, darting his warm and wet tongue out for a quick, light stroke.

With an aching need, I want to grip his face and shove him against my chest, but I refrain. He looks up at my face, smiles softly with that sexy mouth of his and then connects his lips to my rose-covered collarbone. His hot tongue flicks and licks a trail all the way to my jaw, his lips nibbling the entire way. Unable to withstand another second of this torture, I grab his face and yank his lips back to mine, swirling my tongue into his mouth to taste the path he so gloriously sucked.

Groaning loudly in my mouth, he murmurs something about a condom and without warning, he's off of me and leaning over to the nightstand. "Fuck, I want to do this, Rey. I want to do this with you so bloody badly. You're just so…fucking…stunning in every way."

Grateful he didn't call me perfect, I nod my approval and watch him push the condom over his throbbing erection. I bite my lip as his muscular body crawls its way back between my legs. He grips his condom-covered dick and firmly strokes the tip on my wet and slickened center. He releases himself and decides to first plunge two thick fingers deep inside of me.

I turn my head sideways and moan at the unimaginable pleasure his touch has on me. God, it's just his fucking fingers and I'm positively writhing beneath him. Noticing how strongly I'm reacting,

Liam continues pumping me with his two digits, grunting sexily, as my cries grow louder and louder.

"God, Liam! Liam!" I scream as I tighten and climax around his fingers. Holy fucking hell.

My eyes flutter open as he pulls his hand out and strokes his moistened digits over my lips. His mouth crashes down on mine and he pulls my lower lip into his mouth to suck my arousal off.

The whole thing is erotic as fuck.

As he stops sucking on my lip, his hand returns to his dick and he guides it slowly into me. The stretching his size causes in the wake of my orgasm is overwhelming. I'm raw and oversensitive and the desire shooting through me is positively carnal. I reach up and grab his face, pulling him back to my mouth to put action onto the ridiculous effect he's having on me.

"God, you're so beautiful," he says against my mouth as he rests his forehead on mine. That delicious cinnamon breath on my face has me pulling him inside of me further.

"So are you," I pant out because he is. He so fucking is.

"I prefer ruggedly handsome," he murmurs as he thrusts into me at a deliciously slow pace. I can feel the smirk on his lips.

"Shut up and fuck me." I reach up and bite his perfectly pouty lip.

His chest vibrates with laughter, but that's exactly what he does. He quickens his pace—his face intense as he brings me to a place that I'm not all together comfortable being in. Confusion washes over me with every thrust of his hips. I attempt not to slip deeper into those thoughts—to just enjoy the feel of him sinking into me and hitting that exceedingly tantalizing G-spot.

But I can't help it.

I begrudgingly gaze into his eyes and know without a doubt that this act we're performing right now feels so much more intimate than anything I've had before. What we're doing is for a pure and intense connection. It's not just a coping mechanism. It's not a raw, carnal need to fuck. It's a deep, burning urge to *feel*. And despite myself, for the briefest of moments, I allow my heart to feel the sensation of being the object of someone's love.

True, *unconditional* love.

CHAPTER 21

Meaningful change is always painful. It's always resisted. And it's always awkward. Add in a sexy British blond alpha and it's downright confounding.

In grad school, I was always careful around Liam. The feelings I would get in my chest every time I saw him were so poignant, avoidance was necessary. He would drop subtle hints, like he saw me for something more than I was, but I would shut it down every time. I even tried to avoid listening when he'd tell stories about his upbringing or fun things he did with his friends and family. The more I knew about him, the more I would care. I didn't like caring. I didn't like feeling.

I never wanted to end up with anyone. That much I knew. The loss of my sisters is something I carry with me every day. And the loss of my father when I was finally beginning to store memories of him was like a sick, cruel joke that destiny played on me.

My father died of a fluke heart issue when he was only thirty-six-years-old. He was extremely fit. I remember him running on our treadmill every single night because it used to be where I'd have to go to kiss him goodnight.

Now, my lasting memory of him was my mother dragging his limp, naked body out of the shower and administering CPR on our white tiled floor all while screaming at me to dial 911. It was a sight no child should ever have to see of her parents. And no matter how hard I try to hold onto the good memories, all that really stuck was the image of my mother's short body wailing over the top of him as the paramedics came on the scene.

The sight was stained on my mind.

The doctors said it was probably something he lived with his whole life and never knew. And to this day, I still couldn't decide on a tattoo to memorialize him. I went a few times to the tattoo studio, but I always turned around. Nothing worked.

Then slowly, through the years, I became expert at pushing people hard enough to keep them at arm's length. It was survival. The only example of love I had was the warped and frustrating and completely unbelievable devotion that my mother gave me.

I hated it.

I didn't want it.

It wasn't for me.

To be loved…truly loved…was a distinct impossibility for me.

When Liam said those words to me that night we slept together in school, I was blind. Just like last night. I got caught up in the moment and allowed myself to forget that Liam belonged with someone who was like Marisa. Marisa was wonderful. Marisa was good.

And nothing about me has changed. If anything I've only gotten more dark and twisted since losing my best friend.

Allowing the water to cascade down my skin, my mind wanders back to everything Liam and I did to each other last night. The soft sway of the boat as he rocked himself into me was completely mind-blowing. How he had me taste myself was unlike anything I have ever experienced sexually. Then later when he flipped me over and pulled my back against his chest and squeezed my breasts so hard I thought he'd leave bruises.

Fuck it was hot.

Liam didn't fuck like a college boy anymore. Liam fucked like a man.

And damn if it didn't turn me on like crazy.

I had my fair share of sexual experiences back in high school. That didn't stop when I came to London. I was the interesting American so the boys at university were all keen to get to know me. Nothing ever lasted much more than a night. Except for Toby Brentano. He was vile and had a habit of saying the worst things to me while we fucked. Things like 'worthless bitch' and 'dirty whore' and 'ugly twat.' I tolerated it all because Toby wasn't saying anything that I didn't already think of myself anyway.

I kicked Toby to the curb soon after I started my masters. At that point I became more interested in my education and less interested in rebelling and pissing my mother off. Plus, I met Marisa. She was really good for me. She didn't completely change my wild ways, but she made me feel different somehow.

Then Liam came along and it felt like all I was doing was fighting a crazy attraction to him that I had zero interest in pursuing. Regardless of my distaste for all things beautiful, watching Liam and Marisa together became a new kind of emotional cutting for me. They were so happy and at ease with each other. Natural. I would have my ear buds in, blasting my weird indie hip hop and just stare at them sitting near me, giggling together. It made me sick in so many ways because I knew I'd never feel like that with anyone.

And right now, all I wanted to do was bolt. I wanted to walk to the nearest train station and get the hell back to London where I could keep myself locked away in my own urban bubble. This fresh air was messing with me. But last night Liam had asked me not to think. He said "we needed this." So perhaps sleeping together this weekend is something we both can do to get ourselves back on track. Sow our wild oats. Explore the curiosity we had for each other in school and then forget it.

A guy like Liam doesn't end up with a girl like me. No one does. Not even close.

"Stop thinking!" Liam's voice growls. Suddenly the shower curtain is ripped open on me to reveal Liam in his glorious birthday suit. "I swear your thoughts woke me from a very contented sleep just moments ago."

My hands awkwardly attempt to cover myself and he rolls his eyes knowingly. I glance down at his body as he steps over the tub edge and into the shower. He immediately dips his head beneath the hot stream. The large waterfall showerhead in the center of the ceiling soaks him as he scrubs his hair and face. I can't help but ogle every single inch of him as the water finds sexy, muscular divots to ride down the length of his body.

Following the water path, I see that Liam is definitely wide awake this morning. I look up to find him watching me staring and I can't help but crack a grin. He shoots a lopsided smile at me that almost immediately vanishes all of my dark thoughts from earlier.

"I was sleeping really well you know. Better than I have in years until your thoughts started barreling through the thin boat walls."

"Whatever," I explain. "It was those damn swans that woke me. They are a neighborhood nuisance!"

His brows waggle in that charming boyish way. "Yeah, who bloody likes swans?"

"Not me! Too perfect." I turn my back on him and stick my head under the water to rinse the last bits of conditioner out.

His whiskered chin slides down from my ear to my neck as he murmurs, "I like imperfect."

My body goes tense instantly. I turn my head to take in his expression and he's eyeing me inquisitively, clearly waiting for my reaction. I turn to face him and his gaze lazily slides from my mouth to my body.

Without looking at my face, he says, "Don't get squirrely on me, Rey, or I'm going to fuck you right now to get you to stop thinking. And I didn't bring a condom in here with me."

"Liam, I just don't want you to get the wrong idea—"

I cry out loudly as his head ducks low and snatches one of my nipples into his mouth. Sucking hard, he then taps his teeth lightly on the pebbled nub in a gloriously threatening manner.

"Ah!" I exclaim and pull his face into my chest to stop him from pulling back on my nipple any further. "They're kind of attached!"

He instantly relaxes his bite and begins suckling and licking in a completely pleasurable way. His hands find my rear and pull me into his hard on.

"I thought you said you didn't bring a condom," I shamelessly moan, bracing my hand out on the wall for support.

He looks up at me with a ferocious expression as the water pours heavily over his face. "I don't need one for what I'm about to do," he says through the stream. Then, he drops to his knees before me. He slowly slides his hand from my right ankle to my knee, lifting it up and placing it on his shoulder. He looks proudly at my center for one brief second before burying his face in me like a man on a mission to find my deepest, darkest secrets.

I scream out instantly when I feel his teeth brush my clit and grip my other hand on the shower rod. Balancing myself, I move one of my hands to fist in his hair as he assaults my vertical slit with his skilled mouth. Feeling him moan between my thighs sends shooters all down my legs, and I swear they're going to give out. Liam supports my balance with his hands on my backside as they stroke and fondle my crack the entire time.

In only moments I break apart all over him and he pulls his face back to look up at me. His winded and awed expression is sexy as fuck. I pull my leg off and slide down to kneel, mirroring his stance. I bend over and take him in my mouth and he leans back on his heels to give me better purchase of his dick. His groans of my name along with the man he worships are echoing off the walls as I greedily return the distinct pleasure he brought me only seconds before.

"Does this mean you're done thinking?" Liam asks breathlessly after I swallow down the entirety of his climax.

"It means I sucked your dick, Liam. Let's not dissect every decision I make today." No matter how poor they might be, I think to myself.

"Fair enough." He plants a sloppy, satisfied kiss on me and grins while he cuts the water off. "Fuck that was hot."

His mood is contagious as we both towel dry ourselves. We eventually separate to our prospective areas to get ready. I toss my wet hair into a topknot and throw on a pair of black jogging shorts that I stuffed in my bag. Rummaging around, I find a dark gray tank top. I throw on a pair of flip flops and I'm ready.

After a somewhat awkward breakfast, Liam informs me that we are going to take a couple of bicycles into town to sight see. Moments later, I step onto the deck of the boat to find Liam pulling the bikes out of the garden house. They're antique with wicker baskets on the front. He's dressed in a green pair of cargo shorts, black athletic sneakers, and black polo. He looks sporty and sexy with his tousled blond hair and nearly full, trimmed beard now.

"You ready?" He strides over and helps me up out of the boat.

"Yeah, sure. Where are we going?" I ask, eying the bikes dubiously.

"Everywhere." He shoots me that proud boyish smile again and we're off.

We peddle around all day, stopping at various spots and taking in the gorgeous sights. The awkwardness we had at breakfast is completely gone as we focus on the beauty that is Cambridge. It's full of museums and art galleries. There are tons of quaint cobblestone passages situated amongst stunning architecture. Several of the roads are narrow and old, so bicycles are very popular even with the locals. We park our bikes and take a ride on a small punt down the river canal. It's like a page straight out of a Venice brochure.

For most it would be incredibly romantic. For Liam and me, it's just serene and peaceful. We silently take in our surroundings without even looking at each other. It's almost like we both needed a minute alone with our thoughts.

CHAPTER 22

Finally, we stop at a quaint pub for an early dinner and I realize that I haven't stopped smiling since we started our adventurous day. Something about today feels so…healthy. So…replenishing.

Liam orders us two pints and we sidle up in a cozy booth. "Drink up," he mumbles, downing half of his beer in one large swallow.

"What's your deal?" I arch my brow curiously.

He looks off nervously. "No deal. Whatever do you mean?"

"Why are you acting so nervous all of the sudden?"

"I'm not, I'm fine. Let's talk." He pierces me with his stunning eyes and I feel that familiar pull I always have with him.

"What do you want to talk about?" I ask, averting my eyes and gazing out the window to watch a young boy throw rocks off a small bridge.

"How about Frank? He seems safe," Liam offers helpfully.

"Frank," I let out a hearty laugh. "He's…interesting."

"That he is," he replies knowingly.

"How do you know him?" I ask, "We haven't ever discussed it."

Liam presses his plump lips together in the way he always does when he's trying to come up with the right words. Finally, he replies, "Frank was just sort of there for me at a really awkward time and we became mates after that I guess."

"What sort of awkward time?"

He grins. "I met this girl named Finley at a club one night. Not Club Taint. But yeah…I sort of fell for her. She was really the first person I'd been interested in since…"

His voice trails off and I nod knowingly. Clearing my throat I reply, "I met Finley you know."

"You did? When?" His eyes widen with surprise.

"She stopped into Club Taint to see Frank one afternoon."

"Ah. Yeah, her and Frank have a special friendship, too. Frank has an uncanny way of being exactly what you need right when you need it."

"I'm getting that impression." I take a sip of my Guinness. "So what happened between you and Finley?"

"She was never on the market, not truly. She wasn't cheating or anything—" His voice stops mid sentence and his jaw drops in horror as he realizes what he said.

"We save that type of little transgression for the true gems, like me." My voice is hard and flat as my eyes cast downward into my beer.

"Hey," he reaches his hand across the table and touches my bawled up fists. "You weren't alone there, Rey. If I recall, I was the one that pushed you."

I shake my head sadly, feeling a familiar ache erupt beneath my chest. An ache for something I can never atone. And an ache for wondering why I always seem to put myself in these situations. "Finish your story."

He looks at me sympathetically for a moment like he wants to dig deeper but has mercy on me. "There's not a lot more to say, really. Her boyfriend surprised her from America. They had some bumpy roads I guess, but I've seen her since then and they seem genuinely happy."

I nod and look out the window feeling oddly bereft. Would anyone fly over an ocean for me? Even if I wanted them to?

"What about you, Rey? Any romances since Oxford?"

I laugh maniacally. "Definitely not. Nothing for me has changed there. I'm not interested in anything serious with anybody. Ever. I hope you realize that, Liam. I know we're complicating things right now, but this is all temporary, right?" Anxiety pulses over me as I take in his hardened eyes.

"Right. 'Course." He nods his head and downs the last of his beer. He hops up and orders us two more even though mine isn't even half gone. "We better order our food. I made a six o'clock appointment."

"For what?" I ask.

"You'll see."

***

Just as the sun is setting, we pull up to a tattoo shop. You could knock me over with a feather I'm so surprised. I actually look across the street to see what else we could be doing in this neighborhood, but Liam grabs my hand and pulls me inside, squashing all my doubt.

"So who's this surprise for? You or me?" I ask, staring at him as he bounces nervously on his feet.

"Me, but I need you here to do it or I won't be able to follow through. I have a horrid fear of needles." His voice is shaky as his eyes dart all around the room.

I laugh heartily as I take in the waiting area of Tattooing by Fabio. It's a small tattoo studio with huge, colorful murals painted on every wall. Several retro, black and red vinyl loveseats sit around the perimeter of the waiting area with scattered photo books.

"Do you need to look at a book?" I ask.

"No, I emailed them the image I want."

"Was there a reason you picked Tattooing by Fabio specifically?" I have to bite my lip to hide my urge to giggle.

"I read it was the best," he mumbles haphazardly as the buzz of a tattoo gun in the back sends him practically leaping through the air.

A short, hipster-looking guy with a full beard, two eyebrow piercings and a slouched beanie comes strolling out. "You must be my six o'clock. Liam is it?" he drawls in a thick, Liverpool accent.

Liam stares at him without saying a word, his jaw moving but no sound coming out. "Yes, this is Liam," I answer, moving up next to him and squeezing his arm. "Are you sure you want to do this?" I whisper up toward his face.

He nods silently and coughs. "Yes."

"My name's Skin. Come on back. There's room for your girlfriend." The guy turns on his heel and strides toward the back rooms.

Liam's jaw muscle ticks uneasily as he lowers himself into the tattoo chair. He avoids my eyes as he pushes the short sleeve of his polo up onto his shoulder. Skin puts on a pair of black surgical gloves and brings the prepared temporary tattoo sheet over to him and they discuss the perfect placement. Liam wants it on the inside of his inner arm, right alongside his bicep. His muscles flex sexily as the seat reclines and he rests his hand on the back of his neck. It's a hot location for a tattoo on a guy.

Skin rubs cleaning liquid over Liam's arm and then places the temp on the area with some water. When he removes the water-permeable paper, it reveals an intricate compass with a black rose woven subtly inside the center. It's incredible. I move to get a closer look as Skin turns to prepare the black ink inside the gun. I can feel Liam's eyes on me as I drink in every exquisite detail.

"Beautiful," I croak, wanting to touch it. Instead, I gently lift his elbow up more for a better look.

"What's with you calling me beautiful?" Liam's voice puffs warm, cinnamon air on my cheek. I turn my head and his eyes are swimming with mirth.

"I forgot, you prefer ruggedly handsome," I reply sarcastically.

"I am getting a tattoo…That's quite manly I'd say." His brown eyes connect with mine.

"Beautiful is a good adjective I think," Skin mumbles while still messing with his workshop area. "Beautiful can be manly."

Liam and I smirk secretively at each other at Skin's side commentary. "What inspired this? A compass?" I inquire, glancing at the design again.

He rubs his lips together before replying. "I just never seem to know what direction to take. Thought maybe this could help make me more decisive."

I cock my head to the side, gazing at him. His eyes glance down to my mouth and just when I think he's going to kiss me, Skin clears his throat from beside us. Liam's eyes grow wide as he sees the tattoo gun, so I pull the wheelie stool up next to him. His hand shoots out and grabs mine tightly.

"This your first?" Skin asks knowingly. Liam nods and that makes the guy chuckle. "It's not often that the girlfriend is more bad ass than the boyfriend."

"She's not my—"

"I cry like a baby with every tattoo," I cut him off before he finishes. Something about this moment makes me want to feel like Liam's girlfriend. It feels intimate and personal and I don't want him to have to explain shit to this guy right now. I want to be in this moment and not think. I never had anybody special with me during any of my tattoos and I can't help but think how nice it would have been if I had.

Liam looks at me curiously, his eyes swimming over every feature on my face like he's trying to figure me out.

"Stop thinking…and don't get squirrely on me." I shoot him a wink and receive a satisfying, proud smirk back in response.

Suddenly, the tattoo gun clicks on and Liam's face drops as Skin connects the needle with his arm for the first time. He slams his eyes shut and his brows furrow as his body takes a moment for the adrenaline to kick in and the numbing sensation to occur. I try not to smile because tattoos do hurt. It's ink and needles for God's sake. People that say it doesn't hurt are full of it. But watching him flinch, I begin to feel jealous and twitchy to be in his place.

Once Liam relaxes into the pain, his eyes never leave mine. The intensity in them as I hold his hand to my chest becomes powerful and overwhelming. Every stab of the needle on his skin feels like a small stroke on my heart that I can't understand. His gaze on me is saying so much that I can't break eye contact with him for fear of falling. Even when the tears begin silently slipping down my cheeks, I don't move from my frozen position beside him. This horribly, impossible emotion that's overcoming me is holding me hostage. Liam pulls his hand free from mine and wipes the tears off my cheeks with the back of his finger. He bands his hand behind my neck and pulls me down onto his chest, dropping soft kisses into my hair. A pit quickly forms in my stomach at his tender touch.

Because I don't want it.

Not a drop.

And it terrifies me to think of what will happen when we leave here tonight.

CHAPTER 23

Part way through, Skin takes a break to grab a smoke. After using the restroom, I head out to the reception area and leisurely pick up a look book. The very first image I flip to pummels me out of nowhere. Feeling a sense of urgency, I duck outside to ask Skin if there's another tattoo artist around. He says his girlfriend, Bones is available.

I double check to ensure that Liam is fine to do the second half by himself. He agrees, but watches me curiously.

"What are you going to get?" he asks.

"You'll see when it's done."

I readjust my hair up on my head and feel invigorated at the idea of a new tattoo. I also feel extremely grateful for the space from Liam. Whatever was happening between us during his tat was intense and nothing like what I should be allowing to happen.

Bones strides into the other tattoo suite where I'm waiting anxiously. She's a tall, thin, blonde with full sleeves on both sides. She's efficient and makes quick work of the supplies and starts work on me in no time.

The tears fall like they always do. Fresh ink. It's the best pain I've ever experienced. The design I selected is small and being etched into the inside of my wrist. Right along side the pocket watch. She finishes in fifteen minutes. Damn. The girl truly is an artist.

I step out of the room, wiping away my residual tears as Liam comes out of his. He rushes me quickly and strokes his thumb below my eyes. "You weren't kidding about the crying."

I laugh self-deprecatingly and attempt to pull away. "Nope, I cry every time. Even with yours apparently."

"Show me." His hand lovingly cups my cheek.

"Show me yours first."

He lifts his arm and his is truly stunning. It's covered in a clear second skin and his flesh below is just starting to redden and rise around the edges, but damn it's hot. Tattooing by Fabio is legit.

I lift my wrist and pull back the white gauze covering the layer of clear second skin so he can fully visualize it. His fingers dance around the edges of it as he inspects the black Native American dream catcher I selected with the words *"With Every Heartbeat, You Caught Me"* scrawled beneath it. The text was something that came to me after my strange NICU dream, but I didn't have the perfect setting idea for it yet. This dream catcher with four small feathers hanging from it was exactly what I didn't even realize I wanted. As soon as I laid eyes on it, it reminded me of my father and how he'd catch me in his arms every time I ran to him.

"Wow, it's perfect. Four black feathers…for your dad and sisters?"

I smile and nod at how Liam somehow always sees right through me. And how he was brave enough to bring up my sisters in public feels so…peculiar. Having him know this intimate detail about me is chilling.

Skin clears his throat near us, throttling our moment. We follow him up to the front to pay. When we walk out into the warm summer night, the sun has completely vanished along with any warm and fuzzies I was feeling earlier in the day.

"Do you want to pop over and get a drink?" Liam asks, his expression hopeful.

It scares the shit out of me. Suddenly my nerves prickle at all that is going down between us. I awkwardly reply, "No, I'm really tired. I'd rather just go back."

He nods stoically and we hop back on the bikes. The night air is breathing some much needed reality back into my messed up psyche. This weekend was a horrid, horrid idea. Liam and I are anything but 'friends' right now. The way he's looking at me? I don't know what we are, but I know I don't want it.

We both dress silently into our nightclothes, just like the evening before. What is it about the night that stirs up that nerve-wracking tension? It's horribly awkward and completely sexually charged as I look down onto my sex-messed bed and wonder how I'm going to get any sleep in there.

Just as I finish in the bathroom, I step out to find Liam leaning against the wall across from the door, waiting. He's shirtless, and dressed in a pair of lounger pants hanging dangerously low beneath his washboard abs.

I clear my throat and try to feign confidence. "Thanks for a nice weekend, Liam." My voice has a sense of finality to it. "You were right, I did miss you. I'm glad we can be friends again." I'm trying my hardest to be nice right now because my other option is to lash out at him and bring my bitch out. However, I don't want to be mean to Liam. He doesn't deserve it. But I know myself. I can only be pushed so far.

He smiles sadly and ruffles his messy hair. Pushing himself off the wall, he comes to lean over me. I crane my neck back to look at him as his hands slide around my waist and pull me into him.

"Liam," I protest, pushing against his chest and trying to ignore the sexy, smooth ridges of his pecks. "We need to quit now or this is only going to get more fucked up."

"I like fucked up." He nuzzles his mouth into my neck and I flinch away from the intimate touch. Exhaling loudly, he pulls back and his brow furrows in frustration at the discomfort all over my face. "Bloody hell, Rey!" he growls and turns his head.

"What?" I ask, watching the twitch of that pesky jaw muscle.

"You know what!" He releases me and aggressively runs his hands through his hair, stepping back to the wall again. "Why are you doing this?"

"What am I doing?" My voice is forcibly high pitched. My actions shouldn't be a surprise right now. This was supposed to be a casual weekend.

His eyes pummel me with a seriousness that I don't dare look away from. "You're pulling away, I can feel it. I felt it on the whole bloody ride back tonight. For fucks sake, Rey…You were different out there today. Didn't you see that? You were vulnerable, warm, and wonderful in that secretive way that I always saw back at Oxford. Hell, you even did that weird introspective thing you do where it looks like you're smelling the air and debating the meaning of life all inside your head."

"Thanks?" I snap back sarcastically.

"It's a compliment and you bloody well know it," he barks, instantly shooting me down.

"Liam! You don't know me anymore like you think you do. I'm a *ghost* of the person I once was. You have no idea who I've been for the past three years. You haven't been around!"

"That wasn't my fucking choice!" he roars. His eyes are wary. Begging. Pleading.

I swallow down his spot on retaliation. "You said friends. I'm not equipped for whatever you're trying to make this."

"Oh, bollocks!" he shouts and then rushes up to me, trapping me around the door frame. His arms are on either side of my face as he bores wide and tense eyes down on me. "I'm done, Rey. I can't be perfect here. I can't say or do the right thing because that's always serving someone else. Today, I want to be selfish. Today, I want to be impatient. Today, I want to choose the direction my life goes. Today, I want to make you mine."

His eyes flash down to my mouth and before I can protest, he slams his lips to mine and I swear I can taste the word *mine* melting into every part of his sensual assault. His tongue pushes past my lips and takes what it so greedily wants. My limbs turn to mush.

This kiss is entirely different than the kisses we shared last night and this morning. This kiss is powerful, hungry, and demanding. This kiss is taking, not giving. Just as I prepare to grab him by the neck and yank him toward the bedroom to finish the job he's started, he breaks away and murmurs, "Sometimes, nice guys just have to be bad if they want something this hard."

I move my chin up to kiss him again and he yanks himself back from me, leaving me dizzy and breathless against the wall.

"I'm not waiting forever, Rey," he says walking backwards away from me. His eyes have a haunted look to them, like he knows he's leaving way too much power up to me and he's terrified of what's to come. "Even though I'm still *fucking madly* in love with you, I won't…I refuse to wait forever."

And with that, he turns toward the living room, leaving me shattered and completely sickened in his wake.

CHAPTER 24

Sick.

Sick.

Sick.

Not love.

Never love.

Why did he have to say fucking love? He knows so little about the true inner darkness that I have living inside of me. The torturous need I have to be alone. Completely and utterly alone. It's what I crave. It's what I desire. It's what I need for survival.

With my mind reeling and a panic attack settling in on top of me, I throw all of my possessions into my bag. It's not quite nine o'clock, yet. I can still catch a train back to London. My hands are trembling as I physically try to repel the words he spewed at me just now.

Not love. Not me. Never me.

Throwing on a pair of jeans and a tank, I toss my bag over my shoulder and scurry nervously out into the small living area. Liam is sitting on the couch, still shirtless. His head is drooped as his fingertips calmly tap into each other. He looks up at me as I emerge. His normally warm eyes are dark and ominous.

"I need to leave." My voice is trembling as I fight back tears that I have no clue where they are coming from. I purse my lips to hide the quivering. "I have to get back to London."

He nods slowly. "This is nothing more than I already expected."

I glare at him. "What the fuck is that supposed to mean?"

He half smiles but it doesn't reach his eyes. "It means that not much has changed. I saw it in your eyes when I said that I love you just a bit ago."

I flinch outwardly at his words and shake my head, steeling myself, "You can't possibly love me, Liam. This has become too heavy. You said friends, that isn't what this has turned in to."

"I said what I had to," he snarls, rising to his feet and angrily pacing in front of me. It reminds me of the night he tried to convince me of the same thing three years ago. "Tell me, do you run from Hayden every time your *friendship* shifts?"

My eyes widen. "You know *fuck all* about me or my relationship with Hayden!" I scream defensively.

"You can let him get close but not me? It's not hard to tell what you two have been to each other these last few years, Reyna."

"What. The. Fuck. Is that supposed to mean?" My warning tone is unquestionable. "How dare you?"

"How dare I? How dare you, Rey! You're making this into nothing and you fucking know it was more. We've always been more."

"No, we haven't," I shake my head meanly. "We just had a slip."

His jaw drops in shock and he stops pacing and turns to me. "A slip?"

"Yep, a slip. Shit happens." I feel my pulse thundering loudly in my head but I ignore it.

A scary tremor shudders over his facial features. "How often do you *slip* with Hayden?" His eyes are slits. His voice is scarily calm. "Fucking tell me."

I step straight into him looking right up his flared and angry nostrils. If he wants to fight dirty, he's going to lose. I'm the queen of filth. And I've been yielding my words as weapons for years.

My voice is low and menacing. "I'd rather talk about that night you fucked me in my dorm room. It was the same night you showed me the engagement ring you bought for my dead best friend. Or did you forget?"

A sickening expression blasts his face. For a moment I think he's going to crumple to the floor into a fit of sobs. Instead, his lips form a thin line and he breaks our eye contact, pointing to the door. "You need to leave." He turns his newly hardened dark eyes back on me. "I already called you a cab. All you have to do is walk out that door."

"With fucking pleasure," I reply and storm out without so much as a glance back.

***

The train ride back to London flies. I don't know if it's the adrenaline coursing through my veins, but I swear that no sooner do I hop on the train, the announcement that we're nearing Victoria Station blares overhead. As soon as I pop up out of the Underground, I'm practically screaming for release. For oblivion. For nothingness.

I lay my angry eyes on the White Swan Pub. It looks like a cozy beacon of comfort in comparison to the roaring anger in my body. Dragging my duffle along the sidewalk, I ram the door open and charge right up to an open stool at the bar.

"I need three shots. Anything," I snap to the nearest server behind the bar. She's a younger gal that's been here for about a year now. Vanessa something?

"Should I tell Al you're here?" She looks at me cautiously as she sets three shot glasses down in front of me and fills them with a clear liquid.

"Um…no." I close my eyes and tip the glass into my mouth. Schnapps. I fucking hate schnapps.

Just as I'm downing the third, I hear his voice before I open my eyes again. "Reyna, love. You look…"

His voice trails off as I open my hard gray eyes and fix him with a murderous warning to not finish that sentence. Furrowing his brow, his short stature strides over to the bar and stands before me. His bald head has a light sheen of sweat like he's been moving boxes in the back.

"Where the fuck is he?" His voice is deadly serious.

I shake my head. "It's not who you think."

"Then bloody well tell me who. I'm going to set them straight right the fuck now." His fists clench on top of the glossy wooden bar counter.

I groan loudly and snap, "Jeez, I don't need you interfering too, Al. You're just like my mother!"

"Don't get shirty with me! I've picked you up off this bar floor more times than I care to count and I don't care to do it again. I deserve to know who's got you bellied up to the bar getting rat-arsed like your life depends on it."

I lift my eyes to him and sadly shake my head. "He's miles away in a little houseboat of hell."

Al's eyes turn from angry to sympathetic. My vision begins softening around the edges as the liquor takes quick effect.

"I've not seen you like this in a while, Rey. Surely anyone that's got you this upset must be somebody important."

"It doesn't make any difference if he is, Al. I'm not worth any importance." I roll my eyes and tip the remaining droplets leftover in one of the shot glasses into my mouth.

He reaches his hand across the bar and touches mine. I yank my hand away, hating the loving touch he's trying to give me. It feels like razor blades. He ignores my demeanor and says, "Never say that again, lass. I think you'd be surprised how bloody important you've become. At least to me." His wide eyes pierce me with a meaningful look that further inflicts more pain on my heart.

Eventually, he leaves me in peace and I chug two more shots before deciding to stumble home to my flat. Stepping into my living room, I find Hayden face down, passed out on my mattress. Panic prickles my skin at the idea that he could have mixed booze with pills. He's done it before. I rush over to check him.

When I confirm that he's breathing and his pulse feels okay, I relax and begin stripping off all of my clothes. He's just passed out as usual. I cut the lights and crawl under the covers next to him. I tuck my nose into his shirt-covered shoulder. He instinctually wraps his arm around my back and I breathe in his familiar scent of cigarettes and alcohol. It's an odd, comforting smell that I've been using and abusing for far too long.

Drifting off to sleep I recall over and over the green-eyed look that Liam got in his eyes when he asked about Hayden and my relationship. I knew Hayden would be here when I got back. That's the beauty of him. I know when he's going to pull away and when he's going to push in. I can predict him. After our little blow up the other night, I knew he'd be desperate to make sure we were okay. We seek each other out like that. We crave each other's presence no matter how toxic it might be. It's like an addiction.

Liam is entirely too unpredictable. And that scares the life out of me.

This is where I belong—in a bed with someone just as fucked up in the head as me. Someone who uses me for the same reasons I use him.

Someone who will never fall in love with me.

CHAPTER 25

"Mom?" I ask, walking carefully toward her, my hands extended out in caution. "Mom, what are you doing?"

My mother is sitting on her knees on the cold marble floor we had in the living room of our apartment near the Westminster hospital. There's no furniture in the room—only a large bay window with sheer drapes swaying slowly in the nonexistent wind.

"Miracle? I didn't know you were coming by." Her previously tortured face quickly morphs into a smile. "I wish you would have called."

I stare at her in wonder. "Mom, why are you holding that knife?" The shiny blade glints in the sunlight and her gaze drops to stare at it.

"This seemed like a good choice. I'm good with a scalpel. This is simply an extension of that. They're at least in the same family!" She laughs manically and shoves her short hair back away from her face. A layer of sweat drizzles down her forehead all the way to her lips.

"What are you planning to do with it?" I ask, continuing to walk slowly toward her, but not making much progress.

"Miracle, you should know better than anyone." She cocks her head and stares at me.

"What do you mean?"

"Pain. You want me to feel pain, right?"

"Mom, stop. I don't want you to feel anything."

She shakes her head knowingly. "That's not true, you've asked for pain. So I'm fulfilling the request." Her knuckles turn white as she grips the blade and drags it across the skin on her wrist.

"Mom!" I scream and burst into a dead sprint toward her. I'm running with all my might and not moving a centimeter closer to her. "Mom, stop!" My voice cracks as I drop to my knees exhausted.

Blood pours from her other wrist as she creates a matching slit perfectly. Both wounds tight and thin, but the red reaction thick and heavy. I'm kneeling three feet away from her, frozen, watching the red liquid coat the white marble and am powerless to get to her. Loud, riotous sobs erupt from my throat.

"Why are you doing this, Mom?"

"Reyna Miracle. You want me to miss them, I miss them. You want me to crack, I'm cracking. I will see them soon. All of them. My girls. I will be able to hold them where they are. I will be able to feel their skin on mine. Your father, too." Her blue eyes are smiling. Still—sitting in a pool of blood—she smiles.

"But what about me?" I say through snotty sobs.

"What about you?"

"How can you do this to me?" I cry, feeling so at war with my feelings. Part of me knowing this is what I've always wanted. I've always wanted them to have her. My sisters. They deserve her love, not me. But for the life of me, I'm unable to give her up for them.

"Miracle, how can you be upset? You said it yourself. You're only here by accident. Default. A percentile detection by my calculation. The odds don't lie. Three of you had to die so that one could live."

"I didn't want to be right. I don't understand why I had to be the one, Mom. I don't understand. I'm nothing special. I'm not fulfilling. I don't do anything right. I'm messed up in the head, Mom. I ruin everything I touch!" My voice cracks and I crave the ghost of the warm embrace my father used to give me whenever I cried. "I wish Daddy was here."

"I wish Daddy was here, too." Her face purses into a disgusted sneer. "He could have helped keep me safe. So I didn't have to be the only protector."

You protected too much, I want to say, but don't. I can feel her slipping from me and for once I hold my tongue. "Why are you saying all of this?" I slice my fingers through my wild hair.

"I am only saying what you've been screaming at me for nearly thirty years, my Miracle." Her face is calm. Serene.

"I just wanted to know you, Mother! Fuck!"

"This is all I know how to be." She stands up, the bottom of her white dressing gown dripping with blood. She turns her head and I follow her gaze to find Marisa standing there with her hand stretched out.

"No, no!" I rise and am frozen in place again. "You can't have her, Marisa. Stop. Just wait. I need. I need—"

"You need to wake up, Reyna," Marisa's voice sounds like church bells as she pulls my mother further and further away from me. "You need to wake up. Wake up!"

CHAPTER 26

"Wake up, Rey!"

Two firm hands shake my shoulders roughly and I scream out, "No! STOP!"

"Christ, Rey. Please wake up!" Hayden's voice cuts through my dream and my eyes fly open, wet and wide.

"Hayden?" I cry out loudly. "Oh my God, Hayden." I sit up and he pulls me into his arms as sobs pulse through me. His hands rub down my back in soothing strokes and eventually he reaches up and squeezes that spot at the base of my neck. The spot that feels like my lifeline between sanity and chaos.

"What the fuck were you dreaming about?" His voice is hoarse and I look out the window to see it's still pitch black out.

I groan and shake my head crazily. "Too fucked up to talk about." I pull away from his hug and look him in the eyes. They are sagged and glossy in the dim moonlight pooling in from the window. He looks like he's still drunk. So am I for that matter.

"Where were you last night?" he asks, glancing down at my naked chest.

"Doesn't matter," I say and grip his shoulders aggressively. I pull him to my lips. My kiss is desperate and needy. Hard and biting. Anything to get the fucked up shit I was just dreaming about out of my head. Murmuring against his lips, I whisper, "I need to forget, Hayden. Now. Right now." I plunge my tongue deep into his alcohol-tasting mouth.

It takes him a second, but he grips my neck and returns my kiss with fervor. Eventually he pulls back and stares deeply into my eyes. "Always."

The brief expression I see in his eyes is disarming but before I have time to dissect it, he shoves me hard onto my back against the mattress. He kneels before me in a t-shirt and a pair of black boxer briefs. He pushes them down quickly and then hops up to go grab a condom.

I scrub my hands over my tear-stained face, swallowing away the roiling sickness in the back of my throat. I need to forget. I need oblivion. I need Hayden. He returns with the condom already on as he positions himself beneath my legs. He grips my buttocks and says, "I want you on top." He rolls us over so I'm positioned gloriously naked atop him. "Fuck me, Rey. Now."

I nod numbly at his demand, still feeling the buzz of alcohol in my own system. I sink myself down onto him and relish in the fullness our bodies connecting gives me. I gyrate my hips against him in a slow and steady pace. The sensation between us doesn't have the desired effect I was hoping for. Hayden's large hands guide my hips back and forth as he works me toward my climax. Feeling agitated and confused at why things feel differently between us, I reach down to touch myself to help things along. Hayden's voice breaks into my inner turmoil.

"You can't leave me again, Rey." His voice is guttural and tense. "You can't. Ever."

I frown at his odd choice of words. Talking during sex isn't a common thing between us. If we do talk, it's usually just dirty. Nothing like this. We fuck to stop our brains from working—not reconnect them to each other. I shake my head, attempting to ignore him and the strange, niggling feeling that something is missing.

"I need you," he grunts as I pulse on top of him. "I can't…can't live…without you."

My eyes snap open and lock onto Hayden's. Fear rich and deep explodes inside of me. "What are you doing, Hayden?"

"We need each other, Rey. We can't do life without each other. Don't leave me again." He looks down to where our bodies are connecting, still relishing in the sex act we're performing.

I stop moving. "Stop it. Stop saying those things."

"It's the truth." His gray eyes look up at mine, piercing me with a new found intensity I've never seen before.

I slide off of him quickly, curling myself into a ball on the opposite side of the mattress. "Hayden, this isn't what we do. We don't talk like this. We…we—"

"We help each other stay alive, Rey. I don't want you leaving again." He reaches out to pull me to him.

"Don't fucking touch me!" I snap and stand, dragging the sheet with me, suddenly feeling the need to hide myself from him. "And don't tell me what to do!" God. God, God, God! For the first time since waking up, my mind is clear. What the hell am I doing? "You need to leave."

"No!" he barks defiantly.

"Yes!" I scream. "I can't deal with this. I can't deal with you saying these things. If you knew…"

"Knew what?" He reaches for me again.

"I fucked Liam last night!" I scream using my words as a weapon to snap him back to reality. The room turns eerily quiet. The hum of the fridge and the faint sound of London traffic is all to be heard.

"Liam?" His face is horrified. "Marisa's Liam?"

I nod, unable to meet his eyes. He will always be Marisa's Liam to everyone else. The only other person that knows about what Liam and I did three years ago is my mother. And I only told her to hurt her.

I can feel Hayden staring at me for a painfully charged moment before he turns and hops up off the bed. He bends down and grabs his clothes up off the floor.

"Hayden," I say softly, watching him clutch his pants and shoes to his chest.

"Enough!" he roars.

Unable to watch him leave, I turn and freeze, staring at a random smudge on the wall. Tears begin to slide fast and free down my cheeks as I feel painful heartache all around me. I flinch at the loud crack of my door slamming shut.

The sound shoots renewed life inside of me. Hayden is my friend. I can't let him leave like this. I don't know what he'll do! I jump up and throw on a T-shirt and rush out after him. The elevator doors close just as I reach it and I slam my fist against the metal in frustration. I quickly dart down the stairwell, shakily running the four levels.

I burst out the stairwell doors and see Hayden's back exiting my building. I run after him and stop dead in my tracks to find Hayden and Liam standing toe to toe on the side walk. Face to face. Glower to glower.

Liam is in the same lounge pants that I left him in back in Cambridge, but now wearing a white T-shirt. Hayden is standing there barefoot in his boxer briefs and T-shirt, clutching his jeans and boots to his chest. This looks so, so bad.

"Liam," I say breathlessly as the two continue to stare each other down.

Hayden's face flashes to mine like I just committed the ultimate betrayal by uttering Liam's name instead of his. A stony scowl fleets over his hardened gray eyes as he turns his gaze back to Liam.

"She's a fucked up mess. You can have her." Hayden's voice is laced with ominous threat as he moves to walk away. Stopping suddenly he turns back to Liam and adds, "But you might want to know…I was just inside her, mate."

Liam's eyes alight with anger. He pulls his fist back and sends it flying at Hayden, connecting it with his jaw. Hayden drops his clothes and tackles Liam around the waist as they both go stumbling to the ground, fists flying the entire time.

"Stop! Stop! Stop!" I scream, slicing my hands through my hair in helpless pain.

"Oi! Oi!" Alistair's voice shouts from down the street. He comes running up like lightning. "Pack it all or I'll call the cops on the both of ye!"

Liam and Hayden both scuffle up off the ground and separate. Al's small frame stands between the two of them, his arms stretched out to keep them separated. "Get shot. Now."

"I was already leaving," Hayden growls. "Good fucking luck." He turns and walks down the sidewalk without looking back at me once.

"Reyna, are you alright?" Al asks me. His expression is wary as he stares up at Liam. For a short man, he's definitely still able to intimidate even the largest of British men. Liam looks at me angrily, his nostrils flared as he fights to catch his breath.

"I'm fine, Al," I croak out.

"Well, I'm not leaving ya with this bloke," Alistair growls.

"I can take care of myself, Al. Just fucking go!" I snap meanly. I'm sick of people trying to get inside my life. I just want to be left the fuck alone!

He doesn't even react. He turns and punches Liam in the chest with his pointer finger. "I'm just down the street. You do fuck all to hurt her and you have me to answer to. I may not look like much, but I promise you…you will regret it."

Liam frowns seriously at Alistair and then nods. Once Al decides it's safe to go, he shoots me one more withering gaze and leaves us standing there in awkward silence.

"I feel like I could be sick," Liam says finally and sits down on the curb, taking in large gulps of air. His face is distraught and haggard.

I yank down on my T-shirt to make sure I'm completely covered and sit down beside him. "What are you doing here, Liam?" I glance around for people and am grateful I live on a quiet street. The only traffic that comes back here are the residents that live here and it's after midnight so no one is out and about now.

"I came back because I couldn't stand to be in that houseboat after…after." He pauses, swallowing painfully. "I couldn't sleep. I thought if I could just talk to you again, maybe…maybe things wouldn't go so fucking wrong like they did before. I never imagined. I never suspected you'd…" He gestures down the direction Hayden walked away.

"I tried to tell you, Liam. I'm not good. I'm not right. You don't want me."

"I can't wrap my brain around all of this, Rey. All of this pain. It doesn't make sense. I don't know how you don't see how good it could have been between us."

"Liam," I groan. "You bought a fucking ring for her. For Marisa. Were you ever going to give it to her?" I turn to face him to watch his reaction.

He has the nerve to look offended. "That's your question right now?"

"Yes. I need to know."

"I don't want to tell you because it shouldn't fucking matter, Rey! We're living in today. Right now. I thought we could be each other's *salvation* if you'd have just allowed us to be!" He slices his hands up through his hair. "Hell, even after all this, I *still* think we belong together!"

"Stop saying that!" I scream. "I'm not meant for anyone, Liam! Don't you get that? I just fucked my best friend…and kicked him out of my flat. Don't you see? I will *crush* you. I leave a wake of dead bodies everywhere I go!"

"Bullshit!" he roars and grabs me on the arms.

He moves to kiss me and I rip myself free of his hands and stand up. Disgusted by him and myself, I reply while calmly shaking my head. "This is all true. Something about me isn't right, Liam. I can feel myself pulling you down and I need to stop it before it's too late."

"It's already too late, Rey!" Liam's eyes are teary and strained. "That's why the past three years have been such a fuck all mess for me. I've been trying to play the part of the good guy because I refuse to turn into the man that I was that night with you at Oxford. I don't regret sleeping with you and I don't regret telling you that I love you. But I do regret the timing. Always. I don't want this to be another time I regret. I want to fix this. Properly."

"I'm not a fucking project, Liam! I don't need fixing. Especially not by you!"

"Stop!" he cries, standing and moving within inches of my face. "Fixing things is what I do now. It's how *I've* learned to cope. You don't get it. When Marisa died…you were the *only* one who could know what I was going through and you pushed me away. Do you have any idea how that can change a person?"

"Yes! I'm terrible for people. My existence is rancid. I mean…look what I just did to my best friend!"

"Some best fucking *friend*," Liam grumbles beneath his breath. "I'm tired of being a good guy. I'm tired of feeling frozen…like I'm stuck in this state of stone. Unmoving. Unfeeling. Setting life up for everyone around me instead of diving in myself. It's not real!" He grabs my face in his hands. "You are as real as life gets for me, Rey. You are what I still want…after all these years and all this fucked-upness. That means something, don't you think?"

"No," I say firmly, clenching my jaw, completely cold and calculated. My face is the picture of frozen and unfeeling. You could hear a pin drop in our charged silence. His horrified expression only adds fuel to the inferno building inside of me.

"No," he laughs sadly and stares down at my mouth waiting for it to dispute me.

"You need to leave me behind, Liam. We can never be friends."

CHAPTER 27

Deep.

Drugging.

Darkness.

I am sunk. Buried alive. Gone to the world. And vanished from myself. Hours pass before I move from the frozen spot I fell to on my bed. My tears are dry and crusty on my face as the loneliness envelops me. The place in my mind that I've slipped into is a stifling area that even I am not comfortable in.

I pace the floorboards of my small flat…constantly moving, shifting, restless. Unblinking. Unfeeling, but yet overwhelmed with feelings that I can't control. It's as if I'm holding a thin strand of fishing line. I'm stretching it as far as I can between my two hands, desperate to break it, but knowing that if I keep pulling, the string won't break. I will.

My fragile, thin, marked skin.

I stare at my reflection in the bathroom mirror. My gray eyes are wide and haunting. I will myself to cry because if I just get a good cry out, maybe I'll be able to function again.

Nothing.

Not a drop. Not a speck. Not a glimmer of moisture.

How is this my life right now? How did I get to here? In the span of twenty-four hours, I went from feeling good and healthy and on the right track, to fucking and shoving anyone who gave two shits about me. I have truly pushed every single person in my path as far away as humanly possible. Including my mother and Alistair. I pushed and pushed until I hit rock bottom and then somehow, the rocks gave way beneath me.

As night falls on Sunday, I call Frank and tell him I'm ill and can't work tomorrow. I tell him I don't know when I'll be in next. I tell him I can't estimate if I'll ever come back. He's pressing and pushing for answers. I push back until finally I hang up on him. Cold and calculating. Moves and counter moves against myself. Every step I've taken forward in the last couple weeks, I've yanked myself back from now.

If alone was what I wanted, I have achieved it.

Three days pass. I survive on random bits of food and alcohol. When I run out of all of those, I don't bother replenishing any of it. I just let my body eat away at my insides for nutrition. It can feed on the agony just as my mind has been.

I ignore several calls from my mother. She's out of town at a medical conference or I'm sure she'd be pounding down my door by now. I venture to guess that Alistair called her the minute I left the White Swan a few nights ago. He thinks I don't know he talks to her, but I do. I knew that the first night I met him, he called her from my phone. The night that I drank to oblivion and passed out in a booth. I don't know what they said, but I discovered in my call log that they spoke for almost an hour.

Frank's has called three times a day every day since I called him and told him I didn't know when I'd be returning. He leaves voicemails but I don't check them. They all want to know how I am. What I'm doing. I haven't a clue.

I've heard nothing from Hayden or Liam. My artful pushing skills have proven efficient this time. I sliced them both to the quick and neither want to go round two with me.

I can't blame them.

Loud hollering pulls me away from my internal warring. "Oxford! Oxford, where are you?"

I frown and rise from my mattress, making my way over to my kitchen window. I pull it open and step out on the balcony to find Frank down below.

"Are you fucking kidding me?" he shouts as his eyes land on me. His tall, gangly frame is standing on the sidewalk in an all denim ensemble. Slim denim shorts, a denim jacket with the sleeves rolled up and a white tank top underneath. His wild red hair is messily styled into a rooster like comb on top of his head.

"Frank?" I croak. My voice is harsh and cracky. I realize I haven't spoken to anyone in three days. Suddenly, I realize I'm dressed in only a thin white tank and a black thong. Nervously, I cover my chest to hide my nipples.

"Let me the fuck up, Oxford." Frank's face is pinched and more serious than I've ever seen it.

"Frank, what are you doing here?"

"I've been calling for three days and buzzing your door for hours. You let me up right the fuck now or I'll shout down this entire neighborhood until someone calls the cops. I'm not to be trifled with, woman."

"I'm not up for visitors. How did you even find me?"

"You're my bloody employee! Use that fucking Oxford brain of yours. I have paperwork on you. Now, buzz me in!"

He's mad. Like raging mad. And since I'm standing outside nearly naked, I decide that arguing isn't the best idea right now. I turn around to step back inside my apartment and over to my buzzer. I buzz him in, crack my door and then rummage through my clothes for some pants. I slide on a pair of gray sweats and before I have time to find a bra, Frank is standing in my living room staring at me in all his fiery red-headed glory.

"This is even worse than I imagined." His jaw is dropped as he looks around my small flat.

I look around to assess what he's seeing and for the first time I can see just how deeply I've slipped. My kitchen is littered with several weeks worth of dirty dishes. I ate little to nothing these last few days aside from alcohol. Empty wine and liquor bottles are scattered throughout the entire flat. My bed is dirty and covered in spilled wine, crumbs, and tissues. I shudder to think what the bathroom looks like.

"I told you I wasn't up for company." I cross my arms to cover my large breasts on full display in my thin tank.

"I could give a fuck what you're up for. What the bloody hell is going on?" He rests his hands on his narrow hips, waiting for my answer.

"Nothing."

"This doesn't look like nothing. This looks like you've entered the seventh circle of hell."

"Frank, you're my boss. This is inappropriate."

"I'm hardly a boss. I'm a fill in. Lariza is due back next week and then you'll be shot of me anyway. Now, spill."

I swallow nervously at his menacing gaze. "I don't need to spill. I'm fine."

"The fuck you are." He strides over to me and tilts my chin up to look him in the face. "You need a shower. You need a reset. Do you have a stereo? A Bluetooth speaker? What do you use for music?"

I frown at his odd request and point to the portable speaker on my built in shelves. He dashes over and snatches it up, then comes to me and grabs me by the hand, pulling me behind him. We enter the bathroom and he flips the water on in the shower.

"Strip," he says as steam billows out of the shower. He pulls his phone from his pocket and searches for something.

"I'm not stripping in front of you, Frank."

He looks at me in shock. "Like I want to see your wobbly bit. Fuck. Don't flatter yourself!" Without hesitating he strides over and yanks the shower curtain open and man handles me into the tub.

"Frank!" I scream as the water soaks my clothes.

He shuts the curtain and growls, "Now strip."

Not knowing how else to fight him, I peel off my wet clothes and deposit them on the floor of the tub. Suddenly, music echoes off the walls. It's a haunting, deep, soulful voice.

"Who is this?" I ask quietly as the music begins to invade every cell in my body.

"It's by Daughter. The song is called *Lifeforms*." His voice is close on the other side of the curtain. "I'm going to turn it up as bloody loud as it'll go. Stick your face in the water and just listen. Don't think. Just listen."

"Why are you doing this, Frank?" I ask sadly. This is so weird, but I don't even have the strength to fight off his peculiar demands.

"You need this…a reset. This works. Trust me."

I sigh heavily and do as he asks. Water pours down my face as the music crescendos and swells, moving itself into my body. The dissonance and harmonies push and swirl deep into my chest. The slow building tempo of the song carries my pulse with it. It's otherworldly and completely powerful. When a loud, crying synthetic guitar rift echoes off the shower walls, I explode with un-warning tears. Holding my face under the water, I try to stifle my sobs so Frank doesn't hear, but it's useless. The emotions are too painful. I cry out on a painful sob, coughing—the ache in my chest intensifying with each wail.

Frank doesn't say anything. I don't even know if he's in the room anymore. I don't care. I slump down onto the shower floor and let the music move my tears. Yank. Pull. Stretch. And bend. It's cathartic. It's invigorating. It's healing.

The song only lasts five minutes, but what it's given me in that breadth of time is immeasurable. I cut the water off and Frank's hand appears through the curtain holding a towel.

"I'll be in the living room," he says and I hear his retreating steps leave the bathroom.

I dry myself off and wrap the towel tightly around my chest. I patter out to my living room and find Frank perched on the edge of my filthy bed. He half smiles, his brown eyes warm and welcoming.

"Hiya, Oxford."

"Hi," I say, feeling like I'm seeing him clearly for the first time. I sit down next to him and he watches me thoughtfully. Without saying anything, I lean my head on his shoulder. "Thanks," my voice cracks with emotion and I turn to bury my eyes in his shoulder.

"Nothing to thank me for. Music is healing."

I nod and sniff loudly, pulling away from him. "This feels horribly unprofessional."

He grins. "I've never cared much for boundaries."

"Sorry I've been blowing work off." I look down, feeling ashamed.

"Why don't we talk about it?" His voice is soft and coaxing.

"I don't know if I can." My throat feels like it could close up at the idea of spewing out all the horrid things I've done in such a short amount of time.

"I don't think you have a choice."

I nod my agreement and clear my throat. "I am so weak, Frank. And I'm losing my fucking mind."

"What happened?"

"Everything. All at the same time. It became too much and I couldn't cope. I just shut down and turned off."

"Are you back on now?"

I shrug my shoulders. "There's nothing left to be back for. I've killed off everything that mattered."

"Well, what shall we do about that then?"

"What do you mean?"

"You need to get out of this stinky flat, for starters. I've called cleaners in. They will be here in thirty minutes."

"I can clean my own flat, Frank."

"Please, what's the point of being wealthy if I can't spend it on friends? Get dressed. You and I are going on an excursion. And for God sake, please don't wear more fucking black. Put on something cheerful. Better yet, I'll pick your clothes!"

He winks at me playfully before leaping up and heading over to my closet to begin his rummaging. For the first time in days, I feel a grin teasing at my mouth.

CHAPTER 28

"I've never seen so much depressing black in my entire life," Frank says as we ride the Tube to his house in Brixton.

Much to his dismay, Frank couldn't find anything he liked in my closet that wasn't black. So here I sit in a simple black tank dress and silver statement necklace.

"I need to get you in a store with my Lezbo so we can do some serious shopping."

"Lezbo?" I ask curiously.

"My best mate. She's my partner in crime. My red-headed soul sister. Fellow weirdo. My other half."

"And Finley is a friend of yours too, right? You all live together?"

He scowls meanly for a moment before his face splits into a grin. "Finley and I have a love-hate relationship. The bitch knows how to push my buttons. Don't take fashion advice from her. The girl can't wear anything that doesn't have a hood on it."

Frank continues chattering on about his several roommates and I smile at his intimate descriptions of all of them. Was Hayden ever that for me? Were we ever anything good for each other? He never gave me what I got from Marisa in school. Marisa made me want to be better. Hayden just kept me in limbo it seems.

"So what are we going to your house for?"

"It's just a pit stop. I might have stolen Lezbo's bedazzler and the twat will murder me if she finds it missing. I've got to put it back in her room before she gets home from work. Then we'll be on our way."

We pop up out of the Underground and make our way past a skate park littered with tons of young pubescent teens. Suddenly, a boy no older than fourteen shouts through the chain-link fence as we prepare to cross the street. "Oi! Frank! Who's the sexy bird?"

Frank's eyes flash wildly as he turns, shouting at the top of his lungs, "Get stuffed, Nigel, you prat! I know where your bloody mum lives!"

"Crikey, it was just a joke. Keep your shirt on." The boy drops his skateboard and pushes off.

"Bloody twats…the lot of em. Come on now."

He hurries us across the busy street and we stop in front of a large Victorian house right on the corner. A bright purple door anchors the gorgeous three story mansion complete with a Rapunzel tower. Green ivy wraps up along the brick siding.

"This is mine." Frank jogs up the steps, opening the door and stepping back for me to enter first.

"It's gorgeous," I say as we enter the foyer. There's a large staircase straight ahead. To the right is a formal dining room and what looks like a kitchen back further. To the left is a cozy living room with a hallway leading to what I can only assume are bedrooms.

"Cheers. I'll just be a moment. Wait here." Frank turns to run up the stairs, then pauses halfway up. "If a red-headed firecracker that goes by the name of Lezbo shows up, stall her."

My eyes widen at his seriously nervous expression. I find myself chuckling as he disappears to wherever this beloved bedazzler lives.

"Hey!" a female voice calls from my left. I glance over and see Finley striding out of the hallway attached to the living room. She's dressed in a slim black pencil skirt and yellow blouse. Her brown hair is tied up in a chic, high bun. "Rey, right?" Finley pierces me with her clear blue eyes and bright smile.

"Yeah! You're Finley. Nice to see you again." I pause, briefly scanning the back of my mind to remember what Liam had said about their relationship. It didn't sound like it ever got too serious with her, but I can't help but wonder if he still holds a candle for her. He said she was the first person he was interested in since Marisa. I can so see why. Honestly, she's like painfully beautiful.

Just then I hear a scream from the dining room behind me. I turn to find a petite girl draped over a cute, skater-looking boy's shoulder. He gives her ass a hard crack and then his eyes turn wide as he sees me standing in the foyer with Finley. "Oh, bugger. Sorry. Didn't know we had company." The guy stops in the doorway and slides the girl down his chest. He tucks his blond hair behind his ears, looking decidedly embarrassed.

"You prat, Mitch!" The girl's high pitched voice pierces the foyer once she rights herself. Her sloped eyes glare moodily at her offender as she swats him on the arm. He doesn't even acknowledge her assault. "You could have helped, Brody!" she yells back into the dining room.

Suddenly, this mysterious Brody comes strolling into the foyer. This one is even hotter than the first. He's tall, with dark hair that curls at the ends in a sexily mussed way. His deep blue eyes pop out from his creamy complexion. His accent is American as he says,

"Jules, you know that quoting *Breaking Bad* turns Mitch on. Why do you do it right when you have to leave for work?"

"Guys!" Finley's voice cuts into their arguing. "This is Rey. Rey, this is my husband, Brody, and our housemates, Mitch and Julie."

"Nice to meet you, Rey. You're not taking the purple sheets, are you?" Brody asks as he strides past me and wraps his hands around Finley's waist from behind. Finley's tall and he towers a good four inches over her.

"Purple sheets?"

"Ignore him," Finley shakes her head like she's embarrassed.

"It's what we all try to do," Mitch mumbles.

"You love me and you know it," Brody retorts, glowering at Mitch.

"So, wow, you guys all live here?" I ask dumbly.

"Yeah, there's a whole cluster of people in this Brixton mansion. Frank is basically like our Madame. Our ginger, Irish, sassy, Madame." Brody, Finley, and Julie all bust out laughing. Mitch's smirk is sly and I can't help but laugh along with all of them and their strange dynamic.

"Sorry, but I gotta split," Julie says wiping happy tears from her eyes. She kisses Mitch chastely on the lips and offers me a sweet wave as she walks out the front door.

"I have stuff to do, too. Pub later, right Brody?"

"You got it," he drawls in response.

"Brilliant. It was nice to meet you, Rey," Mitch says. Then he heads up the stairs, leaving me in the foyer with a couple that look like they belong in a magazine.

"So, if you're not here for purple sheets, what brings you by?" Brody asks, his eyes wide and kind.

"Oh, I'm waiting for Frank. We're going on some excursion I guess. He had something he had to do here first. Something about a bedazzler?"

Finley's eyes grow wide. "Oh shit, yeah. Lez will skin him if he's fucked with that again."

I laugh at her serious face. "You guys seem like you're all really close."

She smiles kindly. "Yeah, we're close. For better or worse and all that shit. There's a room open on the third floor if you need it! That's what Brody meant when he said purple sheets."

Her offer stuns me. I eye her to see if it was just a pleasantry but she seems genuine. In fact, it feels like she sees right through me and is trying to figure out a way to pull me out of this swamp that I've found myself in.

"Keep in mind, though, boundaries are almost always an issue here."

I smile, not surprised in the least, especially since Frank just shoved me into a shower only moments earlier. "I have a flat, but thanks!"

"No problem. We should do drinks sometime," Finley adds. "I could use more girlfriends here. You'll love Leslie. Frank's great and all, but his obsession with denim is seriously—"

"You bloody whore." Frank's voice cajoles from the top of the stairs. "Stop trying to nick my new mate! Rey is mine. You and Lezbo have your secret cuddles you think I don't know about. Well, I do. You can't have my Oxford."

"Frank, don't get territorial. We can share new friends." She winks knowingly at me as Frank begins to descend. Brody watches on with a broad grin as Finley continues, "I was just telling Rey about your denim fan club that you're the president of."

Frank pauses in the middle of the staircase, straightening his completely denim ensemble. He pops his hip out and strikes a flamboyant pose. "I'm not just the president. I'm also a member."

Finley, Brody, and I all burst into giggles at his ridiculousness. I laugh even harder when I see Frank seriously coiffing his red hair and completely ignoring our fit of laughs. These people…this house…it's magic.

***

After a full day hanging out at Hyde Park with Frank, I've laughed more than I think I ever have in my entire life. He convinces me to get hand massages from this random pop up stand offering them for ten quid. I told him I thought it sounded dodgy but he pushed me into it, claiming we only live once.

He doesn't press me for information. He doesn't talk about Liam. He just offers his friendship. Unconditional. And comedic as hell. It's a beautiful thing. And not something I've ever allowed myself to have since losing Marisa.

I've been MIA for so long now that I forgot what it felt like to let someone in. Watching Finley, Brody, Mitch, and Julie all banter back and forth comfortably is like nothing I've ever had. Not even before Marisa died. But the state of grief I've allowed myself to live in the last three years is toxic. Yes, I lost my best friend. But instead of grieving her loss, I only grieved my betrayal and how I never had the opportunity to ask for forgiveness. And worse, I suffered all of that alone. That's a heavy secret to carry on your own. It's no wonder I've been sinking.

But I'm done. I'm done sinking and falling. It's time for a change.

CHAPTER 29

After getting back into the groove at Club Taint for a couple of days, I'm pleased to find myself with Saturday night off. I've been twitching to reconnect with Hayden and make sure he's doing okay, but my text messages have gone unanswered. I hate how we left it. I decide to text his sister to check in on him.

Me: Hey, Daph. Hayden is MIA again. Have you talked to him?

Daphney: I saw him a couple days ago. He looked pretty rough. We have the charity ball tonight. He told Theo he wasn't coming…but he told me he was. So I'll let you know if I see him.

Me: Oh, that's right. Thanks, Daphney. Keep me posted. Xx

Daphney: Always.

I completely forgot that tonight is the charity gala the Clarkes host every year benefiting suicide awareness. I know this night is always difficult for Hayden. I offered to attend with him last year, but he said he didn't want me to witness the dreary affair. Hayden's mother, Winnie, is a sweet woman who I know is just trying to find the best way to help her son.

However, Hayden is still in denial about his suicide attempts. I think he sees it all more as self-destructive behavior—not a premeditated motive to kill himself. So my hope tonight is that he's just busy and not spiraling into a scary place that I know he's been before.

I decide to shoot one more text to Hayden.

Me: Hey. I know tonight is the gala. If you need me, I'm here. I'm always here for you, Hayden. You're my best friend. None of that has changed. xoxo

At around seven o'clock that night, the buzzer on my flat goes off. I gaze out my kitchen window to find Hayden there looking up at me sadly. His balance sways and I can tell even four floors above him that he's drunk. Still, my heart breathes a sigh of relief seeing his face again. I rush in to buzz him up.

I wait at the door and as soon as he appears around the corner I instantly run and slam into him, wrapping my arms around his waist. My face buries into his chest and the familiar faint smell of alcohol and cigarettes invades my nostrils. He doesn't hug me back at first, just stands there. Eventually, begrudgingly even, he sighs and wraps his arms around me.

I pull back after a bit and see he's dressed in a rumpled black tuxedo. "You look nice," I say feeling tears prick the back of my eyeballs.

He nods silently and releases me to walk into my flat. His icy demeanor scares me and I can sense something big coming. He ambles into the kitchen and starts digging in my cupboards. He pulls out an old bottle of tequila.

"That's old, Hayden. I haven't touched that stuff in years."

He grabs a water glass and pours an inch of the golden liquid inside. He leans back on the counter with the glass in his hand, raises it to me, and shoots it down in one gulp.

"Hay," my tone is warning.

He cocks his head to the side. "I've always loved the way you say my name. Even when you can't be bothered to say the whole thing…it's sexy."

Nerves bubble in my belly. "I've been texting you the last couple of days. I wanted to talk." He nods simply and pours another shot. "Are you sure you should do that?" I ask and his cloudy eyes harden on mine.

"Let's not pretend that you care about anybody but yourself, Reyna, shall we?"

His words sting. "What the fuck? How can you say that?" I move to touch him and he flinches away from me.

Then he begins laughing. Really, heartily laughing. "You fuck my dead sister's boyfriend and then you have the nerve to look shocked by my words?"

My jaw drops. I'm stunned, both at his harsh words and the fact that he's talking about Marisa. "Hayden. Liam and I…We have history."

He purses his lips sarcastically. "So this isn't the first time you've fucked him? That's so much better. Tell me…Were Marisa and Liam together when you fucked him for the first time?"

My face apparently gives Hayden the answer he was suspecting and he laughs at me again. My vision blurs with tears. "Stop, Hayden. I'm just trying to be better."

"And leave me in the dust."

"Hayden. You and I…"

"We don't work…Is that right? Is that what you're going to tell me right now?" He leans down and pins me with a death stare. "You can't hang out with me anymore. You can't fuck me anymore…because you're better than me. You won't live in my darkness anymore. Some fucking friend you are!"

I clutch my hands to my chest and the tears come fast and fierce. Overwhelmed and completely enraged, I scream, "Hayden, you're my best friend but if you're going to drown me, I need to fucking know! I'm already doing a shit job at life by myself, I don't need help sinking. I have my own damn demons to fight. Don't project your guilt on me!" I shriek angrily.

"My guilt?" He stands straight and drops his chin in horror. "What do I have to be guilty for? Oh…Are you talking about the fact that I was the one who killed Marisa? Is that what you mean?"

Fear slices through me at his cold, calculated stare. "No," I cry. "God, Hayden!"

"Go on, Rey, say it. Shout if you like. I was the one driving the quad that struck Marisa." His voice cracks on her name and my heart completely shatters when his face crumples into confused pain. He keeps going, "I was the one behind the wheel. I was the one who watched her body fly away from me. I was the one who lay there…in the grass…my own leg broken…but I still knew. I knew what I had done. I knew I killed her. Even before the paramedics announced that she was DOA. You have her time of death stamped on your fucking skin but *I'm* the one who felt her die. I felt her leave this earth. Do you have any idea—"

"Hayden, stop! Please!" I grab my wrist to cover the pocket watch ink Hayden's referring to. Devastated by his words, I crumple down to the floor at the tragedy being retold with such vulgarity. Hayden was the driver, but it wasn't the quad that killed Marisa. It was the concrete paver she fell backwards on top of. But that doesn't mean shit when your impact was the one that sent her flying backwards.

Hayden and I were two fucked up crazies that fucked each other. We fucked to feel. We fucked to not feel. We fucked away the deepest, darkest parts of each other's mind. And we knew we were lowly, pathetic POS: Pieces of shit. DOA: Dead on arrival. That's what we were to each other. And that was all we'd ever be to each other. Which was why I was trying so desperately to break away from our routine. Get past the tragedy. The despair. The depression.

His voice cuts into my inner turmoil and growls with emotion. "I killed her then. And I'm killing you now. Death becomes me, Reyna. I'm killing everyone close to me because I'm a toxic, poisonous, nothingness."

"Hayden," I bawl and stand up to run to him as he tries to leave. He grips my shoulders, his hands harsh and bruising, holding me as far away from him as possible. "Please, Hayden, you're my best friend. Don't do this. I love you."

"Love," he laughs. "That's a funny word coming from your mouth. You don't even love yourself."

His words crush me and I stop fighting him. He lets me go and stumbles down the hallway and out the door. I drop to my knees and cry at his final words.

Truer words have never been spoken to me.

CHAPTER 30

I peel my crusty eyes open at an incessant noise that invades the darkness that is comforting me right now. I'm shocked to see that it's nearly eleven and that I've been asleep since shortly after Hayden left. My mouth is dry and my heart aches.

I called Daphney after Hayden left to tell her what happened. Not all the specifics, but that Hayden and I had a big fight and that I was worried about him. I was sick with nerves until she finally texted me later to tell me Hayden had shown up at the gala. Knowing he was there and safe was the only reason I was able to finally let myself pass out from all the emotional exhaustion.

I clamber up off my bed and over to the sink in my kitchen to drink water straight from the tap. I flinch at the pinching headache crawling across my forehead and stumble back to my phone on the entry way table.

"Jesus, who the fuck…" I open my phone and see five missed calls and twelve new texts. They are all from Daphney, begging me to call her. "Holy fuck." My pulse sky rockets instantly and my hands tremble as I swipe across the screen to read the later texts.

Daphney: Reyna, I can't get hold of you. It's about Hayden. It's bad.

No…no, no, no!

Daphney: He's okay now. But, we almost lost him.

No! This can't be happening. He was just here! I just saw him. I drop to my knees and press my head against the door blinking rapidly to clear the tears forming so I can read the next text.

Daphney: Theo said he slit his wrists, Rey! I can't believe I'm telling you in a text, but I don't know what else to do. It's all so awful. We're on our way to the hospital. They said he'll live, but…

But what? But nothing. But…but? But how? How could he do this? When did he do it? Where? Why? Oh my God. Was it what I said? I quickly scan through our earlier exchange trying to remember everything I said to him. Fuck me. I was awful. Truly terrible. I'm the worst. The worst friend. FUCK!

I rush over to the kitchen and grab the stray bottle of tequila to pour myself a shot. I slosh some into the dirty glass of Hayden's and bring it to my mouth. One smell of it and I pause, gripping it in my hand as hard as I can until I hear it crack. I scream and throw the broken glass into the sink, flinching at the sound of it shattering into a million pieces. This was Hayden's glass. The same glass he tried to drown his pain with just moments ago. The same glass we've both been using as a crutch for far too long and now look what's happened.

I squeeze my hand into a fist and wince at the sting of wet liquor on an open wound. Is this even a fraction of what Hayden felt? God, slitting his wrists? How could he do something so gruesome? So permanent? I should have never let him leave! This is entirely my fault. Why do I keep doing this to people? First I pushed Liam away three years ago, and now Hayden, my best friend.

Pushing is the only verb I am one hundred percent effective at.

Compartmentalizing my self-loathing, I look down to survey the damage on my hand. There doesn't appear to be any glass in the small cut—just enough to help make me feel like an even bigger asshole. Feeling frantic to get to Hayden, I haphazardly throw on a bandage, then slip on a T-shirt and jeans. Moments later I'm hailing a cab to the hospital that Daphney said they were all waiting at.

While riding in the back of the taxi, I can't help but feel anger at all the bustling streets of London going about their normal evenings. Do they not realize the hell and torment going on all around us every second? How can they all be so cavalier? Happy even? My best friend is laying in a hospital bed fighting for his life and these people are out laughing and partying.

Walking into the hospital, I do my best to hide my tears and trauma-stricken face. The Clarkes don't need me to be a mess too. My stomach clenches as my eyes land on Hayden's mom, Winnie, his dad, Richard, and his sister, Daphney. They are all in formal evening wear and standing nervously in the hallway by the waiting area. Their faces are almost unbearable to look at.

"Winnie…Daph texted me. I hope it's okay I came by," I say awkwardly, glancing down as I approach. I quickly wipe away the betraying tears that fall.

"Rey! Oh, honey—" Winnie's eyes grow wide as I look up at her and sobs burst out of her mouth. Her eyes dance all around me before pulling me into her ample chest for a hug. It's been quite some time since I've seen Winnie and I'm sure just the sight of me evokes memories of Marisa.

A loud breath from beside us echoes in my ears and I turn my gaze to find Liam sitting in a waiting room next to a couple dressed in evening wear. I never in a million years expected him to be here, and a sick part of me has a split second of hope that he's here for me.

He mumbles something over to Hayden's older brother, Theo. A red head is sitting smack dab between the two guys and she's dressed in a formal, tea-length gown covered in blood and dirt. I blanch, nearly unable to look at the sight of her. Was she the one who found Hayden? I can't stomach the thought.

My eyes fall back on Liam as he suddenly stands. Theo rises with him and places a reassuring hand on his shoulder. They exchange words, but I can't make out anything they're saying over Winnie's sobs.

Finally, Liam looks at me and it's one of those moments where I can hear every single thought in his mind and for the first time, I don't want to. His gaze is haunted and pained, and it crushes me. It's been a week since I last saw him and he looks like he's been carrying the weight of the world on his shoulders. Without thought, I break away from Winnie and make my way over. I am naturally drawn to him, but nervousness takes over as I approach. I look down at my shoes, terrified of everything Liam's eyes are saying to me right now.

"Liam," I croak as he moves to walk past me to leave. I need to talk to him. I need to touch him. I need to tell him I'm sorry. Something!

He pauses just a few steps away and looks back at me. "I hope your *friend* is okay. I'll leave you all to it." He sends an apologetic smile to Theo and continues down the hallway, exiting the waiting room.

I lock eyes with the green-eyed red head who half smiles at me kindly. She looks worried and curious. Nice even. Theo stares me down and I look away, feeling blanketed in shame. Theo is like a shorter, more muscular version of Hayden. He has short, buzzed dirty blond hair and thick black-rimmed glasses. Both Theo and Hayden have that brooding look about them. Does Theo know about me and Liam? I shift nervously, feeling incredibly torn over what to do right now, so I make my way back over to Daphney and Winnie.

After a flutter of desperation courses through me, I suddenly blurt out, "Can I just…I'll be right back, yeah? Right back!" I shout and run down the same way Liam just left.

Nerves trembling, I sprint out the hospital doors to find Liam waiting at a bus stop. "Liam!" I cry breathlessly—not from the run, but from the desperate urgency to fix something between one person in my life right now. I need to fix one thing one time and not be this person who continues to ruin people's lives.

He turns and pins me with a sad shake of his head. His eyes flash down to my mouth and then he moves to walk away from the bus stop. "I don't want to talk to you right now, Reyna. Your *friend*, boyfriend, whatever he is, just so happens to be my best mate's brother and he's in the bloody hospital for something that may or may not have to do with me, but has everything to do with you. Our drama is pretty much null and void now."

His words hit me like a punch to the stomach. "Null and void? No, Liam! I need you to understand what Hayden and I are. I need to explain—"

"I've worked it all out myself, Rey. It doesn't fucking matter. You're a different person. You're not who I knew. I don't know who you are. You've fucked me. You've fucked him. I can't sit here and witness this anymore. I don't need you rubbing salt into the open wound, alright?" He storms down the dark sidewalk illuminated only by the glowing blue signage of the hospital.

"That's not what this is!" I cry and run to stand in front of him so he can stop walking away. "That's not what Hayden and I are. Yes, I'm different. Yes, I've changed…but I need you to know…I'm not right, Liam. I'm not right in the head. I don't see things about me that are good. I only see the bad. And…and…you fucking *wrecked* me!" I bring a hand to my hair in exasperation. "I had my life all figured out. I was keeping everyone at a safe distance and then…three years ago, that night in my dorm room, you just pushed me way outside of my little bubble that I was living in. You catapulted me into a mess of fucking self destruction!" My voice cracks with a garbled cry.

"So you're blaming me for the past three years of your life?" he laments, his eyes flashing with anger.

"Yes!" I scream, realizing for the first time when things in my life started going from bad to worse. "I haven't been able to get a handle on anything since then."

He rolls his eyes. "That's rather convenient, Rey. How nice for you to be able to pinpoint exactly when someone fucked you for once."

He moves to walk past me and I shove him back into place. He hits me with a stony glare that intimidates the hell out of me, but I have to finish this. I have to get my answers.

"Liam, I need to know why. Why did you bring that ring to me that night? You have to explain it. You said it doesn't matter because we're living in the now, but you're wrong. It matters so much. Please." My chest rises and falls with each intense second that ticks by.

The previous anger in Liam evaporates, replaced by a warring expression. He looks like he can't begin to tell me the truth, but he knows exactly what his answer to my question is. "It's fucking crazy, Rey. I'm not even sure it will make sense to you." His brown eyes flash to my mouth in a mass of emotional confusion.

"Liam, my best friend just tried to kill himself. Everything around me is in turmoil. I just need to know this one thing to hold on to a shred of my sanity."

He swallows hard, the muscle in his jaw popping in and out. Nerves overcome his face and he turns away from me and begins speaking, "I told you at the houseboat that I've only ever had one dream about Marisa. Do you remember?"

"Yes."

He clears his throat and continues. "The week before Marisa's death, I dreamt that your roles were reversed. We were in Oxford and you and I were in a relationship and Marisa was the one on the side. The three of us were friends like usual, but it was a ring I bought for you that I showed to Marisa. Everything was exactly the same, but the ring was so different. The style of it was so you. Unique and edgy. I can still picture the thing.

"I was showing her the ring I bought for you, and she was excited for me. She was crying happy tears. And then, she suddenly told me she didn't love me the way that you did."

"Me?" I ask and he turns to look at me finally. His eyes are watery with tears.

"Yes, she was referring to you, Rey. It was like suddenly my dream was real life again and she was telling me she didn't love me enough, but that you did."

"I never told Marisa I was in love with you. That doesn't make any sense," I say weakly.

"Do all of your dreams make sense?"

"No."

He looks at me knowingly. "She said that it was always supposed to be you and me." He pauses as he averts his gaze again. "Then in my dream, she died."

Frowning, I ask, "You dreamt about her death before it happened?"

"Yes. I didn't see the accident or anything. But yeah, this dream happened before her death. It was like her spirit came to me to tell me goodbye before she even left. She told me that I had done a proper job loving her and she died knowing I loved her."

I begin to step away from Liam slowly, my mind firing off all around me. It's all so eerie. Thinking of Marisa appearing in my dreams and now she appears to Liam before even dying. It's too much for me to process. My voice is weak and shaky, "I can't wrap my brain around this."

"Rey." Liam grabs my arm and swings me to face him again, holding me still in front of him. My jaw remains dropped in shock as I look into his earnest brown eyes. "I did love Marisa. You couldn't not love her. But you were in my heart. You were in my head. You were in my pulse. You were with me every breath I took. I couldn't *not* think of you. I couldn't *not* wonder about you. But you continually pushed me away. We weren't even dating and you kept me at arm's length. I thought I was crazy! I thought there was no way you could feel for me the way I felt for you. But after that dream, I had to know for sure…it was like Marisa was pushing me herself!"

"But why the ring, Liam? You had a ring for her."

"I bought it to wake you the fuck up, Rey! To get you to open your eyes. I knew I had to do something drastic to get a reaction out of you! I saw that night as our chance. It was my chance to show you how I've always seen you."

I close my eyes, holding back the tears as I recall the intimate feelings that overcame me that night so many years ago. That night he made love to me and told me that I was the one. It was a tenderness that crept into my very soul and awakened feelings I didn't even know I could feel. Liam saw and loved every part of me—stains and all. That night was the last time I allowed myself to believe that maybe…just maybe…I could be the one for someone.

"And I ruined it," I whisper to no one in particular.

Out of the corner of my eye, I see Liam nod. "You let me in and then you shattered me. That was just the beginning of the breaks. It only got worse after Marisa died."

Liam releases my arms and I cradle myself in my hands. A tremble shakes through me as hot tears run down to the crumbling earth below me.

Sighing, he adds, "I've made peace with what we did. My feelings and my heart were honest. That dream helped me realize that. I wish your dreams could do that same."

I twitch at his knowing words. My dreams? I can't understand any of my dreams. Whatever happens in them just seems to shine a flashlight on how utterly screwed up I am. All I've ever done is shove Liam away. So hard. Even after Marisa died, I literally pushed him out the door. I didn't give a shit about his grief. Or him. He loved me with all he had, and I spit in his face after he lost everything.

"I don't know what to say, Liam." Sorry seems so ridiculous to say after all of that.

He swallows hard. "I had hoped that after our time together on the boat that you and I might have a chance. That maybe we could turn our destruction into our salvation. But you pushed me too bloody far, Rey. And I'm just done. I'm done trying to make you see yourself the way I do. I can't love you after all this."

An aching pain prickles in my eyes as a loud sob threatens to shoot out of me. I turn and cover my mouth to conceal my reaction.

"Good luck, Rey. I hope you find what you're looking for."

I hear Liam's retreating steps, but I can't turn to watch him. I can't bear to watch him walk out of my life once again. Instead, I walk back into the hospital, moving both away from and toward the fucked up life that I've created all around me.

CHAPTER 31

Feeling teary eyed and numb, I return and sit next to Daphney and Winnie for the next two hours as we wait for more news on Hayden. They look a little perplexed as to my disappearance but don't ask anything. I think everyone is too distracted with thoughts of Hayden.

I learn from Winnie that the red head is Theo's girlfriend, Leslie. Leslie was the girl that Hayden mentioned to me a couple weeks ago when he said Theo was falling in love. I can't help but look at her in wonder after learning that she was the one to find Hayden in his office that's connected to Theo's workshop area. Apparently that was where Hayden went to after he left the gala. Drunk. That was where Hayden used a small circular saw blade to…

I bend over to tuck my head between my legs not able to even consider how this could have turned out if she wouldn't have shown up in time. How she's even able to stand right now is beyond me. While talking with Theo for a moment, I sussed out that Leslie is "Lezbo"—Frank's best friend and one of the roommates at the Brixton mansion with Finley, Brody, Mitch and Julie. Then there's Liam's connection to Finley. Theo's connection to Leslie. What a strange, interconnected swirling this group is that I've stumbled into. But they all seem to support each other, wholeheartedly. And here I sit: alone.

Did I ever do that for Hayden? Support him in a healthy way? Hayden struggled with suicidal thoughts in the past, but they were more acceptable things. Things you could yell at him for: *Damnit, Hayden, you can't mix booze with pills! Damnit, Hayden, how could you drink and drive?*

But, this? Slicing his own wrists? This was on an entirely different level. What did I really know about Hayden? What did he really know about me? We were too busy avoiding the dark parts to ever really get to know each other. As we wait, I constantly replay the fight we had before he left my flat. The signs were all there. And I didn't do anything. All I want to do now is see him and hug him and tell him I'm so sorry that I let everything around us continue to stay so horribly dark. I should have been a better friend. I should have helped him face the guilt he felt over Marisa's death. Helped him remember what he used to love about life. I should have done so much more.

I just need to say those two little words that I never got to say to Marisa.

When the doctor finally comes out, I stand on the outer edge as he informs the family that they are keeping Hayden for a seventy-two-hour psychiatric hold. I exchange withering glances with Leslie because we're both outsiders in this situation, but we're both heavily involved, like it or not.

After the doctor leaves, Theo comes over to Leslie and informs her that Hayden requested to speak to her.

"Me, whatever for?" Leslie asks, her face clearly displaying her shock.

I slowly begin to back away from them as they continue their discussion. My heart drops through the floorboards. He wants to see her of all people? After everything? I know she was the one to find him, but still. An incredibly selfish part of me wants to take her place. He doesn't need to see her. He needs to see me! We need to work through whatever it is we're going through. Does he not care about mending our friendship? Do I mean so little to him?

As they retreat through the double doors back to wherever they have Hayden, I feel myself imploding with panic. Panic and self-loathing. Self-hate. Self-destruction. I wasn't the blade that sliced through Hayden's wrists, but I certainly was one of the catalysts. And now he doesn't even want to see me. Daphney pins me with a worried gaze.

Clearing my throat, I say, "Daphney, I think I'm going to go." I'm doing everything I can to choke back a fresh wave of tears.

"No, Rey. We might get to see Hayden before they admit him. You should stay."

I shake my head pathetically. If he wanted to see me, he would have asked for me—not Leslie. "No. No, it's alright. It sounds like he's going to be okay. Just…um…keep me updated, please?"

She nods nervously and I turn to leave the hospital where my best friend chose to talk to someone he barely knows over me. If alone was what I was shooting for, I hit a bullseye tonight.

CHAPTER 32

The following day at Club Taint was painful. It was nearly two in the morning before I got home from the hospital. Daphney has been texting me updates today and said that Hayden apparently checked himself in to a thirty-day facility. I asked her what facility so I could send him a letter or something and she wouldn't tell me. When I finally drug it out of her, she informed me that Hayden made her promise not to tell me.

My pushing skills are even impressing myself at this point.

So here I sit—rotting away at Club Taint—unloading glasses from the dishwasher before we open, and trying desperately to stave off the aching melancholy of my own best friend wanting nothing to do with me. The sadness shooting through my veins is potent.

Suddenly, a familiar figure comes shuffling in. "Mom?" I ask, my jaw dropping in shock. Dr. Elizabeth Miller inside Club Taint. And I thought I'd seen it all.

"Miracle! I just got back from my medical conference. I stopped at your flat and you weren't there. I had to come see you right away. I've just spoken to Alistair." She sounds scared and out of breath, but she smiles as she slides onto the nearest barstool. I assess that her sneakers are still firmly in place beneath her long black skirt. Always prepared.

"Mom, you didn't have to come here." *Alistair the narc,* I think to myself. He must have told her about the fight that he had to break up between Liam and Hayden.

"Well, you're not answering my calls." She half smiles but her eyes are squinting at me.

I huff, "Ever think there might be a reason for that? I'm too busy hating every single part of myself. The last thing I want to do is hear you tell me otherwise."

Ignoring my snide remark, her blue eyes train on me in an assessing doctor way that aggravates me. "Have you been eating?"

"I'm fine, Mom. Just stop." I'm so not in the mood for her fake bullshit.

"Miracle, I really think you should move back in with me. We tried this apartment living thing and it's just not going well. You don't look well. You don't look like you're eating or sleeping enough. Let me take care of you. I'll go ahead and cancel the lease on the flat. Come back home." Her face is beaming a huge, glorious, fake smile as she drops this atomic bomb on me.

"What the fuck, Mom?" I sneer.

"You'll be more protected with me. We can be close," she adds cheerily.

"I don't need you to be so close to me all the damn time. I'm nearly thirty! I don't need to be protected! I'm literally nothing to anybody, so stop acting like I'm some damn prize!" That thought has never felt truer since last night.

"Of course you're special. You're my miracle." She tucks her short dark hair behind her ears, doing her best to ignore my tantrum.

"Why do you keep calling me that? I'm certain that one of my sisters would have fared a far more miraculous life on this earth than I am right now."

Her smiling eyes tighten at my comment pertaining to my sisters who didn't have a chance. "Let's not discuss this. Let's just keep you happy and get you—"

"You tell me I'm a miracle all the time, but I'm not. And I'm tired of being forced into thinking I am!" My outburst is unexpected, but not surprising considering all the self-loathing I've been rocking the past couple weeks.

Her eyes blink in shock for a moment, before she smiles brightly. "You're upset. I'll leave. We can discuss this later." She stands and turns to make her way back out the front door.

Feeling angered at yet another Dr. Miller brush off, I push the bar partition up and jog out after her. I blast through the entrance just behind her and we stand face to face beneath the gray London sky.

"Why can't we talk about them, Mom?" I snap, my voice rising in a challenge. "I've seen pictures of all of them. Sure we were all hooked up to breathing tubes and wrapped in UV blankets, but I was with them. They were a part of me. I was a part of them. They were a part of *you*!"

"Reyna, please stop." Her voice is shaky as her eyes continue looking down the street.

"Why can't we talk about them, Mom? Tell me! I have to know. Do you realize how extraordinary quad pregnancies are?"

"Of course I do, Reyna," my mother snaps, her smiling demeanor dropping momentarily as she gives up her search for a cab. She shakes her head and schools her features to be cheerful again. "I'm who hospitals call with their impossible cases just like my own!" Her voice is shrill and tight as she smiles through her words. "High order multiples are my daily life. I also know all that can go wrong in a quad pregnancy. I knew before I even gave birth to you that the odds of me carrying any of you to term were nonexistent! It just can't happen! But I clung to hope with all my might. Then, all four of you came even earlier than any of us ever expected. Before I knew it, I was trapped in a NICU that I couldn't control. They wouldn't let me consult on your care. They said I wasn't in the right state of mind. So one by one I watched my babies die, and now I live with the guilt and the shame of wondering if I could have saved them! Do you know what it's been like for me to have the career I've dedicated my entire life to be rendered completely useless when it came to my own babies?"

Her words send shivers all the way down my spine. A strange prickling settles over me. "Mom—" I start, but am interrupted.

"You are damn right that I remained close to you my whole life," she says with a fire to her eyes that reminds me of the passion I witnessed in my NICU dream not too long ago. "You are also right that I treated you like a miracle. Because you are! You should be dead right now! But you're not. You're standing here…yelling at me. The pink of your cheeks, the rise and the fall of your chest," her voice cracks with a sob.

I step toward her feeling completely overwhelmed at seeing this emotional side of her. It's nothing I've ever bore witness to and something I've always yearned for. I don't even know how to process it. "I'm nothing, Mom. Calling me Miracle just feels like a self-fulfilling prophecy that I can never live up to."

She pins me back in place with a pinched smile. "What else do you call your existence, Reyna Miracle? You aren't the result of modern medicine."

"Then what the hell am I?" I screech in frustration just as a cab pulls up. "Because I feel like floundering nothingness!"

She holds up one finger to the cabbie and moves up to the sidewalk. Then she cups my face in her hands. Her blue eyes are wide and watery, probing and hopeful. The tenderness of her touch literally hurts my skin because I don't want it. I don't deserve it. I don't deserve the look in her eyes.

"You, my child, are the result of divine intervention and I can only find it all miraculous. And the worst of all of this is that I feel so entrenched in my own fear that I could lose you at any second…and all you want to do is get lost." She turns and strides over to the cab, gracefully sliding in. Her face is serious and sad. The first time I've ever seen her this way. "Please, go back to work. Be happy. We can talk later."

She disappears down the street and takes with it a woman I know nothing about. Whoever my mother was just now was not even a glimmer of the person I've grown to know. How can I even begin to make sense of it all?

"Oxford, how the bloody hell are ye?" Frank's voice croons from behind me.

I turn to find him strolling around the corner in some type of an orange jump suit. Steeling myself with a heavy sigh, I reply, "Not great."

His fair, freckled face turns serious. The mirror S's popping up instantly between his brows. "Who was in the cab?"

"My mother."

"Ghastly! Mother's are like butt holes. We've all got one, but damn do they stink and are a bitch to wipe clean. That's why I have a bidet."

I turn to frown at him. "That's not even funny, Frank."

He crosses his arms in challenge. "I'd like to hear you do better!"

"Why are you dressed like you just got out of prison?"

"That's not a mama joke." His hands drop to his hips to rest on the pumpkin-colored swish pants. I point to his clothes. "Oh," he titters softly. "It's a new workout outfit. Lariza gets back today, so I'm heading to the gym after this!"

I roll my eyes and then inspiration strikes. "Frank, I need to ask you something kind of serious." He frowns at me but remains silent. "I think I need to talk to someone."

He leans close to me and whispers, "What the fuck do you think we're doing right now?"

Despite my gloomy mood, I giggle half heartedly. "No, I mean…like…a therapist. I have so many questions that I need someone to tell me the answers to."

"Oh fuck me, I've got ten therapists on speed dial, Oxford. I thought this was something serious." He throws his narrow arm around my back and leads me back inside the club.

CHAPTER 33

A few days later, I'm sitting on a cushy loveseat, staring at what looks like a teenager. Frank vouched for this doctor, but upon meeting him, I'm not so sure. He looks like Doogie Howser and Mario Lopez had a love child and that love child was entering his junior year in high school.

I'm extra grouchy because ever since the fight with my mom outside Club Taint, I've been reaching out to Liam. Shockingly, he was the first one I wanted to talk to. Aside from my parents, he's the only other person I've been able to open up to about being a quad and the feelings that I have pertaining to my sisters. Sisters that I don't even know. I've internalized and dealt with my emotions by myself for so long that to reach out to someone was huge for me. So, for my texts and calls to go completely unanswered feels devastating.

"You do realize you've been here for ten minutes and still haven't said a word, right?" Doogie says with a Spanish lilt to his voice. He told me to call him Miguel, but Doogie suits him.

I eye him speculatively. Frank said this therapist helped him after his parents moved out of the Brixton house. He told me that being gay in high society London wasn't the happiest of news to his parents and he turned into a bit of a wild child for several years after their less than kind reaction. I could tell that Frank was minimizing something huge and made a mental note to ask him more about it in the future. Frank and I have become really close since my shower re-boot, but I don't want to push my nose where it doesn't belong. I only hope that I'm able to return the tremendous favor he's given me someday. Even obnoxious gingers have demons to fight.

"You have to tell me how old you are," I say flatly.

"I'm thirty-one."

"When I asked Frank for a referral, I was expecting a white haired Santa-looking type." Two dimples form in his cheeks as he fails to conceal a smile. His grin reveals a much needed flaw: One of his front teeth is longer than the other. Thank God. Otherwise he's just too damn hot to be a shrink.

"I'm sorry to disappoint you," he says in response.

I sigh petulantly and cross my arms over my chest. I glance around at the stark white painted walls. It would feel rather clinical in here had it not been for the lush, earth tone furniture and accents peppered throughout the office. The room has a sandalwood scent that you know is completely manufactured because where the hell do you ever actually smell sandalwood anyway? I'm sitting in a cream loveseat and he's situated straight across from me in a brown leather arm chair.

"You know, Reyna…This will go a lot faster if you start by telling me why you are here."

Very well, then. Might as well dive right in. "My best friend, Hayden, tried to kill himself last week. He's in a treatment facility and hasn't called or texted or even asked about me. He's even made a point of telling his sister not to tell me anything about his progress in there or where he's having treatment."

"Well, most facilities don't allow outside calls. If he has seen his sister or spoken to her, it is likely the family is involved in group therapy sessions."

"Why couldn't I be involved in a group session?"

"Why do you think you should be?"

I pull my lip into my mouth and chew away the red matte coloring that I applied this morning. "I think I'm the reason he's in there."

Miguel's eyebrows rise in encouragement rather than wonder. "Why is that?"

Rolling my eyes, I lean forward and pin him with a serious scowl. "Look, I'm not a special person, alright? I'm not trying to turn this into something about me. That's not what I'm here for. I'm here to get answers about my friend. But you need to know how he got to this point and I think that had something to do with me. I have an uncanny way of shoving people away who only want to love me. I'm blunt and to the point. I'm just a loner. I feel better alone. When I let people get close, that's when things get fucked up."

"How so?"

I tell him the entire conversation Hayden and I had before he left my flat for the gala and then what Leslie walked in on. "What made him do that? I mean, I know things were bad between us and he was upset…but like, mentally, what made him do what he did the way he did it?" I swallow a painful knot that forms in my throat every time I think of Hayden's method of choice.

"Those are questions that he will work out in his own therapy. I'm more interested in why you think you are to blame. Why do you think things get 'fucked up,' as you say, when you let people get close to you?"

I sigh heavily. "Look, I'm a somewhat educated person. I've done some Googling on what might be going on with me."

He half smiles, creating a dimple on just the one side. "And what do you believe is going on with you?"

"Don't give me that look, they were legit websites. I guess it all started with my mother, because none of the emotions I ever received from her felt real. They always felt like she was giving me what she should have given my sisters. Like, she bottled up all the love she had for the four of us and shoved it down my throat. It was too much."

"And, how old are your sisters?"

"Dead," I reply coldly, and then quickly stop myself to swallow down my bitchiness. I need to rein in my emotions. I don't need to push this doctor away, too. "They died in the NICU a few months after we were born. My mother was barely twenty-four weeks pregnant, so we were crazy premature. It was bad. I was the lucky one of us four that survived. 'The Miracle,'" I gesture with lame finger quotes.

"So, you were a quadruplet? How does that make you feel?" he asks, frowning and scribbling into his notebook.

I huff at that question. It's so therapist and cliché, but it's also so raw and vulnerable. How does me being a quad make me feel? "Well, I must feel something because these three roses represent my sisters," I finally reply, gesturing to my collarbone exposed by my spaghetti strap tank top.

"Would you say you feel a special connection to your sisters?"

I purse my lips as soon as the NICU dream flashes in my mind's eye. "As crazy as this sounds, I dream of them. Frequently."

"Really?"

"Yeah. Until recently, it's sort of just these dark orby feelings. Almost like we're back in the womb and just sensing each other's connection. I feel drawn to them in my dreams. Safe. Comforted. Like I know them implicitly."

He cocks his head to the side and replies, "You said 'until recently.' What happened recently?"

Choosing to avoid eye contact, I look down and pick at the open frayed holes in my black jeans. "I've always had crazy vivid dreams, and I remember a lot of them, too. But most recently, I dreamt of when we were all in the NICU. My sisters and me. I could hear my mother arguing with the doctor, trying to save us. She's a high-risk neonatal surgeon. She's a genius in her profession so she had a lot to say about our care. Meanwhile, I could feel my sisters beside me in their own incubators. In my dream, I felt nervous and protective…but yet powerless because I was just a baby and I could feel them slipping away."

Miguel holds up a finger for me to pause as he writes something down in his notepad. "Your mother is a doctor you say?" he asks, his brow furrows as his writing turns frenzied.

"Yes. Do I get to know what you're writing?" I ask, my tone dripping with annoyance. I've seen doctors take notes on TV, but if there's information about me in there, I want it.

He glances up and offers me a kind smile. "Not always, but you can know this." Clearing his throat, he moves to the edge of his seat, resting his muscular forearms on his knees. "I get the impression that you are hungry for information, Reyna, so I would like to digress for a moment and tell you about the philosophy of 'ghosts.'"

"Ghosts?" I balk, unable to hold back my incredulous stare. Fucking Frank set me up with a quack.

"Try to bear with me. There are some psychologists who do not believe in the presence of 'ghosts.' However, ghosts do not only pertain to spirits. Rather, ghosts can refer to our past dictating our future. This kind of thinking has an origin with Freud and psychoanalysis. But, I have seen numerous powerful examples in my career that I am a full believer. Knowing our own behaviors and where they come from or why we act the way we do is not an exact science. We are all just guessing based on decades of the research and experience. Going back to your friend, Hayden, or anyone who has experienced a horrible tragedy—there could be several reasons for him attempting to take his own life. It could be a genetic pre-disposition he has or the result of a tragic experience that could have led him there. This is an example of the past dictating our future and actions. Coming back to you and the way you say you can feel your sisters…have you considered the possibility of residual memories?"

"Residual from infancy?" I balk.

"Residual even from your time in the womb." His eyebrows lift helpfully.

"You're going to need to elaborate, because right now you sound like the crazy one," I say, feeling curiously cautious.

He chuckles softly. "You see, Reyna, we all have some kind of trauma from our infancy or early childhood that gets stored in our memory bank. Many perinatal psychologists believe that the way in which our culture gives birth is hugely traumatic for infants. So, the question is: Why do we act out like we do?

"For example, take your experience in the NICU. You said you still feel an intense connection to your sisters. So, might it be possible that your body remembers the horrid feeling of losing them one by one? If so, your body may have a sense of impending doom as it still remembers their loss. If you felt that as a baby, your defense mechanism in your life as an adult could be pushing people away. Also, your mother knew the risks better than anyone of what a quadruplet pregnancy would entail. The fear, the terror, the guilt she felt all had to be intense. Those feelings then get passed on to her babies at the brain chemistry level, causing them the same anxiety. She knew the odds, and you survived them. All of that can be labeled as your 'ghosts.'"

My mind swirls at the crazy amount of information. "So my ghosts are the reason I push her and anyone else away?"

"Not all, no. I think the patterns you exhibit with your mother stem from how she's treated you your whole life."

"So why does my mom treat me the way she does? Why does she idolize me so much and put me up on a damn pedestal with every breath I take?" I ask. "She acts like I'm perfect and I hate it so much."

"Not all of our actions are a direct result of our experience in our mother's womb. Many things can happen over the course of our life to trigger these actions. The point is, we keep living those same patterns and then we hit a wall—like a trauma, or a tragedy, or even just hitting our own rock bottom—and until we find some insight in some other way, like therapy or meditation, we just live in that constant pattern."

I briefly wonder how my mother would have been if she hadn't lost my father? Then I think about Liam. It was him that I opened up to and allowed inside my deepest, darkest secrets…until I freaked out and shoved him away. Was he therapy for me? Self-medication? Why was it Liam I opened up to instead of Hayden?

"So, question. If I hit rock bottom like Hayden, why didn't I try to kill myself?"

"Some people are more emotionally resilient than others. You do not react with suicidal thoughts, but your level of self-hatred and pushing those close to you away can be seen as a form of social suicide."

"Holy fuck," I exclaim, my jaw dropped in shock.

"Is there something more you would like to share or ask?" Miguel chuckles softly.

My eyes swim with emotion at everything he's just laid before me. It's almost like this Miguel, Spanish-Doogie just pegged me in one damn session. How is it possible that I said so few words and he's managed to dig into a place in my head that I have never even been before? "You mentioned before that finding a therapist or meditation can help us break our patterns. Can regular people do that for a person, too? Like friends? Spouses? Can they be a form of therapy?"

He nods earnestly. "Yes, certainly. A solid family is monumental. There are relationships and people who are extremely good for us. But with that said, there are relationships that are extremely bad for us as well. There are so many barriers that prevent us from identifying our own value. Our own self-worth. Finding someone who can elevate you and inspire you is extremely therapeutic."

"This has been…enlightening," I say speculatively, still mulling over all of this new information he's dumped on me.

"Good, I'm glad. But, our time is up for now, Reyna. I would really like for you to come back. I can sense your independence in wanting to gain this knowledge on your own, but I feel like we are just getting started. And having someone unconnected to you personally is huge for expediting your healing process." His face looks hopeful.

Without hesitating, I nod in agreement and set up more appointments with his receptionist. The truth is, this is the first time in my life that I've ever wanted this kind of help. I want to take this time that I have and get better…just like Hayden is.

CHAPTER 34

Over the next couple weeks, I end up seeing Miguel four more times. I chastised Frank in the beginning for sending me to someone so young. Truthfully, though, it's Miguel's age that makes him so much more approachable.

I've prided myself on being honest my entire life and I've never felt like more of a liar. Miguel has opened my eyes to all the elements in my life that have played a part in me becoming who I was…am…or who I am fighting against being. Being a quad and having my mother's unrealistic perception of me shoved down my throat was tough. Then I witnessed my father die at a young age, which only made my mother's behavior more extreme. It was no wonder I started pushing people out of my life. I wasn't comfortable. Ever! Then my best friend, the one person I managed to let in, died in a tragic accident. If that wasn't hard enough, I now live with the guilt of sleeping with her would-be fiancé.

I have been constantly pushing people away because I was terrified of people discovering that I wasn't the "miracle" my name portrayed me to be. Therefore, I felt like I wasn't worth saving or even just getting to know. And, as cliché as it is, a lot of those feelings stem from my mother. I have never been seen properly by her and because of that, I never believed her love to be real. And I still have trouble believing it. Being treated like a miraculous angel and feeling broken on the inside wreaked total havoc on my perception of love. Both for myself and for others.

The dream I had of my mother in the NICU was so enlightening in some ways because I had feelings for that woman. She was real, authentic, and present. She was someone I wanted to get to know—not even close to the mother I grew up with. Miguel suggests I bring her in for some sessions soon, but that's not something I'm comfortable with, yet.

And unfortunately, after Marisa, I only started pushing people away even harder, just to avoid the pain of loss. And I started depending on alcohol and casual sex with Hayden in order to cope.

Hayden is another whole ball of wax. Daphney has informed me that they've had a couple of family counseling sessions with him. She said that Hayden is still really raw and fragile, but making strides. He still doesn't want to speak to me, though.

Miguel says that I am probably a large trigger for Hayden and that I need to respect his space. It's painful to know that I let our friendship get so dark and toxic for him. I want to fix it. But, I can't. Instead, Miguel asks me which of my battery of issues I want to address first and without hesitation, I say Liam.

****

"This better be good, Oxford," Frank drawls, strolling into my flat on my day off. I called him over after my latest session with Miguel and am feeling nervously anxious now that he's actually here. "I can tell your brain has been noodling lots of gooey thoughts as of late and I want bloody in."

Between the multiple therapy sessions, I've still been busting my butt at Club Taint. I'm working daily with Lariza now that he's back. The first day he showed up in full Liza Minnelli drag. The man is a hoot! I can so see why Frank likes him. But I still miss Frank. Luckily we've been texting regularly, so that helps me with my ginger jonesing. Of course Frank sang my marketing praises to Lariza, so now I'm taking on even more responsibility at the club. As a result, I'm feeling pretty good about my professional life. Confident and excited, even. As for my personal life, my heart hasn't been feeling so good. Something is missing and I think I know just how to mend it.

So I'm calling on Frank and Beans for help. I conceal the snide comment I want to make regarding Frank's outfit of brown, ankle-length trousers and a denim button down shirt with the sleeves cut off. The truth is: I need Frank right now. And the fact that I'm saying I want anyone to help me is…colossal.

Hayden used to be my security blanket when things got rough—when my feelings became overwhelming and I wanted to forget. Now I don't want to forget. I want to relish in them. Bathe in them. Shout them from a damn mountaintop if I have to. I'm tired of living in the melancholy of the past. I'm ready to bask in the brightness of the now, and being honest with my heart is a huge part of that.

Frank follows me into my living area and makes himself at home picking through my makeup on the floor by my floor-length mirror. "Do you want something to drink? I have…water."

Frank's red eyebrows rise. "What kind?"

"The faucet kind."

His face screws up in disgust. "God, you must be joking. Just get on with it Oxford. Then we can get out of here and go to Chelsea for some real refreshments."

I drag Frank over to my bed and he eyes the mattress nervously before sitting down. "I know you and Liam are friends and I know you probably think I broke his heart…and I did. I know I did. Like…more than once. But Frank, I have to see him. I have to talk to him and see if the shit I have swirling in my head has any chance at being as amazing as I think it could be."

"What are you going on about?" His red brows furrow in confusion.

"I'm talking about the fact that I feel like I am breathing for the first time in twenty-eight years! And with the first real breath I take, I want it to be with Liam. I need to see him. He's not answering any of my texts or calls. I don't even know where his office is. I'm begging, Frank. Can you help me with this?"

I search his gaze for any glimpse of sympathy, but he schools his features to look critical. "Well, what's your plan? Show up to his place of work and profess your love for him?"

The word *love* sends shivers up my back. I'm not sure I'm ready for all of that, but I'm ready for something more. And I'm done waiting. I don't want to waste another second of letting Liam walk the streets thinking that I don't care about him. I care about Liam more than I've ever admitted to myself and now I'm finally ready to tell him. Waiting is NOT an option. I nod my head to Frank in silent answer.

"Oh, for fuck's sake, Oxford. You're hopeless." He stands up and shuffles quickly over to my closet. "You're not going to his place of work. You're coming with me to Ethan's party."

"Who's Ethan? Frank! I have to do this. I'm like bursting to do this and I'm scared if I don't do it now, I'll lose my nerve."

"Scrumpette, you're so lucky I actually like you because what I'm about to tell you is going to positively floor you." I'm hanging on his every word as he pulls out a black dress on a hanger and holds it out to examine. "Ethan is a mate of Liam's and he's having a birthday party tonight and I'm on the guest list…and guess who I'm taking with me."

"Your favorite American?" I grin broadly and stand.

The two S's slice between his eyebrows at my statement. "Honey, with all the American heroines in my life, how could I possibly ever choose a favorite?" His serious expression turns into a wry grin as he adds, "But you'll earn extra points if you let me take you shopping for an outfit for tonight."

I'm pretty sure I'd let Frank throw out all my black if it meant he could get me in front of Liam right now.

***

"This was a terrible idea," I groan, staring at myself in the mirror.

"No! Oxford! I've never seen you look more stunning!"

I stare incredulously at my reflection. My dark hair is loose down my back with soft, large curls and my makeup is dramatic and sexy with magenta matte lips. It's the dress I'm trying to come to terms with. It's a one shoulder magenta mini-dress Frank selected at a posh shop that I never would have even walked in to. The bust is completely covered in glittery crystals and anchored by a magenta belt that flows into a slim skirt. The fit is perfect for my short curves, but the color…I have literally never worn this color.

"I'd rather wear what you're wearing," I say, eyeing his expensive, tailored black tuxedo. He paired it with a purple deep V-neck muscle shirt and a purple and white polka dot pocket square. "Frank. I like black. This is so not black."

"Magenta is magic. The color even compliments your ink."

I glance down at my sugar skull and sunflowers and have to nod in agreement. "But I feel like I'm going to stand out so much."

"Oxford," Frank says coming to stand in front of me. His brown eyes are wide and serious. "You have to stand out if you are trying to stand up."

My eyebrows rise at his insightful words. Standing up is exactly what I'm trying to do. I'm trying to stand up for myself, for Liam, for all the pain I've caused to everyone that's ever given a shit about me. Frank's right. I have to rise to this challenge. I'm ready to exorcise my ghosts. My watery eyes shutter closed and before he can stop me, I pull him into a hug.

His body stiffens. "Oxford, I'm British. We don't hug. We do posh air kisses on the cheeks and even that is only because we're trying to be pompous."

"I'm hugging you, Frank. Just sink into it." I grin as I feel his hesitant arms wrap tightly around me. "I think I might love you, Frank and Beans."

"I think I might hate you, Oxford," he sighs and I giggle into his wild, red hair that he's stylishly mussed haphazardly. After another moment, I release him. His face is stark serious, but his eyes are twinkling with mirth.

"Is my makeup okay?" I ask, touching Frank's masterpiece.

"It's perfect. Now, let's bloody go before you start writing sonnets about me."

A short while later, a cab is dropping us off at a red carpet outside of Cirque le Soir, a posh nightclub in Soho. I've never been to it before, but I know it's a place where the elite and famous frequent regularly. Frank and I pile out of the cab and a mass of photographers swarm us, shooting pictures in a frenzy.

"Do they think you're Prince Harry?" I yell to him over the roar of people shouting. Just then, my question is answered when I finally hear what they are all yelling:

"It's Frank McElroy! Over here!"

"Who's your date, Frank? What's her name?"

"Where have you been, Frank? Haven't seen you out much!"

"Frank! Can I get a shot?"

Frank tucks me under his slender arm and covers himself as we walk quickly to the entrance. The security guards open them instantly as we bypass a huge line of people waiting.

As soon as we're inside, I pull away and stare at him in wonder. "Who are you?"

He shakes his head dismissively. "That's from another life, Oxford. Don't ask. Come on, they are in the VIP room." Frank moves us through the club, like he knows the place easily. The mystery behind Frank's background is niggling at me, but I want to respect his privacy…for now. Not to mention, Cirque le Soir is completely diverting my focus with all its splendor. The posh club is bursting with colorful lights and red velvet cushioned seating and drapes. There are various stages throughout filled with a mix of circus-looking performers. Burlesque dancers, fire-eaters, a woman with a snake. It's freaky and fabulous, and I love every bit of it.

We reach a concealed doorway and Frank gives his name to the security guy, who motions us through. We walk through and the hallway darkens as we move further away from the club lights. Finally, we reach a roped off area that leads up a private, narrow staircase. We head up the long flight that is illuminated with rope lights and leads to a small VIP area. It's filled to the brim with young Londoners dressed to the nines and clearly already in full party mode. Frank offered me a drink while we got ready at my flat, but I said I wanted a clear head for tonight. I have been using alcohol to self-medicate for far too long. Yes, this was a party, but tonight I had a purpose.

Nervously chewing my magenta covered lips, I ask, "Are you sure he's coming, Frank?"

"Yes, he'll be here. You need to relax, Oxford. And keep chewing on your lip like that. It's sexy as fuck," Frank says into my ear as my eyes continue to dart around looking for Liam. "And if you're trying to show Liam that you've changed, the best place to start is by showing him how sexy and fun you can be."

I frown at him. "Sexy and fun?"

"Yes, I know it's a foreign concept to you. You prefer that misunderstood rebel girl vibe. But seriously, show him the girl you were in Cambridge. There'll be time for serious discussions later."

His advice is sound and I nod while earnestly snagging a glass of champagne off a clown server's tray. Just one. I can't risk any mistakes tonight. I grab another for Frank and we do a quick cheers.

Let's hope Frank is right and Liam actually shows up tonight.

CHAPTER 35

"Ethan, this is Rey. Rey, this is the blessed birthday boy."

A tall, caramel-skinned man with blue eyes stares back at me and I actually have to remind myself to breathe. He is breath-taking. He's dressed in a slim, light gray suit with a white button down open halfway down his chest.

He huffs out a cocky laugh, "So, this is Rey. Well, I can see what all the fuss is about." His blue gaze is taking in every curve of my body and every detail of my ink, and it doesn't take an educated person to gather that he likes what he sees.

Frank puts a protective arm around my waist. "Where's Liam?"

"On his way. What is it you do, Rey?" Ethan asks to my chest.

"I work at a club. Bartending," I reply coolly. This prick is definitely not a part of my mission tonight.

"Of course you'd have a hot arse job." His gaze is lazily drinking me in still and it's annoying me.

"Nothing hot about mopping up vomit. I've had to do that twice in only a few weeks." I smile at Frank who gives me a tight grin. "What do you do, Ethan?" I ask even though I really could care less. But if this is Liam's friend, I want to at least attempt to play nice.

"I own an IT business," he replies dismissively and then leans into me. "Rey, what do you say you and I have some fun before Liam gets here? Wanna dance?" His tone is low and seductive.

"I'd hate to take you away from your party. How would they ever survive without you?" I quip with sarcasm. Looking around, you'd hardly know any of these people were here for him. I wonder how close Liam is to this guy?

His grin is arrogant. "They'll manage. But I don't think I will if I don't get a birthday dance from you." He reaches out and seductively pushes my hair off of my shoulder, revealing my black roses. His eyes flare appreciatively on my skin. Just when I'm about to put my nice girl act away and unleash my inner bitch, a thunderous voice behind me sends my heart up into my throat.

"She's not a fucking stripper, Ethan. Back. OFF," Liam says, coming to stand beside me. His jaw muscle ticks angrily as he shoots daggers at Ethan. "Being the birthday boy doesn't give you a hall pass to be an arrogant arse."

I gaze up at Liam and my pulse picks up just by his close proximity. He's dressed in a trim, black suit with a white button down beneath. He is wearing a thin pencil tie on and his blond hair is full and wild on top of his head. It's a little longer than the last time I saw him and I'm definitely a fan. His gaze diverts from Ethan and he glances down at me quickly. I swear I see an ember of heat in his brown eyes before he looks over and gives a quick head nod to Frank.

Ethan begins to launch into a retort, but Frank cuts him off by the balls, "Let's get you a birthday shot, shall we, Ethan?" He throws his arm around Ethan and leads him away.

"What is it with you and other guys?" Liam asks and I turn to find him staring down at me accusingly.

"Excuse you?" I exclaim. I have to bite the inside of my cheeks to prevent myself from going for blood like I want to right now. "I was just standing here. Ethan's supposed to be your mate, isn't he?" I seethe.

He scoffs and then says, "What are you even doing here, Rey?" His eyes flicker with sadness as he looks down at my dress. He returns his gaze to mine and schools his features to look angry.

"Frank invited me."

"Of course he did," he glances at my mouth and then looks away. "He's a meddling ginger—"

"Don't blame Frank for this. If you would have replied to any of my texts or calls, I wouldn't be ambushing you like this."

He looks off to the dance floor down below, that muscle in his jaw ticking violently. "I don't have anything to say."

"Nothing to say?" I reply, my eyes wide.

He pins me with a smoldering and complicated look. His eyes glide down to my magenta lips, clearly conflicted with what he wants to address. The familiar scent of cinnamon washes over me as he leans down closely to my face and replies, "I think we've said everything there was to say, Rey. Let's not lock the gate after the horse has bolted."

I steel myself to take Frank's advice. I need to keep this positive even though every part of me wants to scream at Liam how I feel. "Fine then. Want to go to the bar and get a drink with me?"

He jerks his head back, clearly taken aback. Nearly laughing, he replies, "No thanks. I'm good."

"Come on, Liam. It's been over two weeks. Surely you can have tea with me." I half smirk at him in challenge, throwing the words back at him that he threw at me outside of Club Taint.

His lips form a thin line like he wants to go off on me for what I did. And I wouldn't blame him. What I did with Hayden after just having been with Liam was inconceivable. Instead, he purses his lips and begrudgingly gestures for me to lead the way. When we reach a thick group of people, he places his hand on the small of my back to help guide me through. The sensation of his warm palm against my thin dress sends shivers up my spine. As if sensing that his touch is affecting me, he pulls his hand back quickly when we reach the bar.

"Well, what'll it be?" I ask looking up at Liam next to me as we both sidle up to the small bar.

"I'll just do a beer," he replies without making eye contact.

I nod nervously as we wait for the bartender to finish with the other patrons. Attempting small talk, I ask Liam how his tattoo is healing.

"Good as far as I can tell, but it was my first so I have nothing to compare it to. How about yours?" His eyes glance down to my wrist.

"Fine. The little ones heal quickly." I touch my dream catcher gently. A few small scabs formed, but nothing noticeable.

Just then, a man dressed head to toe in fishnets approaches us to take our order. I glance down and see he has just a patch of fabric covering his man bits. He's got short buzzed hair and a Mediterranean look about him. "What'll it be, love?" He winks at me and then his eyes rove over Liam in appreciation. Can't say I blame the guy.

"I'll do a water and my friend here will take a pint of Fosters."

"Water?" Liam asks, eyeing me curiously. "That's not like you."

I nod and smile. "You'd be surprised." He frowns briefly as the bartender hands him a glass of frothy beer.

Just as Mr. Fishnets hands me my bottle of water, I lean over and shout so he can hear me, "Hey, can I ask you a question?"

"Absolutely, pretty eyes." The man's brows lift in kindness.

"How do you pee in that thing?" My face screws up into playful, worried expression and I gesture down towards his crotch.

His mouth splits into a beaming smile and he lets out a hearty laugh. "Very carefully."

"No, I mean, specifically. Do you have to take the whole thing off?"

"No," he says, clearly knowing this will only intrigue me further.

"So is there a trap door?"

"Nope."

My eyes alight. "So does this mean you just hold your pecker perfectly so the stream shoots between the netting—"

"Please ignore her," Liam interrupts me while wrapping a hand around my waist and pulls me back a bit. He's shaking his head with a grin that reminds me of Oxford. "This is so none of our business. Cheers," he adds apologetically.

"She's alright, mate. Cheers." Mr. Fishnets smiles genuinely and waves us off as he attempts to take the orders of a large group that squeezed in beside us. I turn in Liam's arms and suddenly our bodies are flush against each other in the crowded bar area.

"Bloody hell, you can't be left alone in public," Liam's voice is low and husky as he stares at my lips.

"What? I wanted to get to the bottom of that. It'll keep me up for days!" I smile innocently.

Liam sighs heavily and attempts to conceal his grin. The tiniest of a dimple forms on his chin every time he tries to hide his laughter.

"I remember that." I say, touching the circular dot with my finger.

"What?" he asks, frowning and rubbing his chin.

"At Oxford. That little dimple would show every time you and I would have a private joke or conversation that Marisa was never aware of." My belly flips at the butterflies I used to feel for Liam from afar even back then.

His face flickers with a variety of emotions before he replies, "I'm surprised you noticed."

"I always noticed you." My smile drops as I stare up at him in wonder. A flash of the way he used to be at Oxford hits me. He used to always make sure I had dinner plans before going out with Marisa. Even just the way his forehead creased when he looked at me before leaving. If only back then I could have believed in myself enough to believe in him.

Smiling again, I say, "Do you remember how Marisa harassed that German bartender at O'Malley's Pub?"

This elicits a genuine smile. "She couldn't believe he'd never heard of The *Sound of Music*. I had to remind her that the film took place in Austria, not Germany."

"And then I had to show her on a map that Germany and Austria aren't the same country!" I burst out laughing at the memory of her confused blonde expression as she looked at the map in horror. "She was mortified that she had teased that guy so much."

"I don't think he could understand most of what she said anyway," he says with a huff of laughter.

"I know, right? Everyone always just agreed with Marisa." I shake my head at the power that girl had over people by being herself.

"That they did." Our laughter dies down as reality sets back in.

"I miss her," I say softly.

"Me too."

"Do you think what we did makes it possible for us to miss her properly?"

"What's proper?" Liam shrugs his shoulder with an edge of defiance.

"In a way where I can think of her without thinking of you and me."

His face drops with sadness and he closes his eyes for a moment before opening them again. "How's Hayden?" He takes a long drink from his glass effectively pummeling our moment.

My cheek bones twitch at his sudden change of subject. I care about Hayden, but he's not where I want Liam's head to be right now. "Good, I think. He checked himself into a facility for thirty days, but I haven't heard from him."

"I heard something like that. Why haven't you heard from him? I thought you two were close." Liam's face is hardened and cold again.

"We were, kind of. But, not in any of the ways that matter. Whenever things got heavy between us, we just pushed each other away. We weren't ever really good for each other." I look down and shake my head at that sad realization.

Feeling Liam's eyes on me, I glance up again. The intensity behind his glower scares me. As if snapping out of his trance, he blinks his eyes and shakes his head. "It was nice seeing you, Rey."

He pulls away from me and sets his beer down. Shock and confusion wash over me as he begins shuffling through the crowd toward the staircase. I glance around, looking for Frank, my eyes wide and fearful. As if sensing me, his red head pops up over the throng of bodies and our gazes collide. His eyes dart from me to a retreating Liam and he motions with his head for me to go after him. The fire behind his look ignites me and with a quick head nod, I'm pressing my way through the people toward the staircase.

Just as Liam begins his decent, I shout, "Liam, wait!" He pauses halfway down but thinks better of it and continues. I hurry down the steps and rush into the dark hallway close behind him. "Please, Liam," my voice is pained and shaky as I stare at his back. The lights pouring in from the doorway illuminate his hunched silhouette.

My plea stops him and I take the opportunity to move past him to block his retreat. "So that's it? We're done? You're just running away?" My voice is strident, as I look straight up at him.

"I'm *walking* away." His head hangs as he reaches out to move me to the side. Without thinking, I shove him hard in the chest with all my might. He stumbles back, his head only drooping further with sadness.

"Why? Why walk away? What are you scared of?" I prop my hands on my hips, clutching the thin fabric of my dress nervously.

He looks at me knowingly. "I can't even trust that you're here right now because of me or because you don't have Hayden to disappear into."

My jaw drops. "How can you say that?"

"Well? Is it true?" His expression pierces me for the truth.

"I'm here for you. No one else has even come close to the place you've reached in my heart. I've never lied to you, Liam. Not on purpose at least. You are the one person I've never lied to."

"Please stop acting like I was ever anything special to you."

"You were! You are. You always have been. Even Marisa didn't know all that you know. I never told her—" I stop myself, completely unable to finish that sentence and swallow hard to broach the subject that brought me here in the first place. "You told me I was the one. You told me I was worth something. Was that all a lie?" I ask, my hands shaking out in front of me.

"Just leave it." He moves past me again and I jump in his way giving him another shove. His eyes glance up and he flinches as if just the sight of my face hurts him. "Please step aside, Rey."

"No!" I scream, shoving him back down the hallway. I can't let him leave. Letting him leave again feels like we truly are saying goodbye this time. "I'm tired of saying goodbye to you, Liam. You can't...you can't just...make me *believe* and then take it all away. Push me back! Please? I'm begging you. You have to push me!" I suck in a loud and shaky breath.

"I'm done pushing, Rey," he says with a painful groan. "I'm done trying to make you believe. Don't you see? I never made you believe anything. Ever. I pushed you and you ran. That's all you've ever done." He sniffs loudly and looks at me with tortured expression. "It took me too bloody long to recover the first time. Doing this again will fucking kill me."

I shove my hands into my hair, panicky tears puncturing the surface at the painful truth behind his words. "I know I'm messed up, Liam." A guttural sob erupts and he looks at me with sympathy. Sympathy I fucking hate but I have to keep going. "I'm working on it. But you have to know…I have to tell you." Deep breath. "You made me fall in love with you!"

I cry at the deep and intense shock that smears over his face as the raw truth tumbles out of my mouth. I want to crumple to the floor at the fear coursing through me with that admission.

"Love?" He laughs, his glistening eyes searching my face for something I can't possibly show him.

"I saw the way you saw me. The way no one else had ever seen me, and it made me fall in love with you."

He looks away, gazing down the hallway in exasperation and then he pins me to the wall with ferocity in his expression. "You fucking *broke* my heart, Rey!" he roars and I flinch at the agony in his tone.

Tears pour from my eyes with every frenzied blink. I cover my face with my hands as a loud sob breaks through my chest. His warm arms wrap around me, but the touch is almost more painful than the space. The touch isn't one of a lover…it's one of sympathy. I sob even harder at that realization and at just how truly broken I am inside. I'm sobbing because the first time a person tells someone they love them shouldn't feel this painful.

This bruising.

"This can't be for nothing, Liam," I croak, a knot in the back of my throat aching. "We can't have betrayed her for nothing,"

"One person shouldn't break someone like this, Rey. We tried to turn nothing into something. But nothing is all we ever were." He kisses the top of my head and a chill washes over me as he releases me and walks away.

I slide down the wall and drop my face into my chest and cry like I've never cried before. "Nothing is all we ever were."

CHAPTER 36

"It hurts, Marisa," I cry out while digging my bloodied fingers into the biting rock. "I'm not getting anywhere."

"Sure you are!" she replies in her typical cheerful, singsong voice. "Just look."

I turn to look down the huge cliff that Marisa and I have been climbing up for hours and see that we must be thousands of feet above the ground right now. Hot sunlight bakes my skin as panic sets in.

"Marisa!" I scream, trying to find a better grip. "Holy shit, we're too high. This is way too high. We need help. HELP!" I scream at the top of my lungs while scratching frantically at the jagged cliff wall.

Marisa begins laughing. "You are ma lady and I love you like mad, but you can't honestly be this dense."

"What do you mean?" My wide, terrified eyes ask as I cling helplessly to the bluff.

She looks at me knowingly. "'The higher you climb, the farther you fall.' 'No cliff is so tall it cannot be climbed.' I'm sure there are a million other cliff proverbs out there to draw inspiration from, but good Lord, I don't have time to Google. Come on!"

Suddenly I look up and watch her take one more step as she reaches the top, looking down on me. Relief washes over me as I clamber up to the flat surface. I drop down to my butt and take in huge gulps of air. Looking down over the edge, a woozy sensation overcomes me. I can't see any land down below. Only wide open sky and soft, buttery looking clouds. It's eerie not being able to see the bottom of what you're sitting on top of.

Marisa flops down beside me, her blonde hair blowing freely in the wind. She brushes the rock off her palms and asks, "So you get it then, right?"

"Get what?" I ask, still out of breath.

"The message and blah, blah, bloody blah." I frown, clearly lost as to what she's going on about. Rolling her eyes, she replies, "It's like this: Slow and steady wins the race. You keep climbing and you'll find what you're reaching for. Or…oh, it could be like this: Stop climbing away from your problems and face them head on. Take your pick. I like option one better personally, but dreams are entirely subjective, so it's whatever you've decided is most helpful."

"I'm not sure what problem you're referring to," I reply nervously.

"You and Liam!" she crows at me. The sunlight orbs around her head momentarily. "Come off it, Rey. It's bloody obvious. Just get it all out. Tell me what you wouldn't even admit to yourself back then."

"I was in love with Liam," I whisper. Just saying the words, my chest concaves and a sense of relief washes over me. "I was in love with Liam the entire time and I never admitted it to a single soul. Even myself."

"Honestly, I don't know why you waited three years to admit it to yourself." Her brown eyes flash with challenge.

I bite my lip, feeling sadness envelope me. "It wasn't that easy after I lost you."

"Why the hell not?"

Gazing down, I reply, "You built me up in Oxford, Marisa. I'd never had a true friend before and you made feel special. *Loved.* But, you loved me for who I was—not just because I existed. You actually picked me to be your friend, you know?"

"'Course I did! I have excellent taste." She flashes a megawatt smile at me and I can't help but half smile at her in response. "So if I did such a top notch job building you up, why have you been such a mess the past three years?"

"Isn't it obvious?" I say, painfully aware of what's coming.

"Say the words, Rey. Scream it if you have to!"

I swallow down the painful knot in my throat and blink away the fresh tears collecting in my eyes. "'I'm sorry' sounds trivial at this point. The reality is, I fucking spit in all the beauty you gave me! You were great and kind and loved me. Like, really loved *me!* You were my rescue ship and I repaid you by sleeping with the man you were in love with! I'm fucked up. I'm not right. I'm sick! After all of that, how couldn't I just fall apart?"

"There. Feel better?"

"What?"

"You got it off your chest. Now stop harping about what you did. Do you not remember any of my rants from back at University? We do not conform. We take our soapbox and we shout our convictions until we've convinced everyone around us of our stance and why it is important. Now suck it up and open your damn eyes, Rey." She grips my cheeks in her hands firmly and says with wide, serious eyes, "And please see that I wasn't the only one loving you in Oxford." I look at her incredulously as an image of Liam appears beyond her.

She nods knowingly, releasing my face. "And I also wasn't the only one building you up either."

My heart lurches at the sight of my mother stroking lovingly on her large, taut belly. That orby sensation I get every time my sisters appear in my dreams clouds my vision. "What do you mean, Marisa?"

"You've always felt close to them for a reason, Reyna. That wasn't by accident. They gave you what they could because they loved you. They believed in you so much they gifted you with their entire lives. Don't waste it, ma lady."

Emotions overcome me and hot tears slip down my cheeks. "This is overwhelming," I say gazing up into the sky above me. "What if I've pushed him too hard, Marisa? What if he doesn't love me like that anymore and I wrecked any chance we had?"

She shakes her head and stands up, pointing down to the nonexistent ground below us. "Do not sink down to mediocrity, ma lady," her voice rises in declaration prepping for another one of her epic ranks. Clouds billow up around her dramatically as she continues, "You must shoot for greatness! You're marked now. Be the badass your ink portrays you to be. You are finally beginning to love yourself for what we've always seen in you. This is only the beginning!"

CHAPTER 37

After waking from my dream in the middle of the night, I was completely unable to get back to sleep. I thought I would have spent the night bawling my eyes out and slipping into a depression to rival all other depressions. Instead, as the sun rose, so did my determination. As I sipped coffee from my balcony and watched the gray London dawn emerge, I reveled in the fact that Marisa was still able to inspire me even after her death. I guess that death doesn't always mean the end for everyone. Sometimes, the spirit of someone special is only the beginning.

All night my mind was reeling with ideas for what I could do next to win Liam back. I had rejected him time and time again, so it was expected that he had his guard up. The painful words he spewed at me last night were horrid…but true. My time in therapy was proving all of that. But this couldn't be the end for us.

Already, I've impressed myself with my renewed strength. After Frank pulled me up off the hallway floor of Cirque le Soir, he offered to spend the night, but I refused. I didn't want to use Frank as a Hayden security blanket replacement for when things got rough in my life. I wanted to deal with this heartache on my own. The fact that Frank looked like he wanted to chase after Liam with a broken Ginge on Top beer bottle and shank him in the neck only made me smile. Frank loved Liam, so if he was so ferociously mad at Liam's decision, maybe all hope wasn't lost.

First order of business was making amends for everyone I've fucked over. Frank's words about Liam just living his life as a bystander these last few years broke my heart. He took a risk when he asked me to go with him to Cambridge for the weekend, and I only spit in his face as a thank you. Then the kicks just kept on coming when I left there. The worst part about healing is finding all the massive battle scars left behind.

Dressed head to toe in black, I clamber off the train in East London. Facing Hayden's brother, Theo, scares me. A lot. He and I have never talked much…ever really. I knew he and Marisa were really close growing up and I think we both avoided each other for that very reason. It was just too painful.

But Theo is Liam's best friend. If I can get him to see how very real my feelings are for Liam, then I can get anyone to see. Theo probably associates me with the same fucked-upness Hayden is. But that's not me anymore. I need him to see that I've changed. If he does, then maybe I'll have a chance with Liam.

I reach the white industrial building that Theo lives in. It's a two-story building with a single stall garage door, a workshop, an office, and up above is Theo's flat. A shiver runs through as I recall that this is where Leslie found Hayden that night nearly three weeks ago. My how life has changed in such a short span of time.

The storefront part of the office is closed, so I press the buzzer and wait. I see Theo through the window planing a large coffee table of some sort. He stops when he hears the buzzer and adjusts his black-rimmed glasses. His buzzed head tilts as his eyes zero in on me.

A moment later, he opens the door. "Reyna?" he asks. "What are you doing here?"

"Hi, um, Theo," I stammer. "I wondered if you might have time to chat?" I look down at my black boots nervously.

"Right, yeah. Come on in." He holds the door open and I follow him into his work studio. He gestures toward a tall stool and I sit on it. His large arms cross over his chest and he eyes me warily.

"You know Hayden doesn't get out for another week, right?"

I swallow and nod. "How's he doing?" I look up and see his pale brown eyes staring at me sadly.

"He's doing quite well, all things considered. Making good progress it seems."

"That's good. I've wanted to get in touch, but Daphney said it wasn't possible."

"Yeah, I think it's just best if he doesn't do things on his own for now."

I nod and feel an emotional knot form in my throat. "Listen, Theo, I don't want to beat around the bush. I hope you know that I really do care about your brother. I want him to get better. I have made huge strides recently in getting better myself."

Theo drops his chin and nods, "That's a good start."

"But, I'm not here today to talk about Hayden and I suspect you already know that." I stare him right in the eyes, shoving down all the nerves and anxiety I feel in this moment.

His serious face morphs into humor as he huffs out a laugh, "You've got bloody nerve, I'll give you that." Theo presses his tongue to the side of his cheek, as if attempting to reign in his reply. "Look, Liam is my best mate. I've watched him struggle a lot the last few years…and not in an obvious way, like my brother. Liam is a good person. He doesn't deserve half of what life has dealt him. I can't sit by and watch you turn him into Hayden."

My jaw drops. "Fuck off, Theo! You can't blame me for your brother. Hayden and I were there for each other. We were friends. Yes, we made poor ass decisions, but we did them as adults. Hayden made his own choice and I'm making mine."

"And you're telling me you choose Liam? Is that it?" Theo's eyebrows rise in challenge. "What happens when my brother gets out of rehab?"

"I will do everything in my power to help Hayden…even if that means leaving him the hell alone." The words uttered out of my mouth burn on my tongue, but I know there's no other way. Theo stares stonily at me, not revealing any shred of emotion, like one of those pathetic lions in Trafalgar Square. Fucking British.

"As far as making a choice, there was never a contest," I continue, "You have no clue what Liam and I were…what we still can be! I fucked up. For three damn years I fucked up. I can't take that back. But my feelings are real and major and if there's even a shred of hope for me with Liam, then I'm going to fight for it."

Theo tilts his head to the side. "What do you need from me then? You seem well-equipped."

I laugh at the smirk playing on his lips. "Can I count on your vote then?"

He nods subtly. "I'll see what I can do. I'm sick of the whiny bugger myself. So if you two could get bloody sorted, it'd be a load off my arse. I just hope you're prepared for battle."

I most definitely am.

***

Just as I'm walking past the White Swan Pub, my cell buzzes in my pocket. My heart lurches when I see Liam's name illuminate my screen.

"Hello?" I answer, trying to squelch the scream of excitement in my heart.

"I know what you're doing and it's not going to bloody work, Rey," Liam groans.

I duck into the alley behind the pub and lean against the brick wall. The cadence of his voice moves me to close my eyes and picture his gorgeous mouth. "Hello to you too, Liam. I think this is the first time we've actually spoken on the phone since Oxford."

"Rey, I mean it. Just leave my friends out of this, alright? Especially Theo. And Frank. I don't need to hear it from the both of them."

"Liam," I start, schooling my voice to sound stony serious. "I'm just getting started. You slung a lot of shit at me last night. Shit I deserved. But now it's out of your system. You have to just—"

"I don't have to do anything, Rey!" he cuts me off. "I have to bloody protect myself from the likes of you. Stay the fuck out of my life. And away from my mates. I mean it."

"I'm just trying to get you to see, Liam. We can do this. We can make this work."

"We can't, Rey. You're just somebody I used to know, that's it."

"Now who's the liar?" I ask, my voice rising in challenge. "At least I'm admitting my lies now."

Silence stretches out before us. Eventually Liam replies, "Leave it, Rey. I mean it."

The line clicks dead and I pull my lip into my mouth, chewing nervously. Anxiety prickles down my spine, but I know I have to follow through with Plan B next.

***

I knew that calling Betha and Alden Darby out of the blue was a risk. It had major potential for just pissing Liam the fuck off even further. Not to mention, very likely estranging people that were incredibly important to Liam. But I had to do it. I felt compelled to do it. Liam acting this way scared me. Perhaps I messed him up even more than I even thought possible.

So the next day, I took it as a sign from Marisa when good old Google revealed Liam's parent's phone number in Kent. As I waited for one of them to pick up, I couldn't help but picture them at that pub back in Oxford, sipping beers and slinging cards. The two of them were at the Oxford graduation, but I was too angry at the world to even say hello to them.

It's never too late to say "I'm Sorry," right?

"Hullo?" Alden's voice croaks through the phone line.

"Hi, is this Mr. Darby?" I ask politely.

"Yes, bloody hell," the phone muffles as I hear Liam's dad shout, "Betha…it's a bloody telemarketer from America again. Probably selling something. Should I tell them to get stuffed?"

"Alden!" I shout into the phone as I hear it muffle again.

Alden's voice is deep and firm. "Listen here you, we didn't need double glazing during the war and we certainly don't bloody need it now. Take your windows and get stuffed."

"Alden!" I exclaim, trying my hardest not to laugh, "It's Reyna Miller. From Oxford. I'm a friend of Liam's."

"Oh, bloody hell love, why didn't you say so?"

I let out a laugh, "I meant to. Sorry. I was um…just calling to see how you are?"

"Are you the one with the tattoos?"

I purse my lips. "I am."

"You knew how to play Cribbage!" he roars happily.

"I did. Do you and Betha still play a lot?"

"Every night at tea. And we try to whenever Liam gets home, too. Though that's not as often as his mum would like. Do you still play?"

"I don't have anyone to play with I'm afraid. Though I've run into Liam recently back here in London. Perhaps I can convince him."

"I'm bloody certain you can! He always had designs for you I think."

"Did he?" I ask hopefully, chewing my lip nervously.

"Yeah…pity what happened to your mate, Marisa. Sorry to hear about all that, love. We wanted to come to the funeral, but Betha was still recovering from her knee surgery. She was bloody useless and I still had to push her around in a wheelchair at graduation if you recall. How have you been getting on?"

A moment of pain slices through me at the memory of avoiding them at the Oxford graduation ceremony. "I'm doing better these days, thanks. If Betha is close, I'd love to say hello."

"She is, I'll pass her over. Nice talking. You take care, love."

"You too, Alden."

I can vaguely make out a muffled conversation happening between the two of them. God, I love how utterly normal they are. I can almost picture their oak wooden table with a Cribbage board as the main centerpiece even though I've never even been to their house.

"Reyna love, it's been years!" Betha's voice sings into the line. "Alden and I still have a laugh recalling that day we got pissed at that pub you took us to when we visited Oxford all those years ago."

I conceal a fond smile so I can speak my peace. "That was a lovely day. I'm sorry it's been so long since we've spoken, Mrs. Darby. I suppose I'm calling to make amends. You two were so sweet to me. I'm afraid I just never fully appreciated it back then."

"Call me Betha, dear and you hush. What you children went through back then was positively wretched."

"It was, but it still doesn't mean I don't owe you an apology."

"Apology? Whatever for?" her voice peals straight into my heart.

I swallow before replying, "I could be way off base here, but I just want to apologize for not being a good friend to your son. Liam was nothing but wonderful to me. He was even more wonderful to Marisa. He was in pain, just as I was…more even. I wasn't there for him. I pushed him away because I'm not good at letting people in and that's my fault. Not his. He didn't deserve it. He deserved so much more, Betha. He's a wonderful, wonderful, man. He…he deserves all the best in the world. I just…I wanted you to know that I guess."

Betha's voice catches, "My, my dear. You sound as if—"

"I sound as if I'm sorry. That's all. And I'm sorry for ignoring you and Alden at graduation. That wasn't right of me either. I hope you can find it in your hearts to forgive me."

"There's nothing to forgive, love."

I smile. "I'm glad to hear that. Perhaps if you and Alden ever visit Liam in London, I can be your fourth?"

"We'll bring the board," she says, her voice still in a state of awe and shock. "Take care my love."

"Take care."

I smile, hanging up. Even if nothing ever comes of Liam and me, I'll never regret that phone call for as long as I live.

***

CHAPTER 38

The next day, when I hear nothing from Liam, my heart begins to sink. All day at work, I stared at my phone and nothing. I wanted to call him myself, but the familiar self-loathing in me is strong. It's telling me that if he's not calling to chew me out, then he doesn't care anymore. Maybe he's actually given up on me. I even try to fool myself with the idea that we weren't ever anything special. *Nothing is all we ever were.*

When I cry myself to sleep that night, no inspirational dreams come to me. No signs of hope from Marisa. No orby feelings of connection from my sisters.

Just deep, drugging darkness.

I wake with a jolt to the sound of my flat buzzer going off over and over and over. My eyes are swollen and tender from crying most of the night. "What the hell?" I gasp, glancing at the clock to see it's just after five in the morning.

My door buzzer blasts again and I launch myself off my bed, pulling down my black T-shirt to cover my bare ass. I dash to the kitchen and yank open the floor-length window. I step out onto the wrought iron balcony to see who's buzzing at this time. Leaning over the railing, my stomach roils at the sight of Liam standing there in the gray, London dawn. He's dressed in jeans and a loose T-shirt with his head pressed against the wall in slumped defeat.

"Liam?" I croak, my voice dry and hoarse from all the tears I've shed.

His head snaps to attention and he swerves to look up at me. Even from four stories up, I see agony swirling in his eyes. "You called my parents, Rey." His voice sounds like a pained cry.

"I'm sorry, Liam. I just…had things to say to them," I offer helplessly. "What are you doing here?" I ask into the quiet corner of my street, my heart soaring with hope.

"I don't want it to be for nothing, Rey," he says simply. His face is tear-streaked and tired, like he hasn't slept all night. "What we were back then…it can't all be for nothing."

My chin trembles as the desperation in his gaze mirrors my own. "Come up. Come up!" I cry, and rush into my flat to press the buzzer. I run to the bathroom and shakily brush my teeth, all the while yanking a hairbrush through my tangled dark locks. I'm focusing on the menial tasks before me instead of the screaming avalanche of optimism raging inside my heart.

I run to the door and yank it open just as Liam rounds the corner. His cheeks look hollow and depleted, his brown eyes dark and grave.

"Come in," I say, stepping back.

He pauses and spreads his arms out to grip the doorway on either side. A faint security light in the hallway illuminates his face just enough for me to see the trepidation buried in his eyes.

"I'm fucking terrified, Rey." He releases a shaky breath. "I've been up all night trying to get my head around never seeing you again. Trying to accept the idea of losing you forever. As scary as that feels, this right here," he points down to where his feet are, "feels even scarier."

I move to grasp him around the waist. My eyes look up at his as he shudders in reaction to my sudden touch. "Please, give me a chance to show you that I'm different."

He shakes his head sadly. "I'm so sick of not understanding you, Rey. I'm sick of not knowing why you wouldn't let me in. And then you call my parents and you show me the girl that I fucking fell in love with at Uni. It fucking petrifies me."

"Your parents were important to me, Liam. As weird as it sounds, they meant something to me back at Oxford. That day I spent with them was so gloriously normal. Seeing a glimpse of where you came from. All of it was special to me. They actually liked me. The buttoned up Brits that they are. They somehow saw me for who I was and they liked me."

His eyes swim with emotion and a gentle fondness that he only gets when he speaks of his parents. "They did, Rey. They saw you like I saw you. They spoke of you for a whole year after graduation." He laughs sadly, then swallows, "And…as much as I know I've never been what you want, I can't stop thinking about everything I know we could be."

"You are, Liam! You so are what I want! I want to let you in more than anything. I know I've walked away from you way too many times, but I am different now. Or at least…I want to be. And I've never wanted anything like that before." My watery eyes swim back and forth between his. "Don't give up on me. You are what I want."

His gaze shifts from tortured to hopeful. "You want me?" he asks, like he still can't believe anything I'm saying.

"Liam, there is no one else I want to come out of this mess of my life with. You are my salvation!"

He tilts his head and his expression becomes fierce and determined. In a flash, he drops his hands from the doorframe and grips my waist, rushing me back into my flat. The door slams behind him and he pins me against the wall. "I'm trying to believe you, Rey. I'm trying to believe the words coming out of your mouth." Cupping my cheeks in his large hands, he continues with urgency, "I don't want to miss another second with you. I want to make up for lost time. I want to make up for missed chances. I want what I've always known we could be."

"I want that, too," I reply breathlessly. "More than you can imagine."

Staring at my lips, he adds, "We've always been more. You've always been special." His eyes drift up to mine. "You saw that right? I wasn't alone there, was I?"

I nod woodenly, my chin quivering at his hopeful words. "I was asleep then, but I am awake now and I see everything so much more clearly now. I saw it all…I promise you."

He exhales a shaky breath. "Are you sure, Rey. Because I don't think I'll survive you pushing me away again."

I grab his face in my hands and school my features to look determined. He needs to hear the words. He needs to see my soul. "Liam, I am in love with you. I always have been. You saw me better than I ever saw myself and you pushed me back. Just when everyone else would give up, you would push through. I want to be everything you see in me. I want my insides to match my outsides…perfectly imperfect…just as long as it's with you. I am so in love with you," I say again, teary-eyed.

"I—" he starts, but then slams his lips to mine before he can finish. He tilts his head and fiercely swirls his tongue with mine. His thumbs rub away the tears on my cheekbones as he holds my face just where he wants it. "Fuck," he groans, pulling away and pressing his forehead to mine, breathing his delicious cinnamon scent on me.

"I've waited so long to hear you say that, Rey. I've dreamt of it…and it just fucking blew those dreams out of the water."

"I love you," I reply again because I can say nothing else.

Desperation fleets over his face as he connects our lips again and wraps his arms around my waist. I let my legs hang lifelessly as he lifts me and walks us deeper into my flat. "Where is your bedroom, Rey?"

"You're in it," I giggle against his lips. He sets me down on my bare feet and looks over to find my rumpled mattress in the middle of my living room.

"God, I missed that sound." Leaning down, he nips at my lip and then quickly softens his bite with a warm and wet kiss that swirls all of my senses. He pulls away and grabs the bottom of my long T-shirt and lifts it painfully slow up over my body.

My hair cascades down my naked back as his hungry eyes drink in every exposed inch of me. Bare. Unprotected. Vulnerable and wanting.

I close my eyes as he strokes the back of his hand from my cheek, to my rose covered shoulder, to my nipple, my ribs, my hip and then his caress moves more central to a place that's screaming and so ready for some type of connection.

"I'm going to enjoy this, Rey." His voice is husky and confident.

"Oh!" I cry out as he plunges two thick fingers inside of me and crooks them to a place that makes me feel like my legs will buckle any second. Suddenly, he pulls them out and my eyes snap open, ready to beg, but my voice gets caught in my throat as I watch him bring his fingers to his mouth and suck off the signs of my pleasure.

"I'm going to enjoy this so much more, knowing everything I know now." He reaches for his shirt and yanks it off, mussing his messy, golden blond hair.

"Knowing that I love you?" I ask, my eyes feasting on the sex god before me. The words send a pang of anxiousness through me, but it's a pain that I am prepared for. A pain I'm not going to run from.

His eyes grow darker and his tongue darts out and sucks the remaining taste of me off his lower lip. "I don't think I'll ever tire of hearing you say that."

"It's new for me," I say as he slides his jeans down his legs.

"I know," he nods, while stepping out of his underwear. "And I'm going to bloody savor it."

"I love you," I whisper again as he steps close enough for me to feel his naked erection nudge my belly.

He exhales and leans down, kissing me ferociously while walking us back to my bed and coming down on top of me. I wrap my legs around him, pulling him in as close as I possibly can.

Feeling him on top of me, kissing and licking and sucking every bare part of me, exposed and raw, bring me back to our time together at Oxford.

"I'm not the one, Liam…I'm no one's anything."

"Bollocks," he replies, grabbing my face in his hands.

"This is so wrong, Liam. You can't do this. I'm not worth it."

"The fact that you can't see that you are just shows what a fucking liar you are."

The moments after he told me I was the one. The moments after he told me he loved me. The moments where I allowed myself to believe in my worth, for just those precious moments…they can last forever now. There's nothing holding me back anymore.

I am loved. I am loveable. I am the one. "I want you to tell me you love me, Liam." He pauses his assault on my nipple and looks at me in confusion. I grab his cheeks and continue, "While we make love, just say it to me, please. I know you feel it. I don't want you to be afraid. I'm not going anywhere. You said it when we slept together at Oxford, but I blocked it out. I want to feel it this time. I want to hear your words as you make love to me."

He licks his lips and nods seriously. After grabbing a condom, he places himself between my legs and looks straight into my wide and teary eyes. Fear courses through me at the serious expression on his face.

"Reyna Miracle," he whispers and drops a soft kiss on my quivering lips. "I love you. You are loved. You are so fucking loved. I'm going to spend every day reminding you," he groans as he sinks into me and the overwhelming fullness of our bodies connecting and my heart filling with his words brings a shaky sob up my chest. "Your heart is mine to cherish."

CHAPTER 39

"Good morning," Liam says as he catches me watching him sleeping in my bed.

"Hi," I smile knowingly. I'm lying naked on my side, facing him, my head propped on my hand. "Although it's not morning anymore."

His eyebrows rise. "Well, we had a busy night."

"More like morning," I giggle and he smirks proudly.

"You feeling alright?" he asks, rolling onto his side to face me. He props his head, mirroring my position. "You're not getting squirrelly on me are you?"

I shake my head confidently. "Not in the slightest. I'm quite comfy actually." I reach out and push a wayward strand of blond hair off his forehead. It feels intimate and real. I fucking love it.

"Good." He snakes his hand beneath the covers and wraps it around my bare waist, pulling me flush against his body. Lying on his back, he drops a soft kiss in my hair and exhales deeply.

"Nervous?" I ask, feeling a small wave of melancholy cast over us.

"A bit," he murmurs into my hair.

I pull back and look up at him. "I understand. But I plan to make every day easier for you."

He nods. "I can take it. I'm big and strong." He shoots me a cocky smirk and winks playfully.

"You're definitely big," I reply, reaching beneath the covers and gripping his morning wood.

He groans, dropping his head back against the pillow. "I'll have you know, this is probably going to be a constant problem for us. We have a lot of lost time to make up for. That will probably mean some serious overtime."

I giggle at his cheekiness. "I'm all for putting in the time." I drop a soft kiss to his chest and then shuffle off of him to sit criss-cross. I pull the sheet up to cover my naked chest and chew my lip worriedly before continuing, "But I really want to talk first. I just…I don't want this to turn into just sex."

"Neither do I." He frowns, his eyes wide and accusing. "That's not what I meant at all, Rey."

"I know, I get it." I clutch his cheeks in my hand and drop a reassuring kiss to his lips. I look nervously into his eyes and add, "I want to share some things I've been doing the last couple weeks. I started seeing a therapist."

He rolls over onto his side and gives me his full attention. "How's that been?"

I nod encouragingly. "Good. He's young and cool and has really opened my eyes up to a lot of things that I knew nothing about."

"Like what?"

"Well, back in your houseboat I told you about how I've always felt a connection to my sisters, even though they died when we were just babies. He sort of gave me some scientific information that helped me not feel so crazy about all of that."

"It's not crazy to feel connected to them, Rey. They were, and still are, a part of you."

I smile at his knowing words. "I know that. I just never understood that type of connection. I didn't feel deserving of it because of all the self-hate I had going on. As lame as it sounds, a lot of that had to do with my experience as a child and how my mother treated me for being the only survivor. Constantly calling me Miracle and treating me like I could do no wrong. It messed me up. And it's something I know I'll have to work through with her at some point, when I'm ready."

"You'll work through it, I'm sure." He half smiles at me. "I'm glad you're telling me all of this. At Uni, there was always an agony I could see in you. It was painful to watch. I wanted to be there for you, but you never let me in. Now, everything feels different. What you said to me a few nights ago at the club and the past few days…seeing you fight for me…for us." He exhales and smiles. "This all feels special, Rey. For the first time, I am seeing that anguish in you vanish. It's been replaced by hope. You've always been beautiful to me. I've always been drawn to you. But seeing you completely let go with me…it's incredible."

He drops a soft kiss to my mouth and I immediately pull my lip in as he retreats. The words about my agony at Oxford are true. I was standoffish because of all of the issues with my mother. But she wasn't the only cause of it all.

"Liam, part of that agony you saw in me started when you came into the picture and started seeing Marisa." I look at him cautiously, knowing I'm broaching a painful subject for us. But it's important to me to be able to talk through it. I need to feel that nothing is off limits for Liam and me.

With Hayden, we had so many skeletons in the closet and we never spoke of them. I never told him about being a quad or about sleeping with Liam back at Oxford. We never spoke about Marisa, aside from the middle of the night when he'd comfort me after a nightmare. We were best friends and knew so little about each other. I can't go down that road again with Liam. I need to be truly vulnerable and honest.

Liam looks down briefly, clearly pained by the memory. "Marisa and I…we loved each other. We did. I loved her, she was impossible not to love. And for a while, I did want to marry her. But when I went to get the ring and the only person I had on my mind was you, I knew there was something so wrong with that."

"She deserved better love than that," I whisper, picking at the hem of the sheet wrapped around me.

"She did. I may not have gone about things with you the right way, but I just panicked, Rey. The three of us were graduating soon and planning to start a business together. We were going to purchase property in London! I had to know if you were anywhere near where my heart was before I dove into all of that with you."

I nod woodenly. "My heart was with you, but I didn't know it yet. I didn't know how to process or accept it. I've struggled accepting love my whole life because I haven't had a good example of believable love. But I believe it with you, Liam. More than anyone, I believe it with you."

"I see that." He sits up and cups my face, joining our lips together in our most honest kiss yet. Pulling back, he looks at me intensely with his wide, brown eyes that have always seen what I have failed to see. "Everything about what we're doing here feels different this time, Rey. And that excites the fuck out of me. I love you. More now than I even did back then."

I close my eyes and let the beauty of his words wash away all of my painful sins. Smirking, I open them and shift myself up to straddle him. "Let's get busy with that overtime. Your words are wreaking havoc on my libido."

His lazy gaze drifts down my naked body and I feel more exposed and vulnerable than I ever have in my life.

And it excites the fuck out of me, too.

CHAPTER 40

"I'm just not sure this is a good idea, Liam," I say nervously, while rubbing lotion on my arms in my bathroom.

"I told you, babe, Theo is happy for us." Liam comes striding in and slinks his hands around my waist from behind. He gazes at my reflection in the mirror with a smirk. "I mean, bloody hell…how you managed to dazzle him still baffles me. He's intense. So if he's supportive, what's there to be nervous about?"

"I know, Liam, but I told you…Hayden just got out of rehab. I feel kind of funny parading our relationship so soon."

I've still heard no word from Hayden. I meant what I said when I told Theo I'd leave Hayden alone if that was what was best for him. Daphney informs me that he's doing a lot better and the difference in him is positive. But I'd be lying if I said I didn't miss him and long to see it with my own eyes.

"Well, not that it matters, but Theo won't even be there. He ran off to China to chase down Leslie. Who bloody knows when they'll be back?"

My brows lift curiously. Theo chasing Leslie to China sounds a bit dramatic. I almost feel bad about the secret joy of hearing others having similar dramatic bullshit going on in their lives. Not that I want them to break up or anything. It just makes me feel less hopeless when I see that other couples have their own ups and downs, too.

"I'm just still getting used to all of this. Your connection to them is hard." I rest my head back on his shoulder and smile sadly. Liam and I have been through so much. I'm nervous about putting more pressure on us.

Liam sighs heavily, "I know, babe. We'll work it out. But, tonight should be easy. It's just family flick night at Frank's. A movie, some popcorn, that's it."

"Remind me again who all is going to be there."

"Finley and her husband, Brody—"

"Finley, who you've fucked," I blurt out.

"I never fucked her, Rey!" he growls and nips at my ear. I flinch away, smirking. "You have positively nothing to worry about there. Their roommates, Mitch and Julie, and then Frank, of course."

"Frank all by himself?" I inquire, sticking my lip out sadly.

"Frank's love life isn't something I'm really in the know about. He's not very forthcoming there."

"I know, I wonder why that is."

Liam shrugs. "Frank's not my concern. You are. And I need you to know that if Theo and Leslie were going to be there, you know that would be okay. Theo all but gave you his bloody stamp of approval. And I know you and Leslie would get on."

I smile at his hopeful expression and turn in his arms to face him. Linking my hands behind his neck, I kiss him passionately, plunging my tongue deep into his eager mouth until both of us start seeing stars.

Liam growls into my mouth, "If you're trying to distract me from taking you to Frank's, it's not going to work. I know we've been working overtime to make up for lost time, but I'm ready to go out in public with you. Show you off. I want to make this shit official."

The past couple weeks with Liam have been incredible. I didn't know a healthy relationship could feel this good. Making love to him and not feeling a self-hatred blanket over me when we finish is doing loads for my self-esteem. Even Miguel agrees that Liam is definitely having a positive influence on me and my ability to open up. I'm making strides I didn't even know I could make. And it's all because of this glorious man.

"We're already official. I'm yours, Liam. Always."

He kisses my nose sweetly, "Don't you forget it."

***

A short while later we're standing in front of the Brixton Mansion. The green ivy wrapping around the purple door is just beginning to show signs of summer coming to an end. Liam's firm grip on my hand is welcomed as he knocks on the door.

Suddenly, the door flies open and my eyes land on Frank, dressed head to toe in a red onesie pajama set. With footies and all.

"Oxfords!" Frank shrieks loudly and throws his arms out wide, welcoming us inside. He nudges me playfully. "I can call you both Oxford now that I know you both attended! I had no idea until a few days ago!"

Liam's chest rumbles with laughter. "Frank! As always, you look—"

"Ridiculous," I finish truthfully, eyeing Frank's gelled hair that's sticking straight up. Because apparently the childlike pajamas weren't enough, he had to do something extra special to his wild, red hair.

Frank's eyes turn to slits as he pins me with an intimidating glower. Well, he's attempting to be intimidating, I think. "And the all black look on you, Oxford. Did you select that because it matches your soul?"

I smirk and take a step closer to Frank, matching his glower with one of my own. "My soul is rainbow fucking bright and I still wouldn't be caught dead in what you're wearing."

Completely unoffended by my comment—as I knew he would be—Frank's glower morphs to excitement as he says, "Wait til you see the back and you'll really have a laugh." Frank turns and reveals the scripty text.

"OCD." And beneath it in small letters it reads, "Obsessive Cumming Disorder," I say it out loud and Liam's arm wraps around my waist for support as we both crack up laughing. Frank turns to look at us, a triumphant grin on his face.

"Leslie has a cheetah print one in her room if you want to borrow it!" Finley's voice chimes in as she comes striding out from the living room hallway. She's dressed in a teal onesie just like Frank's.

"Um, I think we're good," I say looking back to Liam whose eyes are twinkling with amusement.

"Yeah, best to ease into it," he whispers playfully in my ear and drops a soft kiss on my cheek.

"If I have to wear one, so should they," Brody groans, following in Finley's footsteps. His tall, broad frame is clad in a matching black onesie of his own. I'm surprised they make them big enough for him.

"Oh my God, I feel like we've entered an alternate universe!" I exclaim, laughing heartily and glancing back at Liam who doesn't seem all that surprised.

"Come on, let's go find a flick," Frank says, pulling me by the arm into the living room. "And don't worry, Oxford…Mitch and Julie don't have onesies either, so you won't look like total prats."

CHAPTER 41

Two weeks later, I'm at Club Taint, sitting at Lariza's desk, proofing a series of print ads we have going out in the mail when I get a call on my cell. It's from an unknown number, so I screen it and continue working. A second later it dings with a voicemail notification. I pull up the message and press my phone to my ear.

"Hiya, Rey, it's Hayden. I'm uh…out…which I'm sure you already know. Listen, I'm sorry for not getting in touch with you sooner. I'd love to see you today if you have time. It's important. I'm in London for the day, so give me a call or text me. Cheers."

The message ends and my heart lurches at the familiar gravelly tone to his voice. Dread and nerves wash over me at what he might want to talk about. I know from Daphney that he's moved back in with his parents in Essex for the time being and he's working at his dad's furniture distribution center. From what I know, he's doing well. How will this meeting affect his healing? How could it affect my own? I've been doing so well in my relationship with Liam and my sessions with Miguel. Am I strong enough for this?

I wish Frank was here, but he hasn't been around much since Lariza got back. And Lariza is up front training a new hire at the moment. Without thinking, I pick my phone up and dial Liam. I manage to squeak out what Hayden's message said and before I can finish, he says he's on his way to Club Taint to see me.

When he appears in the doorway, relief washes over me. "Hey, are you alright?" he asks, striding over to me and pulling a chair up beside where I've been frozen and staring at the same graphic for the past twenty minutes. He's dressed in smart gray slacks and a button down and looks like home to me. I've gotten so used to those dress slacks rumpled on the floor of my flat for the past month.

"Yeah, I'm fine, Liam. Why wouldn't I be?" I roll my eyes like he's being dramatic, but in reality I know he's seeing right through me.

He spins my chair so that I'm facing him, his legs on the outside of mine. His brown eyes are wide and piercing. "Rey, if you don't want to see him, you don't have to."

I frown. "How can I not, Liam? We were best friends and he tried to kill himself the night we had a fight. I think I owe him a chat."

He puckers his lips out in defiance. "I don't like it. I don't like seeing you get worked up. I can tell this is rattling you."

"I'm not that fragile, Liam. I can handle it." I reach out to muss his hair in playful reassurance.

His jaw muscle ticks nervously as he exhales and says, "I can't lose you again, Rey."

My mouth drops into an O. I grab his face in my hands and look him in the eyes, "Liam! I'm not going anywhere. I'm just trying to help a friend."

He twitches his jaw from side to side as he stares down at my lips. "He's a hot button for me, Rey. I can't help it. He was there for you when I wanted to be and I bloody hate him for it."

"Liam," I groan. "I love you. I've loved you for so long. Nothing is changing that."

He nods nervously and I pull him into a tight hug. I think Liam came here for himself just as much as he came here for me. But in reality, I know he has nothing to worry about. This will be fine. I will be fine.

***

I text Hayden back that I can meet today and we arrange to find each other at Battersea Park on a bench overlooking the River Thames. It's a quiet park with fewer tourists and less of the London hustle and bustle.

After a few minutes, I finally see Hayden walking in my direction. I instantly jump to my feet, nervously jamming my hands into the back of my jeans, nervously. My eyes take in every part of his appearance as he approaches without seeing me yet. He's dressed in a pair of comfortable jeans and a black T-shirt. His dirty blond hair is shaggier and in definite need of a cut. His chin is covered in a trim, dark beard. When his eyes finally find me, I can't stop myself. I rush over and hug him, burying my face in his chest. The familiar scent of cigarettes washes over me and I relish in seeing him again. I can't believe it's been six weeks.

I feel a slight hesitation before his arms tighten around my waist and then he hugs me back. He pulls away and his hard gray eyes are wide and blinking quickly as he nervously looks me up and down. "It's good to see you, Rey. You look good."

I laugh haphazardly. I'm still in my black skinnies and Taint tank, but it's nice of him to say so. "So do you," I lie. He doesn't look good, but he looks alive and that's good enough for me right now.

"You want to sit?" he asks, gesturing back toward the bench where I had been waiting for him. I nod silently and follow him over. He turns to face me, resting one leg up on the open space between us. I can tell this is hard for him.

"How have you been? Daphney says you're working for your dad? That's great, Hayden."

He smiles sadly and then replies, "It's not great, but it's what's best for me right now. You're still at the club, I see?" He gestures to my shirt.

I nod, "Yeah, I'm doing more marketing now than bartending, but it's also what's best for me."

He licks his lips and exhales heavily, "Rey, I don't want to small talk anymore. I have a lot to say and I think it's best if I just get it out before I lose my nerve."

"Alright."

"First, I need you to know that I'm so sorry for going AWOL on you and not including you in on my recovery. I just couldn't have you there. I couldn't have you seeing me that way."

My chin trembles at the pain in his eyes. "I understand."

"I also need you to know that what I did…it wasn't premeditated. It wasn't your fault. That night I came to your flat and we got into that fight about Marisa and everything else. I just…I wasn't coping. I was avoiding. I was running. It wasn't right. I could feel myself doing it—being completely self-destructive—but I couldn't stop it. It was like this sickness that I was powerless against."

My eyes threaten to shed tears, but I force myself to hold it back and listen. Hearing him say Marisa's name without flinching is a massive feat in and of itself. And so much of what he is saying are things I've worked through on my own with Miguel.

"I just got overwhelmed," he continues, looking away. "After Marisa's death, the darkness that I was living in became home for me. It became the new normal for me and my family. Maybe even you," he clears his throat and looks back at me. "Then you started showing signs of wanting things to change between us. You said you weren't pulling away, but you were. Not that I blame you. It was necessary. What we were doing with each other wasn't healthy."

I swallow hard as the bleak memories of our time together fall over me. "I'm so sorry, Hayden."

He shakes me off dismissively and continues, looking out at the river instead of at me, "Then Theo met Leslie and started showing signs of change, too. It seemed like everyone was getting better except me. I started to feel like I was living every day feeling like I was getting left behind." He exhales a shaky breath. "So I thought, if I'm getting left behind, then no one will care if I'm gone."

"God, Hayden. That's so not true." I reach out to touch his arm and he rests his hand on top of my hand and squeezes it while turning his watery gray eyes on me.

"I know that now, Rey. It was stupid because I was blaming everyone else for my problems. I learned a lot in that facility and with the family therapy sessions. I was in denial about my suicide attempts before. I pretended I just overindulged, but I knew what I was doing." He clears his throat loudly.

"I'm glad you got help. I've been getting help, too. I've been seeing a therapist and I'm learning a lot about myself."

He nods nervously. "That's good. I want that for you, Rey. I want you happy and healthy, too. But, I also just want to explain why I've been avoiding you. After everything we've suffered through together, you deserve to know the truth."

My brows rise in wonder as Hayden pins me with a serious expression that scares me. "The truth is, Rey, I was falling in love with you. That entire year we were together wasn't just sex to me. I was so in love with you. Every time we were intimate, I would imagine saying the words to you, but I could never get the courage to do it. I was too much of a bloody mess."

My jaw drops. Of everything I thought we'd discuss today, this was not on my list. I suspected his feelings for me had changed towards the very end. Especially when he showed signs of jealousy when Liam showed up. A sick part of me hoped it was because of Liam's connection to Marisa. Not love! Tears well in my eyes at the pained look in his expression. The last thing I want to do is hurt Hayden even more than I already have.

"Why didn't you ever say anything?" I croak tearfully.

"You never dropped your guard with me, Rey. You never gave me any glimmer that you felt for me what I felt for you. And I was just so fucked up. So I kept it bottled up along with all my other shite. But you're the one that I love, Rey. I still love you." He stops talking and hunches over, resting his arms on his legs and refusing to look at me.

My voice is shaky when I speak, "Hayden." I want to reach out and hold him, but I know I shouldn't.

After a moment, he adds, "That's why I couldn't see you at the hospital after I did what I did. I couldn't let you see me like that." He shakes his head sadly. "But then…you moved on."

I purse my lips and tilt my head, stifling a sob over his sad expression. "Hay, I never knew. I mean…we've been calling each other best friends for a while but…we know nothing about each other. Not truly. Do you see that?" He looks at me from the corner of his eye and nods subtly. "The only real thing we knew about each other was our pain."

He turns to face me again, grabbing my hands with his. He brings them to his mouth and drops a soft kiss on the tops of both of them. "I know, Rey. I also know that if we did have a relationship it would only be a constant reminder of our pain." He releases my hands and faces forward again. "But I have to know. This will eat me alive for as long as I live. If I would have seen you that day at the hospital…or asked you to come see me in rehab…and told you the truth. Do you think we could have had a chance?" His expression is cautious as he turns to look at me again.

I bite my lip and release it slowly before replying, "I'm not sure what to even say to that, Hayden."

His hopeful eyes darken and he plasters on a fake smile. Nodding stoically, he says, "Don't say anything then. What you've said is plenty. I know you've moved on. I just couldn't live without at least asking." He swallows nervously. "And we're okay, Rey. I'm not angry or upset. But, you know it won't ever be the same between us, right? I don't think I can watch you with him."

Two errant tears escape and slide silently down my cheeks. I nod and croak, "Why does this feels like goodbye, Hayden?"

His chin trembles slightly as he watches a tear drift down my cheek. "Not goodbye, Rey Rey. Just 'See ya later,'" he shrugs.

Sniffing, I whisper, "I'm going to miss you."

His voice is hoarse as he replies, "I'd be crazy not to miss you."

CHAPTER 42

For the purpose of being completely honest and transparent with Liam, I tell him about my entire conversation with Hayden. Even down to Hayden's true feelings for me. He was decidedly upset at first, but then said he already knew. In the end, opening up to him about it only reassured him more how utterly and completely in love with him I am.

It crushes me to know that my friendship with Hayden is over. But, I get it. We were such darkness together that remaining close would only drag us down.

My only hope is that he can continue to heal and find someone who can help him the way Liam has helped me these past few months we've been together now. Liam's helpfulness has lovingly pushed me so far that I now find myself sitting cozily next to my mother on a cream colored loveseat, shooting daggers at a dimple-sporting Spaniard who calls himself Miguel. He smiles kindly at me in a way that says he knows I don't want to do this, but that I know that I have to.

"So, Dr. Miller, Reyna and I have done a lot of discussing about her childhood these past few months. The biggest hurdle that I would love to help you two overcome is in finding a delicate balance in your communication. I understand your desire and your extensive knowledge in seeing Reyna for the miracle that she is. She is extremely special. But, the way in which you idealize her does not work for Reyna. Instead, she responds better—more positively—to a more transparent trueness."

"Okay," my mother says, smiling brightly at the doctor like he just told her to keep doing exactly what she's always done.

He smiles knowingly. "Reyna, at this time, I would like you to address your mother with some of the concerns that I told you to write down and we can go from there. Okay?"

"Okay," I reply turning to my mom to look into her clear blue eyes. Clearing my throat, I dig out the piece of paper and begin reading, "Mom, I feel bad for a lot of the things I did as a child. Both to you and to myself. I never treated you, or myself, with the love and respect I should have. Part of the reasons I rebelled had to do with all the love that you poured into me growing up. It just felt smothering. Even now, as an adult, the amount of positivity and love you give me, despite my shortcomings, are hard on me. The countless number of times you call me Miracle only increases my feelings of inadequacy that I battle within myself every day. Somehow, throughout my life, I got the impression that I shouldn't have been the one that survived. It felt like your love should have been pointed to someone else."

"What do you mean? Like who?" Her eyes are bright and smiling.

"Like one of my sisters," I reply in challenge and relish in her subtle blanch. Setting my paper down, I continue, "This is therapy, Mom. You can't hide from that subject. I need to talk about them."

"Your sisters?"

"Yes, I've told you I feel a connection to them and you continue to shut down that line of dialogue every time. I want to talk about them, Mother. I want them to be a part of me. For a long time, I thought that I just as easily could have died that day with my sisters in the NICU and nothing in the world would be different. I've done nothing miraculous in my lifetime." Tears sting the back of my eyes at my vulnerable admission.

"Sweetie, you have a masters from Oxford, for goodness sake. You're very ambitious. But, even if you weren't, your existence alone is scientifically miraculous!"

"It's not, Mom. Fuck! Don't you see? I'm not living in your reality! I'm living in my own. In my reality, I feel alone and lost and incomplete a lot of the time. Since I started seeing Miguel and dating Liam, I've gotten a lot better. But, I'm far from healed. When you constantly call me a miracle, it only adds fuel to the fire that is my self-doubt. I'm a realist, Mom. Your words aren't real!"

"This is ridiculous," my mom balks. "I operate on babies like you were everyday. I know how special you are." Her smile falters slightly.

"Is that why you thought it was nifty that I got a tattoo at fifteen fucking years old? Is that why you never let me go anywhere by myself? Is that why I couldn't attend a school dance without you hovering as a damn chaperone? And, why you lived near me for as long as you possibly could? Because, I was special?"

"Yes!" She smiles, "Exactly!"

"Why, Mom? Why am I special? Why am I worthy of being hovered over?" I exclaim, my voice rising with emotion.

"Reyna Miracle, *you* give birth to four babies and watch them die one by one and then tell me how *you* react, alright?" Her smile looks pained and wrong. Ill, even. "I'm a doctor! I knew the odds of you living or dying. Your existence blows science right out of the water. When you witness something like that you can't help but become entrenched in your own emotions. Your understanding of reality shifts and forever changes you."

"Don't you see though, Mom?" I cry, resisting the urge to reach over and shake her. "That is what's making it impossible for us to find our way back to each other!"

She shrugs her shoulders and looks at Miguel for help. "I don't know what to say! I want to find a path to you, one way or another, but you have to clear one for me. I need you to let me in."

"Well, I need you to be real with me, Mom. Dad's dead. You're all I got. I need you to stop thinking everything I do is perfect! I'm horrible! I'm a shitty person and I've been the shittiest to you most of my life!"

"I know!" she cries.

"Well, how the hell does that make you feel?" I ask sharply, taking the good doctor, Miguel's, words out of his mouth.

"Angry! Confused! Sad, I guess!" she huffs loudly. "When you were a baby I got to hold you and hug you and love you. Then, as soon as you were big enough you squirmed out of my arms, and I've spent the rest of my life running to get you back!"

"Just tell me something real, Mom. Anything. I need to hear something imperfect from you to know that we even have a shot at finding peace."

"I hate your tattoos. All of them," she blurts. "Even the black roses. I think they are dark and twisty and look like something Marilyn Manson would have." She covers her mouth in shock at her emotional outburst.

My jaw drops and before I know it, we're both laughing and staring incredulously at each other. She pauses to wipe laughter tears from her eyes and I reach over and grab a tissue, handing it to her.

I've never seen my mother laugh like this before. "That was definitely something *real*," I laugh and look over to Miguel for approval.

He nods knowingly, "It's a good start ladies. A good start."

SIX MONTHS LATER

CHAPTER 43

"You know we can sleep at your flat more often if you like," I say, nudging my butt into Liam's crotch as I pull my white duvet up over my ear in an attempt to get comfy enough to fall asleep.

"I know, but I like your place." He drapes his arm lazily over my side. I relish in our standard sleeping position that we've perfected over the last six months. "And you work late still. I like waiting here in raptures for you to get home."

I giggle softly. "For a dirty boy, you sure can be sappy sometimes," I say, my voice dripping with mirth.

"I'll show you dirty," Liam growls against my rose-covered shoulder and yanks me back into his chest. His arms wrap around me and pinch both of my bare nipples.

"Ow!" I cry out excitedly. A fight or flight response igniting libido. Definitely fight. This dirty boy of mine refuses to let me sleep in a stitch of clothing. Even after being together for almost a year now I'm still not used to him helping himself to my nipples whenever the mood strikes him. But damn does it feel good when he kneads them like he is now.

"Mmm, mine," he whispers, his hands working magic on my breasts. "Are you wet, baby? Do you want me?"

I pump my hips in response to the tantalizing teasing of his hands and his dirty British accent words. What is it about dirty talk with that accent of his? If I was wearing panties right now, they'd be melting off of me. He takes my body rocking against his as an invitation. His large, warm hands graze down my belly, slowly pressing firmer against me as he reaches me—

"Oh fuck!" I moan loudly as he pinches me right on the clit.

"Name's Liam, but I'll answer to Fuck just this once," he murmurs huskily into my ear. His teeth sink into my lobe and his warm breath sends goose bumps all across my body. He shifts me onto my back and positions himself above me. His sexy, pouty mouth moves down and presses sexy fucking kisses right onto each one of my hardened nipples. I rake my hands through his messy blond hair and press my breasts together to cradle his face in my chest. He nuzzles and nips my skin in a delirious way.

I need to kiss him like I need to breathe right now. I attempt to pull him up to my mouth.

"I have other plans for my mouth, baby. I can smell your wet pussy from here and I'm going fucking wild wanting to taste you."

If hot as hell dirty talk was an orgasm, he'd be named Liam Bloody Darby.

I release an unabashed groan at his arousing words as he continues a path of kisses down my belly. He pauses to swirl his tongue briefly into my navel before situating his face perfectly between my legs.

"God, I love every inch of you," he says and then his lips find my aching clit.

I writhe beneath his touch, relishing in the fact that in this moment, I love every inch of me, too. And any moment I have a shred of doubt, Liam makes damn sure he fixes it.

***

"Three babies?" I exclaim to my mother as she holds the ultrasound probe against my belly.

"Three girls, Reyna!" Her watery eyes smile in genuine happiness. "Multiples run in our family, I've told you this!"

My eyes are wide as I take in the ghostly white room with a simple exam table and ultrasound machine. It's as if we're floating in air. I look down at my belly in shock at the large, round shape. "But Mom, three? What happens if they come early? What happens if I lose them all?" My chin quivers and tears form and fall in seconds. I'm attached to them. Just like that: Instantaneous.

"I'm here for you, sweetie. If they come early, we'll deal with it. But, you're already further along than I was when you and your sisters were born!" She strokes my cheek lovingly.

"I'm here for you, too." I look up to find Marisa standing next to me, holding my hand.

I wipe the tears out of my eyes. "Marisa! I haven't seen you in months!"

"You haven't needed me, ma lady. That makes me really happy." Her smile is beaming as she stands before me in all white, her blonde hair blowing in the nonexistent wind.

"It does?" I ask nervously.

"Yes! It means you're rocking the whole life thing," she winks and smiles at me.

"Marisa, I'm having triplets." My face grows serious as I try to relay how utterly terrifying this moment is.

She shakes her head incredulously. "I know, eerie right? Three black roses. Three new babies. It was like it was meant to be."

"What do you mean?"

"It's like your sisters spirits being reborn or something! Is that reincarnation, you think?" Her eyes grow wide and amazed.

The orby sensation of my sisters fills the room in that moment and just like that, I know they are here with me. I can feel them all around me. I snap my gaze to my mother, all humor and happiness sucked from the room and replaced with a grave seriousness. "I want them all, Mom. I don't want to lose one. Not one. I can't feel them all my life and then lose them at the end." Tears pour down my cheeks as a terrified sob breaks free from my mouth.

She nods, her face drooping in sad sympathy. "I know, baby. I know all too well. We're going to do everything we can to get them all here safely."

"When are you going to tell, Liam?" Marisa asks. I attempt to reply, but suddenly feel myself being pulled away. "Rey. Rey!"

"Rey!" Liam's voice cries loudly from beside me.

My eyes fly open and I'm back in my bed, in my flat. I look around quickly and see it's dark outside. The blue security light is creeping in through the blinds. I quickly reach down to touch my stomach to find that it is flat and smooth.

"Just a dream," I sigh, turning to face a worried-looking Liam.

"Rey, you were crying in your sleep." Liam's hand reaches out and strokes my damp cheeks. "It was crushing, babe. Is everything okay?"

"I think so," I croak, still feeling overwhelmed by the realness of that dream.

"What was the dream?"

"I was pregnant," I reply, gauging his reaction carefully.

"Oh," Liam's eyes turn wide and nervous, then sad. "But, you were crying."

"I was pregnant with triplets, Liam."

"Fuck," he exhales heavily. "So you were crying because you didn't want them." He says it like it's a statement he already knows the answer to.

"No, I was crying because I did!" I reach out and touch his face lovingly. "They were ours. I wanted them all. They felt like this crazy beautiful do-over, Liam. Is that nuts?"

"Doesn't sound nuts to me," he replies, his expression pensive and deep in thought.

An immense sense of peace and hope cascades over me as I wrap my brain around how I feel about being a mother. "Liam, in my dream…those babies made me feel important. The same way you do. I loved them. Just like I love you. I didn't know anyone else could give that to me."

"I'd love to give you all of that, Rey." His glossy eyes find mine in the darkness, probing at me for something specific.

"I want all of it, Liam," I reply honestly.

His lips pucker out in that way that I know he's trying to figure out how to word his next statement. Instead, he gets up and walks, bare ass naked and sexy as fuck, to the new dresser I bought a few months ago. With Liam sleeping over so much, I finally found the urge to buy some furniture for my flat. I didn't go crazy. Just a bedframe, headboard, dresser, and small loveseat, but it all made my flat feel more like a home. Having Liam's stuff inside the new dresser was something special I didn't even realize I'd care about.

After a moment of rummaging, he pulls out what he's looking for and stashes it behind his back. Standing before me again, he looks nervous, and I suddenly realize it has nothing to do with the fact that he's as naked as the day is long.

He drops to his knees beside the mattress and I gasp as he pulls out a square jewelry box. "Liam!" I cry, sitting up, pulling the sheet up over my chest with me. He cracks the case open to reveal four thin bands of platinum silver, anchored together with four princess-cut diamonds, one placed on each band, all twined together.

"Four diamonds," I whisper knowingly. "When did you get this?"

"That's the eerie part, Rey. I've had this ring ever since I dreamt about it in Oxford."

"But, that was before you knew I was a quad." My jaw drops in shock. "How can that be?"

"I can't explain it, but I dreamt it and then I saw it at a jewelry store. I bought it on the spot back then because there was a fear inside of me that if I didn't buy it that day, I'd never see this ring again. And it's so you. It's beautiful and unique, edgy and feminine. Everything I've always seen in you. But, you're so much more than all of that, Rey. The marks on your skin and on your heart are my favorite parts of you. They've allowed you to love me so fiercely that I still can't believe most days that I get to call you mine."

"Liam," I press my hands over his mouth, unable to take another beautiful word from him. Tears slide down my cheeks as I replace my hand with my lips and kiss him passionately.

He returns my kiss, but pulls away much too soon. I see wonder in his eyes as he says, "Reyna Miracle Miller, we had a rocky start, an even rockier middle, but I want to have an incredible finish. Will you please marry me so I can live my life knowing that our marks are ours…to have and to hold, forever?"

I smile and laugh at the moment spread out before me. With my dream and his words, a renewed sense of spirit and place in this world washes over me, pushing me straight into the answer I so desperately want to scream.

"Yes," I reply and giggle as he collides into me, shoving me backwards onto the bed and molding his lips with mine.

His tongue massages against my own and he pulls back suddenly, leaving my wanton lips puckered and upset by the recent vacancy.

"God, Rey, you've just made me so bloody happy. This tender moment calls for slow, passionate love, but I hope you'll settle for the shag of your life because babe, I'm going to fuck you so hard right now, even your pussy is going to be screaming my name."

"Well, when you put it like that," I giggle and he pinches my nipples so hard, I yelp. He swallows my cries with his mouth and that naughty, skillful, sexy tongue of his.

This man, this gorgeous, kind person, who knows exactly when to be bad—gave me all of this.

When you start your life small, like I did, being big seems like an impossible obstacle. But, with Liam Darby, I grew into something so much more.

THREE MONTHS LATER

CHAPTER 44

"You two look bloody perfect back there behind the bar. Not nervous a bit."

"Thanks, Al," I say, smiling broadly and glancing over to Liam who's lining up champagne flutes on the bar top. I pop the cork and begin filling the glasses with the fuzzy, golden liquid.

"There's nothing to be nervous about, Alistair," Liam says confidently. "This is an easy night. It's just our friends coming. No customers, yet!"

I nod nervously in agreement. Tonight is our soft opening of White Swan Pub. It's only been three months since Liam and I got engaged and so much has already changed. I still can't believe this pub is really mine.

When Liam and I announced our engagement, my mom then proclaimed she too was getting married.

To Alistair.

I was a bit shocked at how quickly their wedding all came about. No sooner did she announce it, I was walking her down the aisle only a month later. Apparently they had been seeing each other quietly for years. I always sensed something between the two of them. Alistair was so protective of me right from the start and I'm certain that went a long way with my mother. And the way Al's eyes twinkle when he looks at her…it's kind of disgustingly swoon-worthy.

On their wedding day, Alistair handed me a wooden box with a swan burned into the lid. Inside it was the deed to the pub. Apparently he had always imagined handing his business down to his child. He said that he saw me as his daughter the first day he covered me with his jacket inside his pub.

I may have cried like…a million tears.

"Reyna, are you sure you want to cover the bar top like that? What if people want to sit there?" My mom asks, frowning at the display of champagne Liam and I are working on.

"Mom, there are tons of tables and booths they can sit at instead," I argue.

"How many people are coming?" she asks, squinting to count all the tables.

"Thirty-ish."

"I know, but—"

"Mom!" I snap. "Liam and I got this."

Her frown morphs into a knowing smile and she purses her lips.

"Come on, love, I need some help in the back," Alistair says, tucking my mother into his arm and leading her away.

I shake my head in frustration. My mother has definitely moved passed her annoying concrete smiling stage. Maybe too much! Now we have little arguments almost daily. She's taken her tendency to hover and control into a new nit-picking level. Alistair has become a full time referee. But, the fact that she's questioning me—instead of blindly praising me—is kind of amazing. Ever since she told me about Alistair, I've even noticed that her smiles are different. Believable. She's a genuine kind of happy now.

"The party may commence!" Frank's voice announces from the entrance. He pauses mid-step and dramatically smoothes his glossy red hair to the side, even though it looks like it's made of plastic from the copious amounts of product in it. He's dressed in a sharp navy suit and power tie, and you can tell he's proud of his ensemble.

A gentle shove comes from behind him and my eyes land on Leslie and Theo. Theo is in his standard perfectly-tailored trousers, plaid button down, and thick, dark-framed glasses. Leslie looks stunning. Her long, auburn-red hair is pulled back into a low ponytail and she's wearing a fabulous flowy, empire waist tea-length dress.

"You're not the Queen of fucking England, Frank. What are you waiting for? Trumpets?" she crows obnoxiously. I can't help but laugh at the hilarity of how beautiful Leslie always looks, but how obnoxious her mouth is. Liam and I hang out with Theo and Leslie a lot now since the wedding. Ever since my talk with Theo at his shop, he's welcomed me in with open arms, which is incredibly kind considering the fierce loyalty he has for his brother. Theo's loyalty to Liam runs just as deep it would seem.

"The Queen and I are kindred spirits, Lezbo." Frank's eyes finally land on me. "Oxford! You sex monster. You look like you've been rode hard and put away wet!"

My eyes flash knowingly at Liam. "Liam!" I cry accusingly and run to a nearby beer sign with a mirror in it. Holy shit, Frank's right! My eyes are dilated, cheeks flushed, lips swollen, and hair mussed. Liam said I looked fine. I look properly shagged, so I guess that would be his definition of 'fine.'

Mr. Bad Boy, Liam Darby did a surprise sneak attack on me in the wine room below the pub. God, it was hot as fuck. There was staff upstairs getting ready for the party and he bent me over a stack of kegs, took hold of the crotch of my panties and ripped them off with one powerful tug. Then he pounded into me like we were the last two people on earth and the fate of the human race hinged on this epic fuck. He even pulled my hair at the nape just as I—

"Oxford, you slapper! I can practically hear your naughty thoughts screaming at me!" My eyes swerve to Frank and he's got his fingers in his ears like a child.

I pull self consciously down on my black mini dress. I wasn't half as nervous in it an hour ago when I still had panties to account for. Going commando messes with a girl's confidence, especially when you have an obnoxious ginger tuning into your inner most thoughts!

Just as I prepare to give Frank a tongue-lashing, Finley and Brody come strolling in with Mitch and Julie hot on their heels. Hugs and kisses are spread all around and before I know it, we're all drinking champagne and talking about all the new ideas I have for the pub.

All my favorite people are here for our opening. My mom, Al, Frank's Brixton Mansion family—who I've now adopted as my own. Liam's parents, Betha and Alden—whom we've dedicated a permanent Cribbage corner in the pub for. Betha and Alden even like Ginge on Top ale! Several people, including Lariza are here from Club Taint. They all find it hilarious that I framed my old "Taint isn't for the Faint" tank and gave it a place of pride on the White Swan Pub wall. The only person that would make this all complete is—

"He's good, you know," Theo's voice says from behind me as I gaze out the lattice window into the street.

I turn around and smile knowingly as Theo confidently adjusts his glasses. Aside from his pale brown eyes, Theo looks so much like

Hayden. It's sometimes painful to look at him. It takes me back to those dark years and I still battle with guilt.

"Is he really? I thought he was coming tonight. He said he'd try. I can't help but still worry about him," I say, gazing out the window.

Theo purses his lips. "He still might show. But, if he doesn't, I think it's because he's just trying to be respectful. It's your guys' big night and all."

"I would respect him more if he were here," I reply. "That's what I want him to know. I miss seeing him as much as I used to. I just want to see him happy."

"He is happy. He just moved back to London and we're working together again. He's doing brilliantly."

I nod sadly. "I know. He texted me a few weeks ago. I just hoped tonight he might—"

I stop mid sentence as I see through the window a familiar tall, lanky frame striding down the sidewalk. "Holy shit!" I squeal and dash past Theo to run outside and greet him.

I stop quickly to tell Liam that Hayden is here and I'm just going to pop out to greet him. Liam nods and smiles, kissing me sweetly on the lips before I go. A happy flutter cascades through me at the complete confidence he has in me now. He knows how Hayden feels or felt about me. Who knows where Hayden's head is right now. I haven't feasted eyes on him long enough to determine it yet.

When I finally make my way through all of our loved ones, I step outside, round the corner, and am immediately confused at the image before me.

"Bugger! Fuck-a-duck! I! Crikey! How the! Shit!" A spindly blonde is hunched over the top of Hayden as he lies on his back on the sidewalk, tangled in a huge leash and the large straps of what looks like, a gigantic purse. A huge, furry dog is lapping incessantly at his face as she attempts to pull the animal off of him.

"Everything okay?" I ask, helplessly. Hayden's laughing and petting the dog whilst attempting to untangle the mess he's in.

"Oh fuck! Yes! Shit. Dumb dog. Bruce!" the blonde cries and continues to yank on the collar. The long leash is twisted all around Hayden's legs. "Come off it! He's a horrid animal. I thought it'd be fun to have a bloody Beethoven. He's crazy sweet, but slobbers all over. God, I'm afraid he's completely molested your friend here. Oi! I didn't even get your name, yet. What's your name, mate?"

Hayden finally breaks free from Bruce and stands up, brushing himself clean. He leans over and pats the dog affectionately. "I'm Hayden." When he finally looks up at her, his humored expression falls.

"Hiya," she mumbles and nervously tucks her hair behind her ears. The two continue to stare at each other with a serious electric current being passed back and forth.

Finally I break the heated tension. "So who are you?" I ask, looking her up and down. This blonde is a bit of an adorable mess. She's all legs, arms, and long, straight hair. She seems eccentric, but sweet.

Pausing, she looks over to me and glances at my tattoos, "You're Reyna, aren't you?"

"I am."

"Oh God, yes. I'm Leslie's mate, Vi. We work together at Nikon." She looks back at Hayden with curiosity on her face.

"Oh, yes! I've heard of you. I thought your name was Vilma? That's who I have on the guest list. Are you Vilma?" I reach over to shake her hand and she distractedly returns the gesture. Her light blue eyes are lingering on Hayden's.

"Yeah, well…I go by Vi usually. Leslie's the only one that calls me Vilma. Liam told Leslie it was fine for me to bring Bruce, but I wanted to be sure…He's rather vile with the slobber, but we are a bit of a package deal." She's talking to me, but still looking at Hayden.

Since no one is looking at me anyway, I kneel down and give Bruce a good fondle, mindful of my panty-free bottom. "He's great. Bring him on in." I stand back up and glance nervously at Hayden. "Hayden…you're coming in, right?"

"Yeah," he says swallowing and looking at me, finally. His eyes relax in a way that silently says, 'Hi, it's been a while.' I return the same look.

Awkwardly Vi, Hayden and I turn and head back in toward the pub. Hayden looks good. Really good. His coppery blond hair is still messy, but he's ditched the beard. His eyes look brighter and more youthful. Even his lean body looks like it's gained back some tone and muscle. This wasn't how I saw Hayden and my greeting going, but I feel kind of excited that Bruce and Vi seem to be distracting his thoughts.

"Ah, there she is!" Al's voice calls out from near the bar as the three of us re-enter the pub. "We were looking for you, love."

Liam strides up to me and immediately locks eyes with Hayden. The two of them watch each other for a moment before Liam sticks out his hand. Hayden looks down at it and smiles as he returns the gesture. "Good of you to come, Hayden."

"Thanks for the invitation. And congratulations…on everything." Hayden's voice is soft, but his eyes are sincere as he gazes at me with a small grin. He nods his head and then turns to join Theo and Leslie at a nearby table.

"It's time for a toast!" Al says, his eyes twinkling at me with affection. "Come here, lass." He reaches an arm out in welcome. I grab Liam's hand and pull him over in front of the bar where Al and my mother are both standing.

"Reyna girl, I've wanted you to work here for five years now and I'm a bit brassed off that the only way I could get you to do it was if you were the damn owner!"

Everyone around us starts laughing heartily as I bite my lip in embarrassment. Liam grins and drops a soft kiss on the top of my head.

"At first, I only wanted you here so I could keep a better eye on you. Now that I know you're in good hands, I'm just happy to have you here because you're my…daughter." Alistair's eyes turn red and he looks away awkwardly. A painful knot forms in my throat and I pull away from Liam and rush Al for a giant hug.

He clears his throat, he adds loudly, "Blimey, let's not get all soft. This is a party. Cheers everyone!"

"Cheers!" I echo with everyone else. Just before I take a drink, I lock eyes with Hayden who's smiling at me with all the sincerity he can muster…and I give it right back.

Liam strides over and we clink our champagne flutes and begin finally enjoying ourselves for the night. The evening consists of a lot of drinking and laughing. The wait staff does an excellent job keeping everyone happy and ringing up imaginary bills to ensure the new system we installed runs properly.

As Liam and I stand visiting with Finley, Julie, and Mitch, Hayden joins us and murmurs into my ear, "I'm going to take off. It's a great pub. Congratulations, again."

Without thinking, I reach out and pull Hayden into a hug. I'm usually so careful around him, but tonight I'm feeling all the feels. His arms around me feel familiar, except for the fact that I don't smell a whiff of cigarettes anymore. Pulling back, I notice Vilma watching us. Ignoring her penetrative gaze, I tilt my head and say, "I didn't even get a chance to talk to you tonight. I've missed you, Hay. I hope you're doing well."

A small huff of a laugh falls on my face as he replies, "I've missed you, too, Rey Rey. I'm doing well, though. I'm even doing some of my own design stuff now with Theo."

"That's great!" I smile brightly and look over to Liam to see him watching us. A contented smile rests on his lips. "I'd love to catch up some time," I add. But, before Hayden can reply, Frank interrupts us.

"Well loves, I know I'm the life of this party, but unfortunately I've got to dash." Frank throws an arm around both Liam and Hayden and it's the most awkward man triangle I've ever seen. His red eyebrows rise thoughtfully. "Or fortunately, depending how you look at it. I've got a hot date with a bloke named Jerry. He's in merchandising and no, I won't tell you what he merchandises," Frank chortles and Hayden, Liam, and I all erupt into laughter at his naughty expression.

Frank air kisses me on both cheeks and gives a hearty salute to everyone else. Hayden follows and nearly runs into Vi again on their way out the door, Big Bruce in tow.

When the pub finally empties and all the employees have headed home for the night, I walk up to Liam, who's leaning back against the bar like a damn book cover model.

"Well, we did it." I reach up and twine my fingers into the hair behind his neck. "We're legit business owners, Liam."

His eyes roll briefly at my touch and he responds by lifting me up into a hug and setting me on top of the bar. He kisses me chastely on the lips and replies, "You're the owner. I'm just your skivvy."

"We're getting married in a year and all of that will change then. But skivvy you say? How about sex slave instead? I think we can work with that better." I waggle my eyebrows playfully.

He tucks my dark hair behind my ears and looks thoughtfully into my eyes. "I know it's not a bridal boutique like you and Marisa had dreamed up before, but I think this place is perfect for you and me."

I pause to gaze around the quaint pub that was here to catch me when I fell nearly four years ago. "It so is. I've got big plans for this pub." I tighten my hands around his neck and wrap my legs around his waist. "I'm so ready to get to work and use this damn Oxford education of mine for once!"

Liam's eyebrows lift knowingly, "I think you've got plenty of good use out of that education if you ask me." He kisses me sweetly on the nose.

"How do you figure?" I ask, happily grinning down at him.

"Well," he starts, and then pauses as he takes his hands and strokes them down my face and through my hair, reverently staring at my lips while he speaks, "Oxford brought you to me, so that's a start."

I stare at his sexy, pouty lips and reply back, "And, thank God for that. Because you are the one for me."

ONE YEAR LATER

EPILOGUE

It's always sunny at times like these.

Overlooking the Clarke estate on a hilltop, a familiar wooden swing sways on a nearby tree. It has the potential to feel spooky, yet, it doesn't. Instead, it feels…magical.

A light breeze wafts through my hair and I inhale deeply, closing my eyes and basking in the warmth of the Essex sunlight. I drop down to my knees in the dirt and touch the earth, picturing Marisa in that same yellow sundress she wore in my dream so many years ago.

She stood right here, asking me over and over if I was sorry for what I did. She demanded to know why I did it. *"I think deep down, you already know,"* she said when I failed to answer her.

I did know. I knew why I let Liam tell me he loved me that day four years ago. I knew why I allowed myself to let go for those few precious hours with him. I knew why I let him see me in a way no one else ever had.

I was in love with him.

Maybe even from the moment I saw him. I fell in love with my best friend's boyfriend. In my dream, Marisa seemed to already know it, but I was still asleep.

I am very much awake right now.

"I'm getting married tomorrow, Marisa," my voice wobbles as I speak to the beauty all around me. I glance over at the swing and smile. "I'm getting married tomorrow and I haven't seen you in so long. You don't appear in my dreams anymore and I miss you," my voice breaks at the end and I purse my lips and take a deep breath in.

"I thought maybe if I came out here I could feel you with me. This place you grew up in is beautiful and special. Just like you." I swallow down the knot in my throat, begging myself not to cry, but knowing it's pointless.

"You should be standing with me tomorrow, Marisa. You should be right beside me as my maid of honor. My best friend. I want you there." I sniff loudly, picking up a handful of dirt and tossing it into the breeze.

"That night I dreamt of you, right here…all I wanted to say was I'm sorry. But I don't want to tell you that today." I push my hair back away from my face preparing for my speech that I practiced over and over in my head during the drive here. "Today, I just want to say thank you. Thank you for loving me through all my neuroses and for being my first real friend. Thank you for seeing past the mess that I was and helping me see the person I always longed to be.

"But most of all, thank you for Liam. Thank you for bringing him into our lives. He sees me the way you saw me. And it took me a while, but I'm finally seeing myself that way, too."

I smile sadly as I relive all the mistakes I made. "I did things so wrong and so messed up. With Hayden. With Liam. My Mom. Everyone. And in the end…even you. I'm sure you would have had an epic rant for me about how idiotic I went about things." I chuckle, picturing her standing in triumph over the whole ordeal. "But, I sincerely believe that my end can trump my beginning.

"And, despite it all, I'm happy. Seriously happy. We're getting married on Liam's boat, you know. He named her, *The One*." I grin at the memory of the day we came to Cambridge for a weekend and he surprised me with the new paint on the back end. "It's kind of perfect, right?"

I pause, wishing more than anything that Marisa were sitting right beside me. Sighing heavily, I stand to leave, taking one final look at the Clarke home. "Anyways, I'll be tossing sunflowers into the river for you tomorrow, Marisa. I'm going to close my eyes and imagine you by my side. You were my real life sister. And my real life angel. Thank you for inspiring me, still."

I turn to walk back to Liam, who's waiting patiently for me in the car down the hill.

No more waiting. He's waited long enough.

The End

Thank you for reading *Not The One!*

Are you interested in Hayden's story?
If so, post a review and tell me! ☺

If you're feeling curious about the secondary characters, you'll be happy to learn that Finley and Leslie both have stories available and are all a part of the London Lovers Series. Go back and see where it all began with Finley in *Becoming Us*, a spicy college prequel to the London Lovers Series. Or skip the college prequel and start right inside Frank's house in London with *A Broken Us*. Leslie's standalone is called *London Bound*.

ACKNOWLEDGEMENTS

Not The One pushed me to a new place in my writing that I have never been before. I was literally scared of my characters. I didn't know how it was going to end or who Reyna was going to end up with and all of it terrified me. I could not have got through it without the invaluable, incredible, and immeasurable help from several people!

Firstly, my creative sounding boards. My sister, Abby, and my friends, Kelly and Becky. You three read this story as I wrote it, painful chapter by painful chapter. I pretty much sucked the joy out of the reading experience for you by forcing you to cuddle me through this writing process. Thank you for reading and rereading and pushing me when I needed pushing and cheering me when I needed cheering. I couldn't have done it without you. For realz.

My sister in law, Megan Daws. Thank you for shooting my most favorite cover and for sharing your dreams with me. They helped me with this story more than you know.

To my editing: Stephanie Rose, Angela Pratt and Laurie. Thank you all for your contributions to my story. Special note to Stephanie: You pushed me to make this story even better and I know I wouldn't be half as proud of it if I wouldn't have had you there to help me! And to my proofers: Kirsty and Mercedes for being the final eyes! And Belinda, my British cream puff! Thanks for answering all of my late night Brit-lingo queries!

To my rockin' beta readers who read a big chunk at the beginning and were kind enough to go back and reread when I sent you like eighteen different drafts in two days. Jaci and Jennifer, thank you for your patience on this story!

To Faith and Stephanie, my two special people who helped me out through the mental illness topics that I faced in this storyline. I had to get this right and I couldn't have done it without your insights!

To the bloggers that support unconditionally through all my crazy characters. Thanks for being on my team!

To my hubby. I was horrid at estimating how long this book would take me to write. I was in uncharted territories with these characters. Thank you for tolerating my poor time management and not killing me for never showing up on time for dinner or church! And thank you for my nightly fountain Diet Coke's. Best week of my writing. So worth it.

To my three-year-old, Lorelei Hope. Thanks for coming over and pulling out my ear buds so you could hear what I was listening to. Those special moments are always a welcome distraction when I'm writing. And when those moments erupt into dance parties…that's pure inspiration.

And to readers and my London Lovers fan club. This gig wouldn't work without you. For real. I don't write for the birds. I write to be read. Thanks for loving books. Book nerds are the ceeewlest.

To my angels in the sky. My special six. I wish I dreamt of you more. Stop by sometime and say hi. Your mommy misses you.

MORE ABOUT THE AUTHOR

Amy Daws lives in South Dakota with her husband, and miracle daughter, Lorelei. The long-awaited birth of Lorelei is what inspired Amy's first book, Chasing Hope, and her passion for writing. Amy is a lover of all things British and her award-nominated romantic comedies, The London Lovers Series, are centered around Americans in London. For more of Amy's work, visit: www.amydawsauthor.com or check out the links below.

Newsletter: www.amydawsauthor.com/news
www.facebook.com/amydawsauthor
www.twitter.com/amydawsauthor

MORE BOOKS BY AMY DAWS

The London Lovers Series:
#1 *Becoming Us* Finley's Story Part 1…College Style
#2 *A Broken Us* Finley's Story Part 2…London Style
#3 *London Bound* Leslie's Story…A London Lovers Standalone
#4 *Not The One* Reyna's Story… A London Lovers Spinoff Standalone

Pointe of Breaking, A College Dance Standalone by Amy Daws & Sarah J. Pepper

Chasing Hope, A Memoir
A mother's story of loss, heartbreak, and the miracle of hope.

For retailer purchase links, visit:
www.amydawsauthor.com